Anne of Green Gables
A New Beginning

Anne of Green Gables
A New Beginning

Kevin Sullivan
Adapted from his screenplay

KEY PORTER BOOKS

Library and Archives Canada Cataloguing in Publication

Sullivan, Kevin, 1955 May 28–
    Anne of Green Gables : a new beginning / Kevin Sullivan.

ISBN 978-1-55470-134-6

1. Shirley, Anne (Fictitious character)—Fiction. I. Title.

PS8637.U553A645 2008   C813'.6   C2008-903288-8

ONTARIO ARTS COUNCIL
CONSEIL DES ARTS DE L'ONTARIO

The Canada Council | Le Conseil des Arts
for the Arts | du Canada
since 1957 | depuis 1957

The publisher gratefully acknowledges the support of the Canada Council for the Arts and
the Ontario Arts Council for its publishing program. We acknowledge the support of the
Government of Ontario through the Ontario Media Development Corporation's Ontario
Book Initiative.

We acknowledge the financial support of the Government of Canada through the Book
Publishing Industry Development Program (BPIDP) for our publishing activities.

Key Porter Books Limited
Six Adelaide Street East, Tenth Floor
Toronto, Ontario
Canada M5C 1H6
www.keyporter.com

Text design and formatting: Marijke Friesen

The word mark ANNE OF GREEN GABLES is an official mark of the Anne of Green
Gables Licensing Authority, Inc., used under license.

Printed and bound in Canada

08 09 10 11 12 5 4 3 2 1

Anne of Green Gables
A New Beginning

"Our fate lies not in the stars, but in ourselves."
—William Shakespeare

One

Time stood still as Anne settled into a long wicker chaise lounge in the solitude of the beach in front of the venerable old White Sands Hotel. She was soothed by the tranquil ocean and the tepid light of early dawn.

Anne had arisen early that morning. She'd tread softly down the steps of the clapboard hotel, careful to avoid meeting anyone in the early morning. She needed some time alone, time to think about the play—the same play that had kept her pacing and fretting alone in her room through the long dark night. Once out the door, she hurried across the hotel's wide front lawn and sprinted along the beach, clutching her briefcase full of papers. She craved the ocean's comforting sounds and was beside herself to take in the *spirit of place*—of Stanhope Beach at sunrise. The atmosphere, the tone, the air were all a panacea for everything that disturbed her.

Truth be told, the play was but one of her worries, and perhaps the least of them at that. Primarily she was anxious about Dominic, her twenty-eight-year-old son, whose regiment was still overseas in France. She had written him unfailingly over the last several months, with only scattered replies. Now that the Allies had finally proclaimed victory, Anne was waiting for Dominic to keep the promise he'd made in his last letter and return home to Toronto, on the first Canadian boat to leave England.

Anne had written her son not three weeks ago. Begging for an immediate reply, she had asked him to sail directly to Halifax and join her on Prince Edward Island for the summer. She had no idea whether her letter had reached him, nor what his real designs were regarding returning home. Reading between the lines of his last response, her instincts suggested that perhaps a young woman had entered his life. Still, she wondered if this was just wishful thinking. Worry bubbled up in her subconscious that some disaster might just as easily have befallen him. There were so many frequent reports in the news about accidents and sorrows, about those whose lives were caught in the backdraft of fires that still smoldered across France. Staring out at the gently swelling ocean, Anne found herself frustrated by her decision to move back to Prince Edward Island for the summer. It had left her with entirely uncertain means of communicating with the outside world, and especially with Dominic.

The decision—impulsive and rash, it now seemed—had been made when she committed to write a play for Gene Armstrong, a New York producer and good friend who had undertaken the White Sand's 1945 summer-stock season. Several months prior, Anne, on a whim, had pitched the idea of writing a play for Gene. Over drinks in Manhattan's legendary Algonquin Hotel, Anne had confided that she was looking for a diversion to offset her anxiety over the war. After five horrible years she was worried it might never come to an end; even then, she'd been on tenterhooks over Dominic's safe return.

Looking back on the conversation, Anne knew she'd taken Gene by surprise. He'd had no idea what was in store. He'd merely telephoned when he'd learned she was in the city, and invited her to get together so he could ask about renting a cottage on the Island for the summer. They had known each other for years, through mutual friends in the publishing business, and Gene knew she owned a farm there, overlooking the ocean.

Anne adored Gene's big personality and had always been impressed by his ability to find successful material for the stage. She had been absolutely bowled over by his 1940 Broadway production of *And Then There Were None*, starring Bette Davis. By the end of the war, though, Gene's star had lost its lustre, mostly because of faltering ticket sales.

The meeting had been entirely pleasant. They'd laughed and gossiped about friends and celebrities before Gene mentioned Anne's early novels, which were all set on Prince Edward Island and were still madly popular with legions of readers around the world. While grateful for the books' success, Anne bemoaned the fact that her series of juvenile novels had made her more of a household name than her recent and more serious works. As she swirled the ice in her glass during the sensitive conversation about the war and Dominic, an unexpected and intriguing idea wiggled its way into her mind. Sitting in the foyer of the hallowed hotel—a room that had been graced by some of America's most legendary writers and playwrights such as Ernest Hemingway and Edna Ferber—Anne told Gene that she had an idea for a story set on the Island, an idea she hoped to work up into a play that very summer.

Despite the sleepless night she had just endured as the result of that whim, Anne smiled at the memory. Gene was a very persuasive impresario and recognized an opportunity when he saw one. He immediately and wholeheartedly supported Anne's suggestion. It was a no-lose proposition. Anne's status as a celebrated author would bring an instant cachet to his arrangement with the White Sands.

He claimed to be positively crazy about the idea of premiering a play by Anne Shirley on the Island. Buoyed by her friend's enthusiasm, Anne committed to the project on the spot. Within a week Gene had firmed up the arrangements with the hotel and within two more weeks, in early May, Anne found herself back in Avonlea, just as Gene was assembling his troupe of actors and theatre staff. Anne was offered her own suite to live in and work in at the hotel.

ALTHOUGH ANNE WAS CONTENT to be home on Island soil again, and excited by the creative challenge ahead of her, she felt ridiculous living in a hotel. Her entire life on P.E.I. had been spent rambling across fields and dells, exploring the maritime countryside that had become a fairyland for the imaginative child she had been. Holed up in her sprawling White Sands' suite that agonizing morning, Anne fretted over every aspect of her life as she gazed out through a bay window at the moonlit ocean crashing against the dunes.

She quietly concluded that writing a play was no effortless accomplishment. Gene was a strong-willed producer and he had put her storytelling skills to the test. He was also staying in the hotel, playing the role of dramaturge and assisting her to quickly bring her scenario into existence.

By the middle of June, Anne knew things weren't going well. Gene was not happy with the first draft, and the two of them spent hours jousting back and forth over issues of dramatic impact and how best to let the story unfold onstage. Gene had a very commercial sense of what he felt an audience wanted to see. It pained Anne to admit it but he was often right. Still, a few of his comments had rubbed her the wrong way; so much so that she now had her back up about the entire project. She found her mind constantly drifting from the solitary work of writing to impatiently wondering what could possibly have happened to Dominic. After several weeks she could barely concentrate and thought of nothing else.

Anne worried incessantly. So many difficult events had over-taken her life that she found it impossible to reconcile them. She was secretly anxious that another terrible heartbreak might be lingering just around the corner, ready to catch her by the heels and pull her down. At least she was home, standing safely on the beach in the dim morning light, the sensation of pink sand and the sound of the ocean easing her apprehensions.

At fifty-seven, Anne still had dreamer's eyes. She tried to convince herself she had much for which to be grateful. Two happily married daughters, Rilla and Frannie, kept her occupied with several grandchildren. She was financially stable and lived quite independently in a handsome house in Toronto. She had so many friends everywhere—in Toronto, Montreal, New York, and down East—that she was always travelling and socializing. She had the freedom to devote time to any creative endeavour she chose, whether painting, writing or music. In so many ways, her life was wonderful and satisfying. Even the splendid halo of red hair that had made her so miserable as a child had dark-ened to a handsome auburn. These days she wore her hair up, lending herself a sophisticated and elegant look, even when she frequently felt the opposite inside.

MORE THAN FOUR DECADES had passed since Anne had first travelled to Prince Edward Island at age eleven. An odd twist of fate had brought her to Green Gables farm, and to Marilla and Matthew Cuthbert. The elderly brother and sister had or-dered a boy from an orphanage on the mainland, but the message had been mixed up and the Cuthberts had been sent Anne instead. Anne's early years had been so full of heartbreak that she'd embarked on that first journey to the Island hoping desperately for a perfect family to take her in and care for her.

In an extraordinary decision, the Cuthberts decided to keep Anne, who turned their lives upside down with her overactive imagination and stubborn disposition. Anne was also blessed with a tender heart and she did Matthew and Marilla wondrously proud, as she grew in intelligence, beauty and determination.

Now the Cuthberts, like so many others of that generation, were long gone. That part of Anne's life seemed like nothing more than the mist lying in the cove at the end of the beach. Anne had yet to even visit the Green Gables farm. She had wanted to go, but she kept finding reasons to procrastinate. Somehow, she'd allowed herself to become completely disconnected from the property over the years.

Still, Green Gables had remained occupied, and for that Anne was grateful. At her insistence, Diana and Fred Wright had taken over the farm just after the Great War. Anne and her husband Gilbert had moved to the far end of the Island when Gilbert had taken over a colleague's medical practice. Fred had lost his right arm during the Battle of the Somme and had few prospects for work on his return. Anne and Gilbert had quickly concluded that the Wrights should have the farm and raise their young family there. It had been a perfect arrangement, and for many years the Wright family had made good use of the farm. Twenty-seven years later, however, the house had fallen into disrepair from lack of use, and Anne began considering putting the property up for sale. The Wrights, who now used the place only as a summer cottage, agreed that Anne's decision was prudent, especially since property values would likely be on the rise with the war winding down.

Diana promised that her children, John and Elsie, would clear out all of their things immediately, which would give Anne ample time to list the farm that summer. Unfortunately, she and

Fred would not be able to help: They were staying on in Bermuda and would not be making a trip to the Island this year. Disappointed at such a practical reply, Anne had tried to accept the fact that she and her bosom friend had grown distant over the years. It was yet another reminder of how much things had changed as people's circumstances evolved in life.

Even though her fondest childhood time had been spent in the farmhouse she'd shared with Matthew and Marilla, Anne had nonetheless tried to sweep those memories to the corners of her mind. It would have been so tempting to remain safe and comfortable and protected within Green Gables' walls. No, it was good that she and Gilbert had moved on with their lives, Anne reasoned. It was good that they had gone away from the Island into the world beyond. She also knew that Green Gables was still her responsibility, but she had such mixed feelings about how to deal with it. Her practical side told her the farm would be better off sold and in the hands of a family who could devote itself to its upkeep. Her emotional, romantic side had an entirely different opinion. Despite the passage of the years, and her own efforts to move on, the place still meant the world to her. Selling it would be upsetting, and, in her heart, Anne was inclined to avoid the finality of it all.

The day she contacted the real estate agent in Carmody, though, was the day she'd set her hand to the plow. There was no turning back once the For Sale sign had been plunged into the ground at the garden gate, and Anne had given John and Elsie a mid-June deadline for having the house ready to show. The tourist season would be starting by then—a perfect time to sell.

Anne leaned back in the wicker chaise lounge and looked across the water at the rim of orange and yellow light expand-ing along the horizon like a river seeping onto a flood plain after a heavy storm. All of her worries and concerns preyed on her heart as she sat in the solitude of the sunrise. She stared straight into the light, looking for an answer to a question she was not even certain how to phrase. She knew only that she was at odds with her life, agonizingly unhappy and empty.

After a moment, she rubbed her eyes and pulled a somewhat damp tartan blanket up to her waist. It had been left at the bonfire the previous evening by a group of Gene's actors, but it was a much needed luxury in the cool morning air. It brought back the memory of lying in tall grass, reading one of her mother's many books. Out of sheer exhaustion and anxiety she drifted off into a dream state. The salt breeze and the soft wash of the waves allowed her to travel across time. She saw Green Gables nestled in the soft fields of the Island's north shore. She dreamed of childhood friends running through tall grass. Only half awake, Anne realized that these were not Island friends, but children she had known long before she'd come to the Cuthberts. She saw a red clapboard schoolhouse and heard a gentle voice calling for her, searching for her.

"Anne! Anne Shirley!" Her mother's words flew on the wind, across a field of daisies dancing around the edge of a pond. Bertha Shirley was a modern, free-thinking young teacher whose delicate face was crowned with a mane of fiery red hair. Anne dreamed about her mother as a kind of archetype depicted by a group of nineteenth-century English artists called the Pre-Raphaelites who were consumed with replicating the romance of the Middle Ages. Bertha lived and breathed the arts and allowed her daughter a ridiculous amount of freedom when it came to exploring her own creativity.

The voice trailed off, leaving Anne lost once again in the haze of that hot, long-ago afternoon, sprawled out along a tartan blanket under a willow. In the distance, a bell rang and those children, suddenly familiar, were streaming out of the Boling-broke schoolhouse—her mother's principal position of employment in the town where Anne had grown up. The chatter of voices at the end of the school day hardly reached Anne's ears. So intent was she on Alfred Lord Tennyson's exotic poems that each suspenseful turn of the story left her immobilized. At ten, Anne loved literature as much as her mother, who had been so preoccupied that particular afternoon in her classroom that she'd completely lost track of her own child. Bertha felt guilty and irresponsible as she stood calling and beckoning Anne to come out of hiding.

Anne had not fully extracted herself from the world of jousting knights and fair maidens when her mother discovered her hidden in the tall grass by the edge of the pond just behind the school. Bertha lifted Anne up, kissed her tenderly, and took her by the hand as she firmly closed the Tennyson and concealed it in her satchel for another time. She seemed in a peculiar hurry that day and Anne had to scurry to keep up with her mother's stride. Still, it was blissful to trot along beside her through the grass. There was not a soul in the world whom Anne had ever loved more.

"One day I'm afraid I'm going to lose you completely in those blessed books!" Bertha scolded. "You've been out here since lunch, haven't you? Did you forget to come back to class? You never remember to tell me where you're going. You missed our entire history class—the fall of Rome!"

Even when she scolded, Bertha's voice was full of devotion for her daughter. Anne had inherited not only her mother's flaming red hair, but also her unique curiosity, keen intelligence and intense desire for learning. Anne's sensitive soul and her wildly theatrical imagination were all her own, however.

"It's one of the privileges of having a mother as a school-teacher," Anne said cheerfully as they hurried along. "What a relief to be rescued! This book is a perfect tragedy."

Bertha put the hat she was carrying onto her head and walked even faster. Her face furrowed as she glanced at the gold watch pinned to her blouse.

"It'll be a tragedy if we miss our train! Your father's coming home from the logging camp tonight. Hurry up now, dear." Though Anne struggled to keep up, her mind was still fixed on the gripping tale.

"My, but that book gave me a thrill! It's the story about a daughter of a belted earl, stolen away from her parents in infancy by a cruel nurse who dies before she can confess."

"Come on, Anne. Come on!" Bertha laughed, sharing the child's delight.

Lying on the beach near the hotel, Anne tossed her head gently as she drifted uneasily through memory, remembering the reason for Bertha's hurried steps. Anne's father, Walter Shirley, spent almost no time at home. He was completely absent from their lives during the winter and spring, working in lumber camps up in the New Brunswick woods. For a scant few weeks during the summer—once the big log drives to the mills were finished—he came home to visit his wife and daughter in their Bolingbroke boarding house. For Bertha, her husband's arrival at the train station was a longed-for occasion. For days on end she'd talked to Anne of nothing but his arrival. As a child, the only thing Anne truly understood of her parents' relationship was that absence made her mother's heart long for the return of her husband.

Ironically Anne's memories of her father were filled with ambivalence. She had a vague image of Walter Shirley at the station, his back to her as he greeted her with only an outstretched hand. Bertha took his other hand and together they walked down a dappled laneway.

Almost as soon as it had formed, the image evaporated in the haze of Anne's dream, leaving her with only the memory of her mother's soft and reassuring grip as they walked along the lane from the Bolingbroke whistle stop to their boarding house. She muttered the word "mother" in her delirium, trying to tell Bertha there was nothing lovelier in the entire world than to have a mother to gather her up in her arms, but Bertha was gone—disappeared into the tall grass like mist. The child Anne froze in a panic. Silence surrounded her now, and the summer light faded into long blue shadows of dusk. The tall grass nodded in wisps of swirling air and Anne began to run. "Mother, Mother! Where are you?"

On the beach, Anne murmured in her dream until her cries were submerged in the sound of the ocean.

ANNE OPENED HER EYES and groggily rubbed her forehead. She had a headache from lying too long in the warm morning sun and the sweetness of the bygone time that had occupied her dream quickly melted into her subconscious. Out of the corner of her eye she saw a male figure, backlit by the sun, trundling through the sea grass along the dunes and down to the beach. After several seconds she recognized it was Gene. She picked up her leather case, papers protruding from every fold, and tried to appear as though she was hard at work.

"Hi," Anne called to him with a grand smile. "I got up early to write. Easier to think outdoors!"

Gene dragged over a nearby chair, which he plunked down on the sand next to Anne.

"Oh, sure. I figured you were down here ... any new editorial breakthroughs?"

Anne shrugged, doodling absentmindedly on the newspaper spread out on her lap. "Allies Divide Europe," the headline read, which meant that the victors were deciding on the fate of the defeated nations. Anne was tired of worrying about the fate of nations. For her, victory simply meant the boys could finally come home.

"I've come to a decision." Gene began, interrupting her thoughts. "You know there's a read-through with the cast this afternoon. Well, they have some notes they want to share with you before we get started."

Anne looked self-consciously at the gloves in her lap. "I'm a novelist, Gene. I'm not used to taking notes from everyone, especially when they aren't always diplomatic. Couldn't you just have the meeting and fill me in?"

Gene gazed out at the ocean, where seagulls were diving in search of breakfast on the vast plain of water. He was a good-looking man, with fair hair that was receding just a little and an undeviating, energetic manner that enabled him to inspire and cajole actors, playwrights and all the others required to actually produce a play. What he had come to discuss hit Anne like a punch in the stomach.

"No, I think we should just tell the cast you've decided to hold off for now. It's not a disaster. You just have a different concept. It's not stage worthy, Anne. Not yet, anyway. My concern is that it won't be ready to perform this summer. I can put in another play and you can keep working on it here for the rest of the summer. I'll work it out with the hotel that you can stay on in your suite."

Anne had always expressed her pride and sensitivity openly. She and Gene had had several full-fledged donnybrooks in the past several weeks over plot points and characterizations. However, this time, Gene's words sounded final. There was no room for the discussion that had fuelled their nighttime working sessions in the hotel restaurant. Gene continued, but Anne shrank into the chaise lounge and merely nodded silently. She had known all along that the work was not right. She worried it might never be made right. She wiped her nose, thinking maybe she could just escape on the next ferry back to the mainland— just disappear and throw the ridiculous pages overboard. She managed an inward smile at the thought. This, after all, was familiar territory. In a vivid flash, she recalled throwing the manuscript of her first full-length novel out the window and watching the pages flutter to the street. Gilbert had been with her then, and had buoyed her when she lost her head. Anne needed Gil beside her now more than ever. A lump in her throat made it hard to swallow.

Seeing that Anne wasn't about to speak, Gene reached into his briefcase and delivered a second piece of bad news.

"This came for you." He reached over and passed Anne a postmarked letter. The name "Dominic Blythe" in her own handwriting stood out amid a jumble of postmarks and French instructions. It was stamped, very officially in large letters, with "Renvoyez à l'origine—Return to sender." Anne searched the envelope for some other trace of information but nothing presented itself. She laid it on her lap and nodded "thank you" to Gene.

Anne lowered her head. She was petrified, and her imagination did nothing to help. Dominic could have been lost in the lawless aftermath of a skirmish. He could have hurried across a mine field, encountered a pocket of fighters who refused to give up, or had an accident on a shell-pocked road. Her mind was capable of tossing scenarios at her like the rapid fire of a machine gun.

Gene gave Anne's arm a reassuring squeeze. "Don't worry." He looked over at her, and in his eyes Anne saw both understanding and concern. "It's a big victory. The boys are all off celebrating. You'll hear from him in time."

Anne shook her head. They didn't always come back. Gilbert hadn't come back. Despite his age, Gilbert had been permitted to oversee the set-up of a variety of field hospitals in France, as a result of his extensive experience in the Great War. In that instant, Anne felt as debilitated as she had three years ago, when the military envoy arrived at her door in Toronto with a letter. Anne jammed today's letter out of sight and into her bag as Gene turned and walked away. It reminded her of the many losses she had endured.

Anne had gone to France during the Great War, nearly thirty years before, to search for Gilbert, who had gone missing while serving as an army doctor. The search had been a terrifying adventure, but she had found Gil along with Diana's husband, Fred. She also stumbled into her old nemesis, writer Jack Garrison, who was working for American military intelligence. He had been influential in helping her locate Gilbert in a German prisoner-of-war camp, but by the time the war had ended, both Jack and his young French wife were dead and Jack's young son Dominic had disappeared in the upheaval. Anne followed numerous leads through Belgium, searching for him. She refused to give up because she had promised Jack and his wife that she would care for the boy if anything ever happened to them. Even as she accompanied Fred and Gilbert back to Canada, she tortured herself with this obligation. Eventually Dominic was found. Through the kindness of a New York lawyer, informed of Anne's connection to his client's family, the toddler was brought to her and Gilbert. They immediately adopted two-year-old Do-

minic and raised him alongside their daughters Rilla and
Frannie.

Anne shook her head to clear away the memories. The day
was now well underway, and there were things to be done. It
was time to return to the hotel.

ALL AROUND THE HOTEL, colourful posters announcing "The
Straw Hat Ensemble—Four Exciting New Plays through July
and August at the White Sands Theatre" were being tacked on
the walls. The sight of all this business in preparation for the
summer entertainment made Anne queasy. Careful to avoid
Gene and the actors rehearsing in the ballroom, Anne made her
way to the guest phone by the fireplace in the main foyer. Sinking into one of the plush green lobby seats, she waited patiently
as a long-distance operator made the connection to Boston. Finally, Frannie's familiar voice travelled across the wire. The connection was fractured, but they exchanged the usual greetings
before Anne confessed to her daughter about the letter.

"I know I sound like a typical mother, Frannie, but you
know what your brother can be like. To be honest, darling, I'm
terrified." Anne could barely speak for the dryness in her throat.
"Dominic promised to be on the first boat back from England."

She listened to Frannie's efforts at rationalizing everything.
"I know, I know . . . and I'm sorry to bother you just now with
everything you have on your plate. Is the baby any better? No!
Don't be silly, darling. You can't come all the way here when
Timmy has the mumps. I just needed someone to talk to. Why
wouldn't Dominic get in touch with me?" Once again the words
caught in her throat and her heart.

Anne stopped herself when she heard Timmy wailing in
the background. What had she been thinking, imposing all this

on Frannie—a mother herself with a sick toddler on her hands. Frannie was the kind of daughter who would drop everything and rush to her mother's side. Anne knew she needed to say goodbye. "No, no, go along now. Give the baby a big kiss from me. I'll be in touch the minute I have a bit of news. Love you, Frannie. Don't worry. I'm staying put here at the hotel. Bye."

Hanging up, Anne leaned her head on the pillar behind her—tired and worried and alone.

TWILIGHT FOUND ANNE crossing the wooden bridge over Barry's Pond, where Gilbert had once courted her so earnestly. It was a secret and special place. She gazed out over the familiar estuary. As she watched the mist rise and drift over the river as the day cooled, she knew she needed to be near Gilbert.

She stole away to the cemetery behind the old whitewashed Avonlea church at the edge of town. Anne felt a different kind of consolation there among the many mossy, tilting headstones. A new granite stone stood upright, not yet stained by the weather. "Dr. Gilbert John Blythe," read the inscription, "1890 to 1942. Killed serving at Dieppe, France. Gratefully remembered by his community for defending the faith and his country. Cherished for eternity by his beloved wife, Anne."

The Dieppe raid—an attempt to capture a vital town on the coast of France—had been a disaster for the Canadians, and for Anne. Gilbert had died under fire helping the wounded. That he died nobly did nothing to ease the horror for Anne and her children.

Anne knelt before the headstone then sank down fully onto the mound of the grave. The ground was dry and cool, shaded by gentle ferns. Drawing her knees to her body, Anne curled up as though nestling close to her husband. She laid her hand on the soft moss that had quickly grown across the mound, and in her mind, she touched his chest.

"It isn't right to cry so," she whispered. "It's just that…I never expected this life, Gil. Send Dominic home. Get him back to me."

When she finally rose a half-hour later, Anne's face was smudged with tears and the red earth she cherished. Crossing the old wooden bridge again on the way back through town, Anne leaned over the rail to gaze into the same waters where, long ago, she had acted out Tennyson's "Lancelot and Elaine," and where Gilbert had rescued her from the disaster of nearly drowning in the imagined funeral barge on its way to Camelot. The disintegrating wreck of Mr. Barry's duck hunting stiff could still be seen wavering in the oily depths of the pond, right where it had filled with water and sank, just as Anne aborted her imaginary voyage in a desperate scramble to climb onto one of the wooden pilings that supported the bridge. Anne smiled at the memory. Gilbert had always been there to see her through numerous disasters in her life; and she had saved him, too. They were a wonderful balance for each other for more than forty years. A relationship like that was incapable of disintegrating. It found its own way of transcending time and tragedy.

Images of Dominic as a toddler filled Anne's mind as she stared at the shafts of light wavering in the dark, brackish water. She remembered meeting him at the Bright River Station—the same place that Matthew Cuthbert had found her sitting on an empty bench. In a flicker she heard Dominic's laughter and saw his sweet rosy cheeks as he raced across the platform and into her arms. She remembered their mutual delight as she covered him with kisses. What she wouldn't give now to enjoy that moment again!

"Maybe he's all right and just doesn't want to get in touch with me? You can't let go of the people who raised you, though," she whispered to Gilbert, continuing her conversation. "But not knowing who your real parents were will always haunt you."

Anne's thoughts drifted away from Gilbert and Dominic and back to her own mother and father. That morning's dream suddenly seemed prescient. It drew her back again, deep into her subconscious, looking for answers to questions she had asked even as a child. Why was her father the way he was? Why had her mother loved a man like that?

Two

That evening, Anne was back on the beach, this time with Gene and his troupe, who were enjoying a bonfire. The actors were a high-spirited lot and laughed uproariously as three of them danced a hornpipe to an accompanying fiddle. Their arms were linked and they cast long, cavorting shadows. Sparks flew merrily up into an indigo sky. Perched on a lounge chair, Anne clapped and laughed and shouted, "Bravo!" along with the ensemble. Every so often though, her mind would wander and she knew that Gene had caught the faraway look on her face more than once. When the music finally stopped, Gene seemed irritated more than amused.

"Time to pack it in before my patience is exhausted and we consider recasting," he laughed. "Thanks for coming."

Pleasantly tired after a long day's rehearsal, the members of the troupe began to make their way up the beach. One of them, a young woman, stopped to give Anne a hug on her way past. By now everyone knew about Gene's decision.

"Sorry about all the changes in the play."

Anne shook her head and wished the pretty young actress sweet dreams. The others sauntered off, many still singing and horsing around.

"Ten o'clock tomorrow," Gene called after them. "Learn your lines."

Gene waited until they were all gone, hunkering down and prodding the dying fire before he spoke to Anne.

Anne remained silent, staring at the glowing coals.

"Don't worry about Dominic." Gene broke the silence. "He's a big boy. He'll be home soon enough. Anyway, have you thought about reworking the scenario? I think you should consider rewriting. Maybe make me a big-time producer again?" he said laughingly.

Anne could hardly believe her ears! How dare Gene try to jolly her out of her frame of mind. "Don't be smart!" she said sharply. "The great American impresario, who's about as far away from Broadway as he can get!"

She knew this was an unfair jibe at Gene's distinguished accomplishments. Anne watched Gene's brow crease into a frown.

"I don't get it!" he bristled. "Why did you come here? You tell me you have a great idea for a play, that you want to challenge yourself creatively. What are you doing here?" When Anne did not respond, Gene simply asked again. "What?"

"I came to sell Green Gables," Anne blurted out, stung by her friend's sharp words. "Writing a play for you was just my excuse to get here."

Her response left Gene momentarily speechless. Anne realized he was angry. No doubt he was thinking of all the effort he'd already put into her play.

"Don't waste my time," he snapped.

A log cracked on the fire. Anne's face was ruddy in the light and she drew her arms about herself.

"Go! Just go away from me. Leave me alone."

Gene didn't need to be told twice. He turned in the sand and walked back toward the hotel, leaving Anne silhouetted and alone in the firelight, far from the music and laughter of the hotel guests. As soon as he was gone, Anne regretted her words. A long dormant turmoil filled her with disquiet. She wondered why she was dreaming of her mother after all these years.

"I've always needed to write," she thought. "I've made up

stories about myself all my life. I used to imagine my parents were a perfect couple, living in harmony. I did it so often for so long, I don't know what the truth is any more. I only know I wouldn't recognize my father if I saw him."

THE OLD DREAM SWIRLED in Anne's mind again as the flames of the bonfire danced before her eyes, transporting her back to a tiny yellow clapboard house with white muslin curtains and wildflower boxes under green-shuttered windows. Anne's had been an endearing little house, just big enough for three. Her mother and father came laughing out the door, both holding their arms out to Anne. She ran to them joyfully and her father scooped her up in his strong embrace. Anne was the centre of their attention. Down a sunny path the little family walked, two devoted parents loving and protecting their only daughter from all that was cruel in the world. A breeze set the lilies, snapdragons, and sweet peas nodding in the garden.

"That's where I always imagined we'd live, my parents and I," Anne thought to herself. The newly wakened parts of Anne, stirred from her gnawing worry over Dominic, brought forth other memories—ones she had sealed away since the day Marilla had told her she could stay.

The bonfire crackled in front of her. In the sparks she saw a black mare, lathered with sweat, tearing along on a narrow road, a red-wheeled wagon jolting along in tow. Walter Shirley clenched the reins. Bertha clung to his elbow, trying to resist being tossed out of her seat. She screamed at Walter to stop, but he had fixed upon a scheme to improve their fortunes and he was determined to show off his new acquisition to his wife, even if it scared her half to death. Fortified by the drinks he had just thrown back at the roadhouse in Bolingbroke, he felt he could outrace anything.

"You wanted me to quit the lumber camp," he yelled to his wife. "Now you can build your own place instead of living in boarding houses."

"Walter Shirley, you're an intoxicated braggart. Why do you have to prove this to me in the middle of the night with this crazy nag?"

Walter whipped the reins smartly on the rump of the mare. She laid back her ears and broke into a gallop, cutting through the strands of fog that raced across the road in front of them. Walter had purchased the powerful animal with a bonus in his wages from his last winter's work. A contract to deliver the Royal Mail was his answer to Bertha's constant pleas to leave the lumber camps and stay with his family.

"This mare can do the mail run from Grand Falls to St. John in twelve hours. There's a pretty penny to be made when I get the big contract!"

Bertha shrieked louder and louder as their pace quickened, begging her husband to stop. Her red curls whipped in the wind, her straw hat barely clung to her head. She sobbed as the road took a turn in the dense fog, onto a narrow bridge crossing the river. Unable to make the sharp curve, the mare skidded as her hooves slipped out from under her. Walter yanked frantically on the reins, but to no avail. The whole rig crashed straight down the embankment into the frigid, fast water. The harness snapped, dislodging the mare from the shanks and the wagon flipped upside down, catapulting Walter and Bertha headfirst across the water. Bertha held out her arms to defend herself as she crashed onto the river rocks. She stayed afloat for only a moment before the current pulled her under.

Walter surfaced midstream, choking and sputtering. Twisting sharply, one way and another, he was unable to find Bertha. Within moments, though, he spotted her limp form moving downriver in the powerful stream. With an immense effort, he managed to grasp her waist and drag her, chilled and now shivering, to the muddy bank. He lay beside her, gasping for air and groaning at the disaster he had brought down upon the two of them.

ANNE STARED AT HER MOTHER lying in the pine casket, dressed in her elegant satin wedding gown. Bertha looked like a wax effigy; this just couldn't be her mother, Anne thought. She found it impossible to comprehend that the person she cherished most was gone forever. She would never gather Anne up into her arms again, or share a thrilling exchange about the latest book they were reading. Anne did not cry; she could not cry. She merely stood obediently, stunned and silent. She wondered if her father would come to tell her it was all a mistake—that Bertha Shirley would be coming through the kitchen door of their new home at any moment, her old smile on her face.

Bertha's kindest and very best friend, Mrs. Louisa Thomas, stood behind Anne. She reached around the girl, removed a small gold locket on a chain from Bertha's cold fingers, and slipped it into Anne's hand.

"Your mother would have wanted you to have this," she whispered tearfully. "It holds her wedding picture. She would have wanted me to look after you." Louisa Thomas was the town doctor's wife. The elegant, pretty young woman was about the same age as Bertha, with three children of her own. It was Louisa who'd sat with Bertha through the brief illness brought on by the icy plunge. And it was Louisa who took Anne to stay in her house following Bertha's death. Louisa looked after all of the funeral arrangements, even down to fitting Anne out in a black mourning dress and black straw hat.

Louisa glanced across the funeral parlour, arranged with lilies and floral wreaths. Her gaze was stern when her eyes rested upon Walter, standing alone in the doorway. She knew that he was afraid to approach the casket and that he had been drinking to dull his pain. The townsfolk who had come to pay their respects to the local schoolteacher stared at him as if he were a murderer. From the moment Bertha had expired in Louisa's arms, everyone in the community blamed Walter. The story of Bertha Shirley's tragic end was passed from one household to the next. It changed and grew until Walter's sheer negligence and recklessness became a deliberate plot to rid himself of his wife. The scandalized talk was more than Walter could bear.

Louisa led Anne to a seat directly in front of the minister's podium, beside the open coffin. The Reverend Jones cleared his throat. The tension was palpable.

"Since Dr. Thomas and his wife Louisa were such dear friends of Bertha's, Walter and I have asked Dr. Thomas to eulogize our beloved schoolteacher."

Dr. Thomas, a hefty, black-haired man in a rumpled suit, stood up somewhat unsteadily and made his way to the minister's side. Louisa immediately flushed red with embarrassment. She had prayed her husband would refrain from having a drink on such a solemn occasion, but apparently he had not. With his high colour and swaying stance, it was clear he was as intoxicated as Walter. Dr. Thomas patted the widower on the back as he passed. Taking over from Reverend Jones, he held onto the lectern for support as he watched Walter inch out of the room.

"Seems Walter is overcome with grief," the doctor hiccupped loudly. "Walter Shirley is not at fault in his wife's death. Walter loved his wife."

Dr. Thomas looked out at the congregation's expectant and scandalized faces and groped for suitable words. "Ah. . . . our school teacher and friend, Bertha, has been stolen from our community in an accident of b-b-biblical proportions," he slurred, avoiding the cold, but tearful gaze of his wife. "But the . . . uh . . . the white majesty of death now falls on this beloved woman and sets her apart as one crowned . . . to live forever in God's heavenly kingdom. . . ."

At the word "crowned," Anne looked up at Louisa in a brief moment of hope. The greatest heroines in the books she had read were all crowned for their nobility! If her mother had gone to a place of dignified immortality it would certainly be an improvement on the story she'd heard people mumbling about. Louisa felt like sinking through the floor, she was so mortified at her husband's inability to deliver a dignified eulogy.

The short service was thankfully over and Bertha's coffin was slid into an ornate black hearse with glass sides, drawn by ebony horses waving dark plumes on their heads. The small crowd followed it to the cemetery where the pine coffin was lowered into a shallow grave as rain began to pour. Anne scanned the faces around her, looking for her father. He was nowhere to be seen. The black-robed minister laid his arm across Anne's shoulders, interrupting her search. "The entire community is sorry for your loss. Be strong, child," he told her as though he knew what advice she needed for the future that awaited her.

Louisa, still mortified at her husband's behaviour, tried to ignore the disapproving frowns and whispers as she led Anne away from the tragic tableau. Mercifully, the rain grew stronger, allowing Louisa to at least shield herself from prying looks with her umbrella.

Confused and frightened, Anne looked up into Louisa's

face. Already, her imagination was hard at work. "If Mama's been crowned, that makes her a queen. So what am I then, Mrs. Thomas?"

"A child of God, sweetheart." Louisa replied tenderly and put her arm around the girl. Anne digested this for a moment. She noticed the people around her were eyeing her up and down with a macabre curiosity.

"Don't you think I'd be much better off from now on, telling people I was the daughter of a queen than to endure the notoriety of such tragedy?"

Louisa stifled a sob, but smiled through her tears. What a remarkable little girl, to grasp at such a view of the world at such a bleak moment. The woman took a deep breath and considered the proper response to such a thoughtful question.

"You're better off speaking the truth, dear. Your mother may have had noble dreams but she died of pneumonia with dignity, bless her soul. No thanks to your father." Louisa hadn't meant to speak ill of Walter, but the words slipped out. She patted Anne's hand. "I hope my husband can find him and bring him back."

WALTER SHIRLEY DID NOT SEE his wife's coffin lowered into her final resting place. He had fled the funeral out of fear and shame, trying desperately to outrun the accusing and angry stares. By the time Dr. Thomas found him, Walter was inebriated in the extreme at the local roadhouse—very near the stone bridge where the fatal tragedy had occurred. It took no persuasion at all for Dr. Thomas to sit down and share a bottle of bourbon. By the time the pair stumbled out onto the tavern verandah a few hours later, they were both awash in liquor. Walter was in the grip of tearful remorse, while Dr. Thomas was trying his drunken best to cheer him up.

"Don't be so hard on yourself, Walt," he pontificated as they stumbled down the tavern steps together. "The Almighty thinks better of each one of us. What's that saying? To err...is human, to forgive is...uh, what is it? Oh yeah...to forgive is divine!"

Walter paid no attention. He was weaving toward the menacing stone bridge like a felon drawn back to the scene of the crime. The extensive gouges cut into the embankment by the wagon wheels, several days prior, were still horribly visible. Behind Dr. Thomas, an assorted group of barflies crowded onto the roadhouse steps to stand and ogle at Walter's public repentance. They were not cheated out of an ounce of drama. When Dr. Thomas tried to grab his shoulder and lead him back to the tavern, Walter aggressively flung him off.

"No, no, Doc!" Walter exploded. "I killed her!" He staggered across the bridge and leaned over as if drawn to the river.

"Whoa, Walter...stop!" yelled Dr. Thomas suddenly realizing his friend's intentions. "Oh no!"

He was too late. Walter had taken a single step forward and plunged straight off the bridge and into the rushing current. Boisterous laughter broke out amid the crowd of men behind Dr. Thomas on the tavern steps.

"Drunken fools," they hooted, enjoying the spectacle immensely.

Wobbling through his alcoholic haze, Dr. Thomas valiantly lurched down the embankment and into the water, too, all the while bellowing for someone to help. Luckily, Walter was too far into his cups to thrust himself out into the main current. Dr. Thomas managed to snatch him by the belt and heave him, coughing and soaked, up onto the muddy shore.

Anne heard this outrageous story from the upstairs bedroom in the Thomas house as she peered through a floor grille into the kitchen below. She was in her nightdress and was supposed to be sleeping with Violetta, Louisa's fourteen-year-old daughter. However, Dr. Thomas woke up his entire family, slamming doors and crashing unsteadily on his way into the house. Louisa remained tight-lipped as she attempted to serve him the dinner that had been waiting so long on the stove. Dr. Thomas immediately poured himself a glass of wine to go along with his meal.

Anne got up from her tear-stained pillow and hovered over the metal grate directly above the kitchen table. The grate, meant to let heat from the kitchen stove come up to the bedroom in the winter, provided a perfect view. Behind her, Violetta rolled over in bed to watch Anne, her face sour.

"You're not listening, Louisa! He went back to the river," Dr. Thomas told his wife, trying to placate her anger after the events of the day. "He wanted to drown his sorrow. Literally!"

"And you pushed him!" Louisa accused her husband, infuriated as she cleared away the remnants of his meal. Dr. Thomas knew he was in deep trouble with his wife but was nonetheless pleased by his own heroics.

"I rescued him. But it was a noble performance for the entire town to see. He's taken off. We may never see the likes of Walter Shirley again."

Taken off? Anne gasped to herself, clinging to every word. What did that mean, "never see the likes of Walter Shirley again?"

Dishes clattered under Louisa's furious hands. "Have you any idea how embarrassing it is for a wife to attend the burial service of her dearest friend while the town's esteemed doctor is off on a bender? The entire town knows what the disgusting pair of you was up to!"

Dr. Thomas waved one hand, the other grasping the kitchen table for support.

"'Twas barely a drop. Walter desperately needed my support to absolve himself in front of the town. That's all it was."

"Walter needed a good kick in the pants," Louisa stammered. "And so do you! Temperance will be practised in this house from now on."

Louisa grabbed the glass of wine her husband was drinking as well as the bottle of whiskey sitting beside it and poured the contents of both down the sink. She began to grab every bottle she could get her hands on from the cupboard, underneath the dry sink, and even the parlour. Every ounce went down the sink. She was unstoppable.

Aghast, Dr. Thomas leaped from his chair and wrestled his wife. He knew that in Louisa's mind, temperance meant that all alcohol was to be forbidden forever on her premises.

"Now, Louisa, no ... no ... you're being ... far too extreme ..."

Louisa only shoved him away and kept on pouring. Her husband's tipsy protests drifted up through the ceiling grille. Anne quickly drew back when Dr. Thomas started shouting for the children to come see what their mother was doing.

"There will be no more liquor here!" Louisa commanded fiercely. "You can survive on water if you need to imbibe anything." The anger between the couple escalated into a full-fledged battle. Violetta, and her two brothers, seven-year-old Jock and nine-year-old Keith, were all eyes and ears as they listened from under their bed covers. Violetta had witnessed this kind of outburst from her father before and had always shrugged it off. This time she looked frightened. She loathed Walter Shirley and was beside herself that she was being forced to share a room with his trashy daughter. Her mother may have had a bleeding heart, but Violetta didn't. She wanted Anne out of their house forever.

Anne could sense Violetta's disgust as she crawled away from the grille. Disturbed by the uproar down in the kitchen, she made her way to the dresser mirror. Whenever any disaster

befell Anne, she would try to fancy that her own refection was
another little girl—a friend she could talk to at any time about
anything, as long as she was near a mirror. She'd adopted the
idea after reading *Alice through the Looking Glass,* and had convinced herself that a completely alternate world existed on the
other side of the mirror; a world in which it was entirely safe to
live. She had even named her looking-glass companion Katie
Maurice. Anne felt certain that by keeping up her conversations
with Katie, she would one day find the means to escape through
the glass, just as Alice had. As Violetta continued to stare at this
peculiar girl she had no use for, Anne felt a desperate need to
talk with someone.

"Katie," she murmured to her dim reflection, "I'm convinced
I must have been a disappointment to my father now that he's
not coming back." She couldn't understand why her father had
left Louisa to do everything. She wondered why he didn't want
to see her.

Taking a breath, Anne resolved to face the future head on.
"Mother told me he was a free spirit. So I made up my mind I
could be a free spirit myself. I have resolved that the Thomases
will be my new family and my life need not be a graveyard of
buried hopes."

Anne stared into the mirror, wishing for Katie to agree. She
opened her mother's locket and gazed at the picture of her parents on their wedding day. Watching from the other side of the
room, Violetta could hardly believe what she was seeing. Her
expression evolved from cynical curiosity to outright alarm.
There were already enough troubles in the Thomas household.
No one needed an orphaned girl who spoke to herself in mirrors.
Violetta swiftly made up her mind: As long as she had anything
to do with it, this homeless interloper would not contribute any
further problems to the mix.

Three

As Anne carried her late-evening tea from the inn's kitchen into the lobby, she caught her reflection in the hotel's grand mirror. She paused for a moment, remembering Katie and how much she'd been able to share with her. How glad she would be to have such a friend now. She was embarrassed that she'd been so upset with Gene, especially over issues that were not his fault. She realized she'd been rude and insolent at the beach earlier that night, but had come to the conclusion that Gene's confrontation with her had been for her own good. She knew her original draft had been misguided. It smacked of artifice and the actors had picked up on that immediately. Writing had always been a form of self-examination for Anne. When she allowed herself to write from the heart, about the dramatic parts of her life or about the world as she knew it, writing was a real panacea. She wondered if her unexpectedly vivid memories and dreams were a sign. Perhaps it was as if a sixth sense had suddenly surfaced in her consciousness.

Creeping across the lobby, Anne realized that all of the actors and most of the hotel guests had long since retired. The place was eerily deserted. A smouldering fire in the grate threw long, delicate shadows that danced like apparitions against the dark basswood walls. Anne found Gene half-asleep in one of the plush wing chairs in front of the stone fireplace. Knowing that sleep would not be possible until she'd set things right,

Anne sat down beside him. She debated waking him, but decided he probably knew she was there. "Gene?" she whispered, putting her cup of tea on the table.

Gene didn't move but his eye lids flickered.

"I don't want you to feel pressure to produce my play."

Gene sat still and refused to open his eyes. "Good," he murmured, "I feel pressure to make money this summer."

Anne fell silent for a while, genuinely tied in knots over her decision to explore another avenue to develop her play. One thing she knew for sure: She could not stay on at the hotel. She needed to be at home.

"What would you think if I went to Green Gables to write?" she asked hesitatingly. This drew a smile from Gene. He flipped the magazine lying on his lap onto the side table, beside his drink, and opened his eyes.

"It would do us both a world of good."

The pair fell into companionable silence. Gene fell asleep in the warmth of the fire. Anne stared into the sinking flames and glowing embers, wondering if some force was at work, drawing her back to a place in her subconscious she had avoided for many years.

THE NEXT MORNING FOUND John and Elsie Wright loading boxes in the upstairs bedrooms at Green Gables. Elsie gathered up everything from the room her parents had occupied; a room that had once belonged to Marilla Cuthbert. Moving all of the Wright chattels had proven to be an almost insurmountable job. Over the past week the siblings had already made several trips back and forth to cousins and other family members in John's truck, loaded down with personal treasures. Clearing their parents' bedroom was the last item on their list and they had only a few more boxes to load onto the truck parked at the gate. As Elsie packed away every sentimental little detail, she tried to resist growing nostalgic over too many items. She was overcome with gloom though, on finding a photo of her mother and father along with herself and John as little children.

"Look how young Mother and Dad were when we first came here," sighed Elsie, who had her mother's raven hair and flawless colouring. "I'm furious that they let this place get so run down! No wonder Auntie Anne feels she has to put it up for sale."

"Come on, Elsie!" John urged impatiently. "Don't preach to me. I promised Anne we'd be ready by ten. You know what a pistol she is. The fact that Anne's own kids have never taken any interest in the place is just plain weird, if you ask me."

"How can you be so callous? Green Gables was a wonderful place to grow up in. Besides, it's always been much too far away for any of the Blythes to even visit."

Distracted by the pile of photos she'd been organizing, and trying to put everything away quickly at her brother's temperamental prodding, Elsie knocked over an entire jar of pennies. The coins flew in every direction and Elsie watched as most of them rolled through the door of the open closet she'd just cleared out. Sighing at the thought of cleaning up one more mess, Elsie noticed that several pennies had fallen between the floorboards. As she got down on her knees to put them back in the jar, she had a vague memory of herself as a little girl, assiduously saving them up from sundry sources. Her mother must have put that old jar in her room, out of the way.

"You can't clean out thirty years of living in an old place like this in a couple of days," she said in exasperation as she fished for the coins between the boards of the old pine floor. She pushed one finger into a knothole on the edge of a board. Suddenly, the board popped up under her hand and the board beside it slipped sideways, revealing a cubby hole between the joists. Elsie peered into the dark space in the floor. Dusty papers tied with twine lay on top of the struts and old plaster at the bottom of the gloomy cavity. Elsie reached in dubiously. She drew out a yellowed bundle of letters in Marilla Cuthbert's handwriting, all addressed to a certain John Blythe, Esq. Elsie flipped through the correspondence, mesmerized at the thought of such intriguing personal artifacts hidden under the floorboards for so long, undisturbed.

NOT FAR AWAY, Anne was walking through the familiar Avonlea farm fields, searching across the hills for her first glimpse of the house that had been her childhood refuge. All at once, it simply appeared, nestled in its usual hollow and surrounded by a lush, fertile acreage bordered with spruce trees. The woods nearby were alive with the songs of chickadees, blackbirds, jays and all the other woodland musicians Anne knew so well. Everything looked so serene. The cherry and apple orchards still stood graciously on either side of the field just next to the house. Lombardy poplars guarded the edge of the orchards where the big field ran down to the brook. The poplars gave way to a grove of weeping birches, which grew together, dipping their branches into the dancing water. The old homestead retained an air of enchantment that was as potent as the day Anne had first caught sight of the property, arriving in a horse and buggy with Matthew. Anne smiled. A veritable cascade of memories flooded her mind. It felt as if an entire lifetime had passed since she'd last walked the path across the field. She paused to stand on the last hill, looking tall and slim in her smart brown trousers. Her heart leaped inside her now that she was finally close to the house. She started down the hill walking swiftly, but, unable to contain her eagerness, she soon began to run through the tall grass with unbridled exhilaration.

At first, she only had eyes for the white frame house with its wide verandah where she had whiled away so many happy summer afternoons. It still looked inviting with its curved fretwork adding a note of fancy to the rather plain design of the original building. As Anne rounded the picket fence that wrapped the yard, she was startled to see the building was really quite tired and worn. It was no longer the scrupulously well-preserved farm with gorgeous gardens and vegetable beds that had belonged to Marilla and Matthew. The house was more severely weather-beaten, with shutters falling off and window screens disintegrating. The front yard was churned up and full of weeds. Young apple trees from the orchard had sprung up in the garden that used to be Marilla's pride. Rampant greenery was thrusting itself into all the places that used to be swept clear of a single twig or stick. Hammered into the middle of all this was a big For Sale sign announcing to the world that Green Gables wasn't wanted any more. New owners, please apply. Suddenly, Anne felt responsible for every errant weed and dangling shutter.

She glanced away from the sign and tried to put aside the myriad complicated emotions that welled up inside her. There was a truck parked outside, piled high with boxes, suitcases, and furniture. Diana's family was indeed clearing the place out, just as she had requested.

There was even more chaos inside. Anne stepped into a vestibule filled with so many boxes she could barely find the main stairs. The beautiful, meticulously kept wallpaper from Marilla's day was yellow and water-stained. What a vast amount of repair and restoration would be required for whoever was prepared to undertake the project.

"Hello! Elsie . . . John," she called out. There was no immediate reply. "It's me Anne. . . ."

"Auntie Anne! Come on up!" John shouted anxiously from
Marilla's room. Anne bounded up the stairs and entered the familiar bedroom to the left, where she found Elsie and John surrounded by the confusion of packing. Instead of placing items
into boxes, however, Elsie emerged from the closet dumb-
founded, holding several packets of letters.

"What mischief are the two of you up to in Marilla's old
room?" Anne asked the guilty-looking pair as she stepped over
boxes. John, who had his father's sturdy figure, threw his arms
around Anne. "Terrific to see you, Auntie Anne!" he said as
hugged her tenderly.

The letters in Elsie's hand drew Anne's immediate scrutiny.
"I see your mother's finally written, has she?" she smiled. "I was
beginning to wonder if she'd lost every letter I'd sent her in the
last couple of months."

"I know, Mother's been terrible at responding to everybody," Elsie laughed as Anne hugged and kissed her too. "She's
taken up golf!"

There was a slightly awkward silence after the embrace.
Elsie looked painfully embarrassed as she slowly held out the
letters.

"Um, we were just finishing packing, or so we thought,
when we found these letters in the closet, under the floorboards. Can you imagine? They appear to have been hidden
there for ages. No one in our family ever knew about them."

Anne accepted the old missives with a look of wonderment.
They were dry and yellowed, but the handwriting still stood
out, sharp and clear. It took a moment for Anne to register Marilla's handwriting and to recognize exactly what they were.
"Why . . . these are old love letters between Marilla . . . and John

Blythe." A wistful gentleness passed across her face.

"They quarreled, you know, once upon a time, when they were young and courting. Marilla always wished she'd forgiven him . . . while she still had the chance. He met Gilbert's mother and that was the end of it for Marilla." Anne shook her head. "What a great, well-kept secret! Imagine this! I just can't believe it."

Anne well knew the story of Marilla's youthful courtship with John Blythe. When Marilla realized just how stubbornly Anne was refusing to admit her real feelings for Gilbert Blythe, John's son, she had spoken to her adopted daughter of her own romantic mistakes. The old woman had wanted Anne to understand the devastating consequences of being too obstinate. Fortunately, it was a lesson Anne had been willing to learn.

Flipping through the formal but adoring correspondence between her father-in-law and Marilla, Anne mused on the romance that might have been. She felt a terrible lump in her throat over the turn Marilla's life had taken, and an intense gratitude for the happiness Marilla had made certain of for her.

"Who is Walter Shirley? Elsie interrupted her thoughts. She was holding out another letter, this one in a different-looking handwriting. "And how did Marilla know your family if your parents died when you were born?"

Anne felt as if the entire second floor had just dropped out from under her. The blood rushed from her face and she immediately sat down. Her pulse was racing as she tried to catch her breath. Elsie passed her the ancient envelope, but Anne hesitated as if this one might scorch her soul. She could see full well that the letter was addressed to her! She blinked and then read the address again, wondering if she had seen it correctly: "Anne Shirley, kindness of Miss Nellie Parkhurst, Green Gables Farm, R.R.#3 Bright River, P.E.I."

Very slowly, Anne turned it over and stared at the return address: "Walter Shirley, Old Fort Lane, Fredericton, New Brunswick."

Elsie and John studied Anne's ever-changing expression as she struggled to open the flap and extract the single sheet of velum. The letter seemed to be caught in the haste of an incompletely opened envelope. Anne stopped herself and, without a word, quietly passed the envelope over to Elsie, who quickly obliged and successfully unfolded the paper.

"My dearest daughter," Elsie read aloud. She glanced at Anne, but her aunt seemed unable to look up. "Please accept this note as confirmation that I have come into much better circumstances in my life." Walter Shirley's voice gradually filled Anne's mind as Elsie proceeded. Surprisingly, Anne could now remember the exact timbre of it. "And so I feel it is my duty to try to contact you. I finally had the good luck to marry that wonderful woman." Anne shuddered at the thought of her father marrying another woman. "I have a prosperous hardware business in Fredericton now. It is my sincere hope that you can forgive me for the expanse of time that has elapsed between us and come back to me."

Elsie stole another look at Anne, who now seemed to be completely petrified. In her mind's eye, Anne was picturing a figure, sitting at a table by the light of a hurricane lamp, writing slowly with his one good hand.

"I realize you are likely in much better circumstances," Elsie resumed, "than we could ever provide, and I have entrusted our mutual acquaintance, Miss Nellie Parkhurst, to make contact with you again, and to determine if my approach is acceptable to you and your guardians. For so many years, your mother wanted me to quit the logging camp and build a home for us. Maybe now I can fulfill my promise. If you cannot forgive me for the harm that has come to you as a result of my neglect, I will respect your wishes. Any response would be welcome. Your loving father, Walter."

Tears filled Anne's eyes as she listened to the words of a man she'd thought was gone from her life forever. A ghost might as well have materialized at her elbow and spoken aloud! Inside, her heart was crushed; outside, she was unable to stop herself from shaking. Trying to get hold of her emotions, she got down on her hands and knees to peep into the hole under the floorboards, as if the space might reveal something more. Anne could clearly imagine Nellie Parkhurst—a woman she hadn't thought of for more than forty years—climbing down from her wagon in front of Green Gables and handing the letter to Marilla. Tough and tanned as old horse hide, Nellie would have stood by the picket fence, explaining as personally as she could the circumstances that had preceded the writing of the letter. Marilla's stern face would have betrayed very little to Nellie, but she would have most certainly panicked. After all, she and her brother had come to love the child, and the letter might have had the power to tear the orphan away from Green Gables. She might have admonished old Nellie then gone straight to her bedroom without a word even to Matthew. Marilla had attempted to seal the secret for all time, but not destroy it for some reason.

"Marilla must have felt she needed to protect me or been frightened I might leave ..."

"Protect you from what?" Elsie asked, curious about such a complicated annotation from her aunt's past.

Anne straightened and put her hands to her face, still barely able to speak.

"With Marilla, that would have been an instinct."

Anne sat down on a pile of luggage and tried to remain composed. So many thoughts rushed through her mind. She looked up at Elsie and John, who were watching her with concern and fascination. Apparently, some of the things they had always taken for granted about their mother's dearest friend weren't necessarily what they had understood.

"So you weren't an orphan?" John asked.

Anne gave a tiny shrug.

"As a child, I made up stories about my parents. No one knew a thing about me so it was easy."

For a split second, Anne thought of her days with Mrs. Hammond, with whom Nellie had simply left her: The days of back-breaking work looking after the horde of Hammond children. A place where no one cared how tired or crestfallen Anne was so long as she could fuel the stove or keep Mrs. Hammond's twins out of her hair. It was an awful existence, and but one of numerous unbearable places the child had endured along the way to Green Gables—all the result of Walter Shirley's disappearance.

Anne snapped back to the present, acutely aware that Elsie and John had not moved a muscle. She wiped her eyes, somehow knowing she needed to divulge a little more.

"You see, I'd given up hope of ever finding my father." At this confession Anne lost her composure and broke down. Elsie slipped a sympathetic arm around her, a gesture that allowed Anne to pull herself together quickly enough to change the subject. She simply could not talk anymore about that painful time before Green Gables.

"Come on," Anne urged, turning her attention back to the boxes all over the room. "Let me help. What luck finding all Marilla's letters! What luck!"

Jumping up, Anne helped John with the luggage. Elsie folded the letter, which Anne seemed to want to leave alone, and set it on the bureau.

"Do you mind if we tell mother?" John asked. "She used to say with your imagination you always longed to become a great writer."

Anne remembered only too well the many elaborate fabrications she had been capable of as a child. She broke into a crooked smile, still trying to conquer her emotions. "Yes, I longed to write once," Anne confessed as she followed Elsie and John out of Marilla's room, all three laden with boxes. "Now I do it just to work everything else out."

"You never can tell why certain people decide to write. It's obviously very personal," said Elsie, who had always been in awe of Anne's chosen profession. As they tramped down the creaking old stairs of the farmhouse, Anne laughed.

"Yes, well, I suppose some people like me are 'born to trouble' . . . and others, like your mother, are blessed with the desire to play golf."

Outside, John loaded the last of the Wright's belongings into his truck while Elsie looked back wistfully at the now-silent white house with its green roof and deep green trim. She took Anne's arm as they sauntered a little way along the picket fence that cried out for a whitewash. Gratitude welled up in Elsie's heart as she thought of how important the old place had been to her childhood.

"Thank you, Anne, from our entire family. Mother says she'll call once she knows it's been sold. Truth be told, she hasn't written again because she couldn't bear to discuss it. We had so many wonderful years growing up here. Why did you ever give it to us?"

Anne tilted back her head to catch a wisp of sea air—another reminder that she was home. She handed the final suitcase to John.

"Well, Gil's medical practice wasn't in this area and your mother and dad were down on their luck after we came back from the Great War . . ."

Anne's words trailed off as she shrugged shoulders.

"Don't sell it, Anne." Elsie burst out suddenly, tears in her eyes. John glanced back from behind the wheel.

Anne saw the For Sale sign sitting baldly on the lawn, offering the house to any stranger with enough money to buy it. She sighed.

"Well . . . I have complicated feelings about the place."

"Mother always said you get to a certain point in life when you can't just bury the past."

Anne hugged Elsie then looked at her squarely and smiled. "I remember someone saying to me, long ago when I was very little, that as life marches on one can't imagine how difficult it is to draw a line between the past and the present. I can honestly say I have only just started to understand the meaning of that ancient testimonial."

The truck engine started, signalling that John was ready to leave. Anne helped Elsie into the cab, kissed John goodbye and waved them off. Once they had disappeared down the lane, she turned to look at the house, alone with so many phantoms from her past. Memories of Matthew and Marilla, of her parents, and of her beloved Gil all swirled around her as she stood on the Green Gables lawn. Even the building itself seemed dead; and upstairs lay that enigmatic letter. Anne decided she needed to close up the cavity that had innocently housed that message for so long. If she was going to remain in the house as long as it took her to sell it, she would use the rest of the summer profitably and begin to write again.

Four

losing up a hole in a closet floor could not seal up the past. Anne sat in Marilla's old room remembering the time after her mother's death and wondering how she had ever survived it.

As a young girl, Anne had been entirely unaware of Louisa Thomas's many problems. She simply knew Dr. Thomas was in a great deal of trouble with the town and she began to surmise that he too would affect her predicament. She was right. Not long after her father's disappearance, Anne found herself in a carriage with Louisa, rumbling down a peculiar, out-of-the-way road. Anne pictured herself as being like a prisoner en route to execution. She clutched Louisa's hand as the woman tried to explain that, with three children of her own to care for and money being so scarce, the now-struggling Thomas family could not afford to take her in.

Louisa tried hard to remain calm as she revealed Anne's prospects. The anxious child sitting beside her still wore her funeral black, but her hair was tied tightly in two red braids, incongruous with the mourning attire. Her few possessions had been packed up in the small brown suitcase at her feet.

"The cash from selling your mother's things was given to the town," Louisa explained to Anne. "They'll pay your board here for a time. We're leaving. Sadly, my husband has lost his license to practice medicine in Bolingbroke."

Louisa could barely continue, thinking of the disgrace her husband's drinking had brought upon the family. It had done no good to pour all the liquor in the house down the sink on the night of Bertha's funeral. Dr. Thomas was now openly accused by the townsfolk of an egregious crime. Anne begged Louisa with every particle of her being to allow her stay. "Can't you keep me until my father comes?" she whispered.

Louisa drew in a tattered breath. "You need to know … that your father is gone for good."

Anne struggled to grasp this new piece of information. Her father had always been an erratic figure, showing up for a time before disappearing to faraway lumber camps to find work. "I heard your husband say he drowned in his sorrow. But he isn't really dead, is he?"

Looking down at her knees, Louisa did not even bother to suppress her own anger. "In some respects, he is. Things haven't worked out well for either of us, Anne."

Anne felt her one and only refuge slipping away. Her father was not coming back. Louisa turned away from the desperate, mute appeal in Anne's face as the black carriage rounded a bend along the misty road and stopped at a set of tall, rusty gates. The sign on the stone pillar announced the Bolingbroke County Poorhouse. Beyond it loomed a large, grim building of grey stone with a row of small barred windows. The carriage crunched to a halt on the gravel. As far as Anne was concerned, she might as well have been led to a guillotine.

Louisa stepped out of the carriage first and helped Anne down. Evidently, they had been expected. A substantial middle-aged woman with an air of importance about her hurried down the terrace steps to meet them. She didn't waste a second. Louisa had hardly bent down to give Anne a parting kiss when the woman—the superintendent, it turned out—seized the girl with one arm and hustled her out of Louisa's embrace.

"No need for theatrics, Louisa," she said with scorn, "You've done your duty. God help you keep that sorry husband of yours sober in the next town."

News of Dr. Thomas's downfall, alongside Walter Shirley's dastardly acts, had spread far and wide, creating a deep ripple of scandal. Louisa flushed with shame, but dared not answer back. The last glimpse Anne had of her mother's best friend came as she stepped back into the carriage, a miserable look clouding her face. The superintendent bundled Anne unceremoniously up the walk so fast the little girl clutched her suitcase and stumbled as she tried to keep up.

"Your life is cursed, girl!" muttered the superintendent as she shoved open the front door. "Thank your stars the county just found the room."

Provisions for the destitute were always a problem in Anne's rural hometown. The county authorities had no idea how to accommodate a recently orphaned child at short notice. Often in such closely knit communities, children who had lost their parents were simply absorbed by other families, who always had room in heart and hearth for another youngster. But no one in the Bolingbroke community had been willing to take Anne Shirley under wing.

As Anne heard the iron door of the poorhouse slam behind her, it was the sound of doom. She knew this eerie place was where old people were sent. It was a home for people whose families had given up on them or where vagrants and madmen were taken in order that the county would continue to be a safe place to live. She had heard many rumours about the horrors that lurked inside the establishment. She prayed she would be spared some of them, and that the money from the sale of her mother's things would afford her a room of her own.

The superintendent did not let go of Anne's arm as they marched up a long, dark staircase though more heavy doors and into a sparsely furnished office where another woman, known simply as the matron, awaited them. She was asked by the superintendent to sign a raft of necessary papers, indicating that the poorhouse would undertake full responsibility for the child. The matron, Anne would learn, was the wife of the overseer. She was a gaunt, hard-eyed woman with no hint of compassion in her face. Her grey hair was pulled back into a mercilessly tight bun and she kept a large shawl pulled around her shoulders as an antidote to the perpetual chill of the thick stone walls—a chill Anne already felt.

The last thing the matron wanted was homeless children foisted upon her, and she eyed Anne with annoyance. "A child like this would be much better placed in an orphanage or a foster home."

The superintendent donned her hat and cape in readiness to leave. With a single swift motion, she signed the document committing Anne to the care of the poorhouse. She tossed the pen down emphatically on the table.

"No family will take her after that sorry business with the father," she said with finality. "As a member of the board I can say with impunity that since the Doc Thomases are being asked to leave, the county has a sole responsibility. You have to take her."

Listening to her opponent's sharp tongue, the matron realized she had no leg to stand on in the matter and bowed to authority. She shrugged and signed the document hastily, also throwing down the pen when she was done.

"We'll do what we can," she promised, her voice totally devoid of optimism.

The superintendent gave Anne a single glance, which might

have contained pity had Anne been able to read it. She hurried out the door, leaving the little girl to the rough mercy of the matron and her husband.

Anne realized that the scandal of her mother's death had turned her own fate into a complete reversal of fortune. She followed the irritated matron, who kept jerking her head back at Anne with instructions while she led her into the stone asylum where the inmates actually lived. Clutching her suitcase, Anne glued herself to her guide as they entered a clammy, candlelit corridor echoing with moans and mutterings. Anne was stunned to witness male and female inmates in rags, begging for attention or picking lice from one another's hair. Some shook with the tremors of delirium.

"We don't usually take children at all," groused the matron resentfully. "We're always full up. A little beggar like you should thank the Lord the board took pity on you at all."

Stepping across filthy stone floors covered with straw and waste, Anne wondered if animals in a barn were better cared for. They passed women huddled together on benches and others who drifted aimlessly, either eerily silent or talking to themselves. To Anne, they all appeared old, defeated, and perhaps even deranged. Clearly, the poorhouse was a place of last resort for the abandoned, the incurable, and the insane.

All at once, an ancient figure rose up in front of them, clanging a tin cup on the iron bars of his cell-like hovel at the bottom of the stairs.

"Water! I need water," he wailed in a despondent cry. "Give me water or I shall die!"

A pair of watery blue eyes and a nose that might have belonged to an impoverished nobleman were all that were visible through the man's long grey beard and shaggy strands of matted hair. He looked so old and arthritic—begging to have his thirst

assuaged and barely able to stand—that Anne's heart went out
to him immediately.

"Stop it!" the matron commanded, completely losing her
composure. As the ancient fellow continued banging, she
picked up a rusty cup out of a bucket lying on the floor and
violently threw its contents into the old man's face, making him
gasp and cringe away from the bars.

"Some of them here need to be kept in check at all times."
Her voice was proud and filled with harsh satisfaction at being
able to quiet such a madman. Anne managed a glimpse over
her shoulder as the old man's dripping face came to the bars
again. He stared after her as she disappeared up the stairs into
a kind of ward where the women slept. The large room was
furnished with low wooden bedsteads pushed up against the
rough stone walls. Some of the women sat up, plucking at each
other's hair or staring out the high, unreachable windows. Each
wore a bleached cotton garment like a nightgown with a cap
on her head. As twilight had already descended, many of the
beds were crammed full of several women, trying to catch what
slumber they could amid the noise and mayhem. The matron
stopped beside a large bed that seemed completely occupied by
several snoring women.

"You can sleep with these three."

Anne looked at the bodies jammed into the bed.

"To share such cramped quarters is greater than even my
imagination can abide ma'am," she said, trying to be as polite
as she could. "I understood a room was paid for on my behalf
by the town itself."

The matron glared at Anne as though the bedpost had
opened its mouth. She scoffed. That money had already disappeared into places the overseer and his wife would never need
to explain to a soul.

"We don't harbour royalty here, miss. We are too stuffed as it is. Least these old girls don't have fleas! You either put up or shut up. It's all the same."

The matron shoved a coarse uniform and an even coarser nightgown into Anne's hands.

"Put this uniform on at sunrise when you get up," she tersely instructed as she stabbed a finger at Anne's suitcase. "You won't need whatever's in there. You'll be assigned chores first thing. Move over girls and make room for this little brat."

The matron gave the nearest occupant a whack on her rump, which only made the woman glare more alarmingly at Anne. The matron turned abruptly then stopped herself and threw a cold, disapproving glance at the child standing so forlornly beside the bed.

"By the way, I know all about Walter Shirley. This is the price of atonement for the sins of the father, eh? You understand that, girl?"

"Yes, ma'am," Anne nodded timidly, though she only understood that she was somehow being made to suffer for what these people thought her father had done.

The matron left Anne in the bleak room full of coughs and menacing mumblings. Anne did not even dare to put the nightgown on. She timidly tapped the shoulder of the angry woman on the edge of the bed. "Could you move over, please?"

A pair of cold eyes glared at her from under a tangle of hair. The woman snarled and pushed her away aggressively. Anne waited until the angry woman closed her eyes again then carefully tried to lie down on the few inches of straw mattress protruding from under the woman's elbow. This time, she was shoved violently to the floor. Not daring to try again, Anne put her head down on her suitcase and curled up, shivering from cold and apprehension. She had no idea what would possibly become of her.

The chill from the floor seeped into her tiny frame and the hard stones stiffened her hips as the night wore on. Staring out the casement window at the building opposite the ward, she spied a chandelier-lit room. The matron and her husband were greeting guests and dining convivially. In a warm room with plenty to eat, the merrymakers seemed completely unaware of the suffering barely a stone's throw away.

AFTER A LONG, uncomfortable night, Anne was keen to be fed. She got up quietly and put on her scratchy uniform. It consisted of a plain dress with an even plainer pinafore to protect it. Breakfast amounted to a sparse meal of rough porridge laden with grease. Afterward, she was taken outside and assigned to work with the older women who picked oakum. She soon discovered that this was a miserable task. It involved pulling apart lengths of worn out hemp rope into individual fibres that would be sold for use as ships' caulking. Only the forced labour of poorhouse inmates and jailed convicts made it economically viable, as oakum sold cheaply by the pound. The stiff, prickly strands, sometimes thick with old tar, soon made Anne's tender hands coarse with blisters.

The older inmates worked alongside the younger ones who ground corn or took wheelbarrows to the field to spread the mixture as fertilizer. The work was demanding. Hour after hour, it went on, with punishment from the harsh staff if any of the inmates slowed down at all. They all had to earn their keep. Even though Anne was half the size of the adults, she was expected to work just as hard.

One day, her supervisor watched as Anne wrestled with a corn grinder, grinding the hard kernels of corncobs too old to be good for any other purpose. Her lack of success eventually led the supervisor to assign her to push wheelbarrows. Though they did not dare talk to her, many of the inmates looked at her wistfully as she went about her work, as though remembering children of their own. Whenever she could grab a spare moment, Anne gazed up at the swallows that were free to fly away from this horrible place. She noticed them nesting in the apple tree by the little graveyard with the picket fence and she wondered how long people actually lasted in such a miserable poorhouse.

The last thing Anne wanted was to give up, but as days passed, a sense of dread began to fill her heart. She was frightened that something awful would happen to her, something that would defeat her completely. She prayed and prayed. In the end, though, when no answer came, she decided that God had forgotten everyone in that place, including her.

Five

Something awful did happen—something that once again changed Anne's life completely. Looking back on that dark period from the vantage point of an adult, Anne began to see that a pattern of extraordinary events had moulded her character. Often these experiences also fostered her desire to escape to imaginary worlds. In the end, she refused to lose hope, because she was determined to believe her life was enchanted.

Week after weary week surpassed the next at the poorhouse, until autumn was gone and winter set in. Icy winds and deep snow kept the inmates inside, though the endless oakum picking did not abate. In the dining hall, they jostled to get a seat close to the great fireplace in hopes of warming their tired bones. The main stone over the fireplace of the vast dining hall was inscribed with the words "God is Love," a statement at which neither the overseer nor the matron ever glanced. Preaching to the inmates about a wrathful deity, who punished out of fear, was much better suited to their insidious purpose.

One evening, snow fell thickly outside, muffling the yard and fields in a white blanket. The wind rattled the windows, eager to get in, and breathe its icy breath down those necks not cold enough already. Anne was sitting with her three bedmates on one of the long benches pulled up to a plank table close to the fire. They were waiting to be served their supper of stale bread and thin stew. Frost covered the windowpanes with a frigid tracery that Anne tried to admire, even in her eagerness to rummage for food to eat.

On the whole, Anne was doing her best not to be noticed. She had learned long ago not to pay attention to the petty fights that erupted over food among the more distraught inmates. Her bedmates qualified in that category. Anne's main concern was being able to eat quickly before one or the other tried to snatch her ration away.

Mary, who had pushed Anne to the floor that very first night, was sniggering oddly to herself. Anne had tried to be kind and friendly to the women but their minds functioned so erratically that they often forgot she was even there. Suddenly and quite unexpectedly Mary pulled out Anne's small suitcase, which Anne often kept under her chair at mealtime, and snapped it open. The girl always tried as best she could to conceal the suitcase full of books and mementoes far under the bed when no one was watching, hoping her companions were too unbalanced to notice. Mary caught Anne slipping a book out very late one night, though, and had got it in her feeble mind that the suitcase must be full of treats.

Anne had not even noticed Mary sliding the case from under her seat until it was actually on the table, wide open in front of everyone. Mary began pulling out Anne's clothes and schoolbooks, rifling through her personal items with delight. In seconds, the other women at the tables were grabbing Anne's good clothes and books, and tossing them around the table.

"Stop it!" Anne shrieked, completely appalled. "Those are mine. Leave them alone!"

She might as well have shouted at a whirlwind. Squabbles had broken out all around her as a number of inmates now fought over every last content of the case. Anne's childish efforts

to retrieve her precious belongings were kept at bay by cal-
loused hands and sharp elbows.

"That's pretty!" crowed one, pulling at the nightgown
Anne's mother had made for her.

"Why does she get to keep all this?" accused another across
the table, wrenching Anne's beloved history book from the inmate beside her.

The shrieking and fighting quickly erupted into bedlam that
spread like a wave from table to table. Before long, the overseer
stormed into the hall, followed by his wife and several custodians.

"Silence!" he bellowed with an ear-splitting crack of his
cane on the oak table. The wooden stick nearly sliced the fingers from one inmate's hand as it came down. At once, the
crowd dropped Anne's effects, fear now added to the usual
sullen expressions. Only Anne continued to move, her beacon
of red hair loose and disheveled as she struggled to collect her
precious books. Before she could reclaim anything, however,
the matron and her cohorts had seized every item. Anne looked
up at the overseer, knowing he was more than capable of using
his cane on any one of them.

This stern disciplinarian was a man in his middle years, well
fed and wearing a long, flowing cotton coat that gave him a
somewhat imperial appearance. Now he strode up and down
between the tables. The inmates stared down as he passed, hoping not to be caught by his reproachful gaze.

"God in his wisdom has chosen to make you paupers, not
animals, but dependent on the charity of others, nonetheless,"
he moralized to the room, cane at hand. "And God in his wisdom has chosen us to help you find spirituality with your lot in
life. Harmony is to be maintained here at any cost."

No doubt, over his comfortable stomach, he was about to
point out the spiritual benefits of gruel, but Anne interrupted

his lecture. She stood up with a shriek. The matron was tossing her books, one after the other, into the blazing fire!

"Those are my only possessions," she pleaded. "Please don't!"

The heartless woman merely pitched another book into the hearth's the fiery maw. Without considering the consequences, Anne hurled herself across the table and tried to physically wrest the books from the matron's grip. The overseer pounced on Anne.

"Enough! Come here, *you!*"

He quickly surmised that this red-headed mutineer was the source of all the disorder. The matron pushed Anne roughly in front of her husband. He scrutinized her up and down then stood her on a chair for all to gawk at. He shook his cane at her, gloating at the prospect of being able to intimidate such an easy scapegoat.

"See this young brat?" he shouted at the crowd. "Her father is a criminal who is accused of doing in his own wife. Keep away from her. Be wary of her flowery manner of speech, which she uses to deceive everyone."

Anne's fanciful way of speaking and use of big words had done nothing but fill the overseer and his staff with suspicion. His wife resumed tossing Anne's library into the fire. She waved a notebook in the air at the mob. Educating the poor only made them all the more difficult to subdue. "God knows what illicit writings such schoolbooks contain. They are well condemned to the flames!"

"No," Anne protested, frantic at such a travesty. "That's not true!"

The overseer jerked Anne's head around by the chin. His eyes narrowed.

"See? Innocent as a dove, cunning as a serpent. Only stiff punishment can save this kind."

Followed by his wife, the overseer marched Anne across the room. Every inmate stared at her as she was dragged through the hall, eyes wild and red hair tumbling about her shoulders.

"God chose to put a child in our midst to test our skill at recognizing the difference between good and evil," the overseer added. "We will punish her. No resident gets away with this kind of behaviour here."

The overseer called these last words over his shoulder to the enthralled crowd as he thrust Anne out into the drafty corridor at the end of the dining hall.

"You will remain standing until daybreak." His voice echoed in the darkness. The matron forced Anne up onto a round wooden stool in that solitary hall.

"God punishes the disobedient," the matron spit at her before she turned to follow her husband back to the dining hall, "with eternal damnation."

LEFT TO HERSELF, Anne was full of dismay and too overcome with outrage at the loss of her books to allow the cold to have any immediate influence. As time crawled past, she balanced herself on the stool until her whole body ached and her knees begged to buckle. She gave way to a storm of tears. Then recognizing that such a display of emotion was futile, she stopped crying and put her energy into creating an imaginary world.

Anne's ability to escape the turmoil of the institution through her imagination had grown stronger since Louisa Thomas had dropped her off. It was the only means by which she could sustain herself. She had survived the days of pushing wheelbarrows full of ground corn by imagining she was a nun conveying fragrant, crusty loaves of bread to sorry prisoners locked in a cheerless prison with no one to feed them but the holy sisters of an ancient convent. She picked oakum for hours, imagining she was separating threads of gold for the Lady of Shalott to weave into splendid tapestries depicting a party of festooned lords and ladies beside King Arthur, in armour that shimmered in the sun.

Now, standing on the stool in the cold, damp hallway, it took Anne no time at all to conjure up a most wonderfully pathetic scenario. She lifted her pinafore over head and transformed it into a gauzy bridal veil that floated around her, blowing in the draft. Folding her hands, she closed her eyes and began to play out the story, scene by scene, taking care to wring out every drop of delectable melancholy.

Anne had just managed to transport herself away from her misery when a dire kind of groaning drew her back to reality. Opening her eyes, she listened fearfully. The sound came again. It was truly worthy of a dungeon, though Anne knew it had to be one of the inmates. The groan carried such unimaginable loneliness that Anne could not help but respond. Knowing that the overseer and his wife would be fast asleep by then, she climbed down from the stool, slipped her apron on properly and set out to investigate.

The noise was coming from behind the bolted door at the foot of the stairs, near the end of the corridor. Slowly, Anne approached and stretched out her neck to peer in. Through the iron bars, she glimpsed the same peculiar old man who had clanged his cup for water on the bars of his cell the miserable day Anne had arrived. Now he was rocking and keening, as though there were no end to his troubles.

An awful thought occurred to Anne: Perhaps no one had given him water for days! It would be just like the overseer to deny the man enough to drink as yet another form of punishment for some fancied wrong. The poor soul could have been driven quite mad from thirst, she surmised. Anne dared to step closer.

"I gather no one is supposed to speak to you," Anne ventured, "but the temptation is just too irresistible. Want some water?"

A shaggy head slowly rose up out of the dimness to stare at Anne's sweet young face. The man stopped moaning and nodded. Finding a water bucket nearby, Anne broke through the thin ice with a tin cup lying on the floor nearby. The wind echoed as it battered against the stone wall outside the old man's cell. "You've been here an eternity, haven't you?" Anne commented as she handed him the full cup. With his long white hair and beard, and his gaunt face, the man looked to her like the very sort of prisoner who would have been chained in a dank, dismal chamber for a hundred years.

He nodded gently in response, sipping the chilled water. Perhaps he couldn't talk, Anne thought. His watery, blue eyes looked bright and intelligent, however, and not at all insane.

"I've been standing in the dark trying to imagine I was a bride in a misty veil waiting an eternity for her betrothed, who has left her at the altar," Anne revealed wistfully. "This is a far worse place than even I could imagine, so it was a task to pretend. But a white dress would be my true ideal of earthly bliss. Do you have any earthly ideals?"

The man's gaze met Anne's then dropped sadly. He nodded, and then, upon reflection, decided to speak. "I did once ... once upon a time," he spoke in a broken voice.

Now that Anne realized he could understand her, she apologized for monopolizing the conversation. "I'm sorry for rambling on so ... it's just that I was feeling lonely and ..."

"Oh no!" The man shuffled a little closer, regarding Anne. "Nobody talks to me here at all. Do go on."

It was the first time Anne had encountered anyone in the Bolingbroke County Poorhouse who was actually interested in her. Her kind, romantic heart expanded instantly to make room for this lost and decrepit old soul.

"Well, when I saw how tyrannical the matron was to you that first day, I felt instinctively you must be the product of a lifelong sorrow."

The man's eyes darted sideways. "I dare not say. The walls have ears."

"Why was she so cruel to you then?"

"She's frightened," the man said. "Because I have a higher purpose. I know the secret."

Anne leaned close to the bars, looking around his cell in curiosity. The silvery old head bent closer to her and suddenly his eyes shone with an inner spark. Anne waited while the man considered sharing his profound riddle.

"The secret—to free everyone in this place," he finally whispered conspiratorially, trusting Anne's ingenuous look. "But you see, I'm not leaving until I finish my life's vocation. There's so much to do . . . and I need help . . ."

From what Anne could see, the man's cell contained a cot, a chair, and a small, unstable bench. He turned away from her, got down on his knees, and pulled aside a grate in the far wall. From the dark space behind it, he dragged out an old corduroy carpet bag and set it on the bench, muttering to himself.

"It's all very well to read about sorrows," said Anne, thoughtfully gazing about at the miserable surroundings, "and imagine yourself living through them heroically. But it's ghastly when you really come to have them."

"I have the key to freedom," the prisoner insisted, pulling a rusted iron key from inside a deteriorating book at the bottom of the carpet bag.

Anne's eyes opened wide at the sight of the imposing relic. "Then why do you allow yourself to remain imprisoned?"

She was unable to believe anyone with a key would not use it immediately to get out of such a horrible prison. Harsh as reality was for Anne, the occupant of this cell certainly must have experienced far more sorrow than she. Nevertheless, he brightened with a kind of feverish excitement.

"I am ... ah ... editing a complete history of every word in the English language ... for posterity."

He began to pull out a dog-eared assortment of books, notebooks, and papers from the bag where he'd hidden the key. As he did so, he mumbled to himself distractedly before shaking a disordered handful of papers at Anne, all written in random script.

Anne's breath was momentarily taken away at such a noble, gargantuan enterprise. Here was someone who certainly loved words as much as she did. She realized people laughed at her because she used big words, but she remembered her mother saying, a long time ago, that a person needed big words for big ideas. The man's eyes sparkled with the radiance of a fantastical obsession.

"I'm so sorry." Anne hated to impart unfortunate news, but the thought had begun to occur to her that perhaps he was out of his mind. "I don't mean to be impolite, sir, but I'm afraid the dictionary has already been invented. Did you not know that?"

A frown of concentration crinkled the brow under the tangled hair. The fellow scratched his head in complete puzzlement.

"I've never heard such a ... a word before. Dict-shun-ayr-ee. Do spell it."

His circumscribed life, which he'd chosen to fill with such endless work, told Anne the truth.

"You don't have a single soul in the world, do you?"

The gleaming gaze wavered as Anne struck home. Then the ancient voice fell almost to a whisper as he told her his source of sorrow.

"I had a wife and daughter once. They console me still . . . here." He touched his heart. "As life marches on, you can't know how difficult it is to draw a line between the past and the present." The horrid reality of their situation pressed in on Anne. She and the old man shared a mutual harshness that not even her vivid imagination could ward off. Anne had no one to console her, no one at all. Alone with this elderly prisoner, her sense of hope failed and a genuine despair entered her voice.

"You're ancient, but I'm at the beginning of my life. We are imprisoned here forever!"

She had dreamed so often of someone to rescue her, to spirit her away from these hateful stone walls, to love her and take care of her. Now she saw that no one would ever come for her—not Louisa Thomas, not her father, and certainly not her poor mother. The old man, who had suffered far worse than Anne could imagine, offered the only thing he had to stave off utter hopelessness—a share in his immense undertaking.

"Once this work is done, I will let everyone out. But please . . . so much work . . . notes, memories . . . that all need to be copied . . ." His spidery hands began to shake as he gathered up handfuls of scribbled notes and thrust them at Anne. "Only at night," he cautioned, "when no one can see."

"I will help you," Anne declared, deciding she was prepared to participate in his dream, however foolish. "What's your name?"

"Gabriel . . . Blake. At your service."

Anne felt a shiver. This man's name was a sign!

"Gabriel . . . Gabriel was a heavenly messenger, wasn't he?"

The old man bobbed his head, confused again but still intent upon passing more notes to Anne through the bars.

Anne gathered up the trove of pages and slipped back to her stool to explore them and copy them by moonlight. As she left, Gabriel turned back to his papers and his disjointed mumbling, a new optimism in his shoulders.

"Everything will be much better now . . . with your help. I have the energy . . . so much to do and so little time. . . ."

Anne spread the papers around her stool on the cold stone floor and set to work with the best of intentions. Having spent a day and most of the entire night without rest, however, she soon tumbled into sleep. As she dozed off, she buried her face in her arms.

Anne slept until the unforgiving clang of a distant bell penetrated her consciousness. She awoke with a shock to discover numerous feet shuffling past. She had no idea that the entire populace of the poorhouse had been summoned for inspection by the County Board of Representatives. In fact, it required a long, confused second to even remember where she was. She scrambled back up onto the stool, surrounded by Gabriel's notes, even as Gabriel himself was led with the others into the dining hall. It was the first time Anne had ever seen Gabriel out in the open. With his threadbare garments flapping around his bony frame, he looked even older and shabbier than the night before. Gabriel had only a moment to toss her a worried glance before the matron, who was shepherding the line along the corridor, spotted Anne and came roaring down on her.

"What devilment are you up to!" she questioned, pointing to the pile of papers and pencil which Anne had been unable to hide. "Where did you get these? Surely you don't think you're above rules?"

Anne knew it was useless even to shake her head. She was instantly condemned. The matron's mouth was rigid. She expected complete order for all of the inmates to be presented to the board members, who were already waiting in the hall. In her mind, the county representatives were all substantial citizens who would broach no lack of organization. The matron yanked Anne off the stool and led her to the dining hall.

In the dining hall, the overseer wore his most self-righteous expression as he pointed to row upon row of unmoving, regimented inmates seated at the tables. No matter how demented or confused, every one of them knew instinctively to cooperate as the overseer waved his arms around expansively.

"The county should be pleased at the God-fearing ideals of all our tenants. Purged of pride here, and eager for employment, each one earns their keep."

At that moment, the matron pushed Anne through the arch into the hall with one hand, clenching a fistful of crumpled notes in the other.

"This child has continued her disobedience!" She turned to the representatives. "Our resident lunatic, Gabriel Blake, has been filling her head with foolishness!" She looked to her husband, showing him the notes. The overseer set his jaw.

"I am pleased," he continued to the representatives, "to demonstrate to you our exacting methods of inmate discipline."

Secretly, he *was* worried about this child with the flaming red hair and her ability to rebel. Apparently, a night of standing on a stool had done nothing to cool her dark, insubordinate little soul. Taking out his spectacles, which were strung to his waistcoat pocket, he scanned the notes his wife had thrust at him. He concluded that there was no time like the present to make an example of this wretched girl. Otherwise, the inspection committee might conclude that a mere mischievous child was capable of giving him problems.

Casting the papers on the floor, he glanced at Gabriel, who sat silently at the end of the room. "This sad little demon has fallen prey to the defiant tactics of our resident lunatic."

The overseer instantly marched Anne up to the front in full view of the assembly. "Her flaming hair is the source of her wickedness and evil! Scissors please, matron," He said under his breath, as he shook Anne by the nape of the neck and yanked her loose hair into a knot. Anne tried to break free but her struggles were of no avail against his secure grip.

"No don't, sir! Please!" she begged. "Not my hair!"

The overseer showed no trace of weakness before the row of county delegates lined up in the archway. Nor did his arrogance allow him to notice the shift of discomfort that passed through the entire group at his mistreatment of Anne, not to mention their discontent over the very idea that red hair made children wicked. The superintendent herself clenched her hands at her side when the matron produced an appalling pair of scissors. She half made a move to stop the mutilation but she was too late to intervene. As Anne screamed and pleaded, the scissors cut off a great clump of her hair. Her struggle only caused the scissors to mangle the hair at the nape of her neck, but that mattered very little. The matron triumphantly held up a vivid handful for all to see.

"Take it and burn it," her husband ordered. "Let the county recognize that Bolingbroke Asylum bears witness to Christian principles alone."

With a smirk, the matron tossed the bright hair into the same fireplace that had devoured Anne's books only the day before. The stench of burning hair filled the room.

"You will stand again until daybreak," the overseer shouted at the sobbing child. "And no one dare to rally round this girl either!"

The board members looked about with particular awkwardness. The superintendent caught their sober expressions as she turned and quickly led them out, Anne's cries ringing in their ears. The overseer strutted out behind the group, pleased at having shown his complete authority.

The matron stood in the dining hall, solely in charge now. She eyed her assembly, who mumbled among themselves.

"You heard him," the matron ordered. "No one acknowledge this guttersnipe!"

Anne was frightened. All around her in the dining hall, the inmates glanced at each other uneasily. The only one who never bothered to look once at the overseer or his wife was Gabriel. His eyes never left Anne. He rose and, in an act of calm and magnificent defiance, he walked between the tables, past the astonished matron and directly up to Anne. In his hand he carried his own tin cup full of water. He gently offered it to Anne, as though she were his own daughter, reciprocating her kindness from the night before. His courageous insubordination astonished her. She took the cup and she patted Gabriel on the shoulder in mute thanks.

The Matron was flummoxed but recovered enough to go on the attack. This dreadful old man was trying to make fools of them all.

"Seeing as you crave freedom, you'll be less constrained outside, Mr. Blake!" She nodded sharply at the two muscular custodians standing in the hall. "You know the routine, men."

The matron concluded the order by snatching the cup out of Anne's hand. The burly custodians took Gabriel by the elbows and hauled him out of the dining hall.

Anne remained on the stool, her hair chopped and disheveled around her sweet face. Once the matron and all of the inmates left, she felt she could finally look out the window to see what had happened to her friend.

In the centre of the wide courtyard was a platform with a post rising in the middle. At the top of the post was a heavy

wooden crossbar hung with chains. It was an old place of punishment that had been left as an example for anyone who became too unruly. But now, Gabriel was chained there. He leaned
with his arms over the cross piece, his head back, and the chill
wind blowing his hair off his old face. He had no gloves or coat
against the winter cold. Lightly falling snow accumulated on
his shaggy head and dampened his worn shirt. He shouted and
swore defiantly, but no one aside from Anne seemed to hear.
For a long time, Gabriel just stood there, roaring into the wind
like some beast trying to face down a storm with sheer
willpower. His cries were of defiance—sometimes clear words,
sometimes jumbled nonsense, sometimes just inarticulate bel-
lows. By noon, however, a bell was clanging and Gabriel could
be seen rocking on his feet in rhythm to it. He was shivering
severely, snow accumulating on his head and sitting on his
shoulders, the spirit within him refusing to be crushed.

ANNE STOOD HUNGRY and with aching feet. All day she'd imagined that she would soon take Gabriel's frails hands and warm
them with her own. By late afternoon, Gabriel's age and the
damp cold began to win out. No longer able to stand, he
slumped to the ground, his back against the post and his cries
replaced by an occasional moan. As evening advanced, he sank
lower and lower in the wake of the biting wind. Finally, in the
darkness, he slumped, nearly lifeless, from the crossbar. He had
been reduced to a wintery effigy, only an occasional shiver indicating he had not completely succumbed.

Anne watched the great clock in the hall, wondering how
much longer he would be forced to suffer. She was unaware that
the superintendent had just returned and ordered the two custodians to release Gabriel from his chains. They had to carry

the frozen, spent old man back into the asylum, for he was beyond walking or even moving.

Anne, too, was finally taken down from the stool. After seeing to Gabriel, the superintendent herself had come to determine whether Anne had also been left without reprieve.

"I declare you're a little scrap," the superintendent called to her, not unsympathetically but in astonishment. "Just worsening your trial here by inciting calamity."

"I'm devastated," Anne burst out wretchedly, voicing the thought that had been tormenting her all day. "It's all my fault!"

"You are entirely naughty. Never mind. There is a darkness here which needs to be rectified." The woman continued enigmatically. "Your innocence may assist me, if I have my way."

AS GABRIEL LAY DEPLETED and feverish in the poorhouse infirmary, the superintendent had started forces working to improve matters at the insidious institution. The overseer had had no choice but to obey the superintendent and call in the doctor. The doctor, who was also one of the county representatives, was shocked to learn what brought on Gabriel's condition. He had seen Gabriel just that morning in the dining hall, able and sound.

Anne could not sleep even when she was finally allowed into bed. She had managed to claim a strip of mattress as her own and was grateful to be on the opposite side from Mary, as well as for the warmth of the other bodies. The wind still whistled about the eaves and drove pellets of snow against the small windowpanes. She lay quiet until all the others were snoring, certain she could hear Gabriel moaning far down the hall. She knew he was in the infirmary and was certain he needed her help.

As soon as she dared, Anne pushed back the flimsy blanket and crept silently out of bed. Peeping in the infirmary door, she could see Gabriel, perspiring heavily and barely breathing. She saw the superintendent leave with the doctor. The woman drew the doctor into the shadows of the corridor while Anne flattened herself against a wall, close enough to listen.

"We really have no alternative, doctor," the superintendent whispered. "We must condemn the building, annex the institution to the neighbouring county, and expel the overseers. But I indeed want to have this child speak to our entire board at the right opportunity."

The doctor nodded gravely. Still commiserating, the pair walked away in the opposite direction, leaving Anne free to find her way into the near-empty infirmary.

Anne entered the room, which was lit by a single oil lamp, and slipped over to Gabriel. His eyes were closed and his breath rattled in his throat. Sometimes a shudder racked his body. Anne touched his shoulder.

"Gabriel? Are you awake?"

His red, feverish eyes blinked in confusion.

"I overheard the superintendent. She wants to help," Anne informed him, full of hope that he could recuperate.

"She wants ... the doctor ... to send me away," Gabriel whispered. His glassy eyes stared at Anne affectionately.

"I'll fetch all your books and notes," Anne promised, thinking they were going to take Gabriel to a place where he would at least receive proper care. Gabriel had something else on his mind.

"The secret ..."

"The key?" Anne asked.

"It's under the boards ... in the bag. It's all yours now. Go...."

With barely a nod he urged Anne away, his eyes following her until she vanished. Swiftly, Anne ran down the hall to

Gabriel's cell. Testing the door at the foot of the stairs, she found it unbolted. She entered stealthily, taking care not to make a sound. In a flash she pried off the grate in the wall. Opening Gabriel's carpet bag, she found the heavy, old iron key just where he had indicated it would be. She pocketed it and stuffed all his books and papers inside the bag.

Back in the infirmary, she presented both key and carpet bag to Gabriel, who smiled weakly. "Freedom ... whenever you need it."

"I won't go ... till they bring you back," vowed Anne.

Gabriel reached over to touch Anne's delicate face. It took all his strength. His head was sunk deep into the pillow and his hair was spread all around, still matted from the snow that had soaked him to the bone.

"Hold my hand. So splendid to have a friend. You're a true kindred spirit."

"What's that?" whispered Anne ingenuously.

A flicker of brightness showed in Gabriel's eyes.

"A kindred spirit ... is someone you can rely on, right to your innermost soul."

At that moment, Anne thought perhaps she understood the meaning of a person's "soul." It was the one part of Gabriel that no one could ever harm. It was the innermost part of him that was noble and true, that had allowed him to survive all these years despite insurmountable hardships.

The brightness in Gabriel's eyes passed and a faraway look took hold. His breathing was laboured. Anne felt a lump form in her heart. There was no longer any strength in his hand.

"I feel so tired," he sighed with a shallow breath.

Gabriel closed his eyes and his fingers dropped away. Anne held the wizened hand tightly. She felt something in her own soul just then, too. She had been given a delicate gift. Witnessing the sanctity of Gabriel's strength as it left his body into the safety of his soul, Anne was determined that she would seek out other kindred spirits for the rest of her life. Still, the notion did not dull the ache she felt inside, and tears came quietly, in relief.

ANNE MIGHT WELL HAVE taken Gabriel's name as that of a heavenly messenger—a sign that she was not forgotten after all. His horrible punishment and subsequent death was the last and worst of a growing string of complaints against the Bolingbroke County Poorhouse. The County Board of Representatives called a meeting, which gave the superintendent the opportunity she needed to compel Anne to speak out. It was a solemn day as Anne stood before a long table of older gentlemen taking notes. With her mangled hair pinned into a tidy knot, Anne spoke straightforwardly and answered each question as fairly as she could, thinking about all of the people in the asylum who were unable to speak for themselves.

The superintendent knew it was the right thing to do. She was energized by Anne's articulate ability to speak the truth. In the wake of all the injustice she'd experienced, it was the first time any adults, besides her dear mother, had ever really understood her. The child rediscovered inner strength and spoke about her father and her own misfortune. She described the tribulations of the others she had witnessed in that horrible establishment. The tyranny of the overseer and his wife would come to an end. Perhaps the proverb, God is Love—so eloquently carved into the stone over the fireplace—might not have been in vain after all.

Six

Standing in the yard at Green Gables, Anne gazed up at the sun through the dappled leaves of the billowing aspens. She searched through the memories of that dire period in her life with a kind of wonder. Turning to look back across the lawn at the wide verandahs where she had spent so many wonderful hours with Marilla, and then up at the window in the upper gable, where she first had a room all her own and where Matthew had once confessed to her how heartbroken he would be if she ever left, Anne pondered the enigma of her life.

"Angels *have* watched over me," she thought to herself, "rescuing me. Each one a different kind of kindred spirit. Making me feel as if I had a voice." Anne began to pace back and forth across the lawn. She always did her best thinking outside. Green Gables had made her mind fertile with all sorts of fresh ideas about the kind of drama she would really like to write. The letter from her father still lay inside on the bureau. It had unleashed a deluge of memories and secret emotions. She began to walk through the orchard next, enacting scenes in her head that might prove to be good for a play. She even began to speak lines that sprang to mind, just to hear how they would sound if someone were to act them out.

SUNSET FOUND ANNE IN THE ORCHARD, thinking about the carpet bag that had contained Gabriel's life and then her own.

The gate key to the Bolingbroke County Poorhouse was the source of Anne's freedom. Once the measures voted on by the Board of Representatives were duly instituted, the poorhouse was closed permanently. By spring, the building was condemned and the inmates were prepared for a move to a far healthier place in the next county.

When the transfer day finally arrived, a paddy wagon belonging to the local police drove into the yard. The more confused and demented inmates were loaded aboard in order to facilitate a safe journey. The wagon was really a jail cell on wheels, but it provided a relatively easy means for the custodians to assemble the initial transferees, who, one by one, were helped up and into the vehicle.

Anne knew her name was yet to be put on a list. She took the opportunity to steal away to the tiny graveyard on the poorhouse grounds. Here rested those on whom the world had given up. Anne knelt beside the most recent grave, one that still lacked grass on its mound of earth. A simple white cross stood at its head with "Gabriel Blake" inscribed in black paint. Anne laid down a small handful of wildflowers, plucked from the grassy verge beside the mound. She didn't see the matron until the woman had walked directly behind her. The expression on the woman's face was one of resigned disgust.

"The county board has found a special foster home for you in Perth, girl. Consider it an honour they've gone to such trouble. You'll leave tomorrow."

Anne was still so consumed by the injustice of what had been done to Gabriel that she struck back with spirit.

"It's no honour having you be the one to tell me so."

The matron's face grew pinched. "Who would have thought a child so cunning as you could have brought about the downfall of everything we built."

Anne imagined her comment to be the eternal cry of the petty tyrant, watching her empire collapse. The matron and the overseer had carefully organized a very comfortable nest for themselves, living well off funds allotted for the upkeep of the indigent and enjoying the intoxication of power that came with the belief that they were both unassailable. Now it was all over.

"I'm glad I hurt you," Anne threw back, her eyes blazing in defiance. "You've hurt me more than my own father. You and your husband haven't a spark of kindness in you! I'll never forget what you did to Gabriel. You . . . you had no right!"

The matron moved toward her angrily. Anne turned and ran off as fast as she could; she knew better than to let the matron try to catch her.

The interior of the poorhouse was beginning to look quite open and empty. Anne could slip through the silent corridors unseen and unimpeded now. She had made up her mind about getting away, long before the matron told her of the foster home. She had been given the key to freedom and she meant to use it.

For the last time, Anne crossed the ward where she had spent so many nights being elbowed and kicked by her larger bedmates and wondering what would become of herself. She hurried into the corridor where the door of Gabriel's old cell stood ajar. It only took a moment to pull back the grate and locate the carpet bag.

Through a window, Anne could see the last paddy wagon rolling out to the road. The superintendent locked a wooden gate in the wall and hurried off across the courtyard, looking pleased that her efforts had helped improve the lot of the most defenseless of the county's population. Anne knew she could wait no longer, especially when she overheard one of the attendants indicate that they would be back for her and several others within the hour.

When the yard was completely deserted, Anne put the carpet bag under her arm and ran down the stairs to the dark, dank basement. She knew of a small door that led from the coal bin into the yard. Looking about cautiously, Anne managed to slip outside and to bolt across the yard to the side gate. She thrust Gabriel's iron key into the heavy metal lock, and struggled with the stiff mechanism. For one awful moment, Anne feared Gabriel had given her a key that did not work. Then the key turned and the lock fell open. In an instant, Anne was running down the lane with all her might, the carpet bag bumping against her legs. She could not see the matron spying on her from a high window.

The woman stood frozen, initially refusing to move a muscle to stop the last inmate from getting away. Then she decided otherwise. She went to seek the superintendent to let her know that Anne had escaped.

The lane joined the road at just about the spot where Anne ran out of breath. She began to walk quickly, with no plan except to get as far away from the asylum as possible. She was about to venture across a narrow stone bridge when she heard the sound of hooves and the clatter of large, wooded wheels. The paddy wagon was moving so fast that it threatened to mow her down!

Anne froze. If the police saw her they would surely catch her and throw her inside. Before the wagon advanced onto the bridge, Anne flung herself and her bag down the embankment, flattening her body against the bridge's old stone foundation, not daring to take a breath until the dreaded wagon had passed. As it disappeared into the distance without stopping, Anne breathed easy. Still, the encounter forced her to reconsider her route. The open road was far too risky. For all she knew, word of her escape might already have spread. In another half hour, officers could be scouring the roads for a red-headed escapee who would be easy to spot. With a sigh, Anne realized she hadn't thought beyond her actual escape. Now that she was away from the asylum, she had no idea where she was supposed to go.

She followed the river in the hollow, tramping along the embankment in the direction of the current. Anne had not reckoned on the dense bush. As soon as the road was out of sight, the woods enveloped her like a prehistoric jungle. Thick foliage towered high above, cutting off the sky with its heavy green canopy. The piercing cries of unidentified birds and animals echoed around her, sounding frightening as well as disapproving of any human intruder. Thick ferns, hummocks and fallen branches impeded her progress. Brambles caught at her clothes as though actively trying to pull her back. Eventually, she became thoroughly confused as to her direction, and just as thoroughly frightened listening to twigs snapping beside her or birds flapping up as though startled by some unseen figure. It took no effort at all to imagine bears, wolves, or even the overseer fast on her heels.

With the river as her only guide, Anne hoped to reach a village or town. Trying not to look back, she steadied herself for a while by pretending she was the only daughter of a prince, stolen away and abandoned in a savage wood by wicked cousins who wanted to steal her inheritance. Abandoned so that she could be torn apart by wild animals!

Anne began to fight her way faster and faster through the undergrowth. In a thicket so dense she could barely see through it, something grasped her ankles and held tight, pitching Anne nose first, into the muddy, musty leaves of the forest floor. Almost passing out from sheer panic, she lifted her head; nothing at all had happened. She lay panting, but no sharp teeth mauled her flesh. Finally, she dared to glance back to see what exactly was holding her. It was a tangle of creeping vines.

Once she'd twisted round to free herself, she had calmed down enough to get up and look around her. Not only did the trees thin out beyond that spot, but there was a building not far away—a hotel overlooking the river at the edge of the ravine.

As Anne stared at the welcome beacon of hope, she wondered briefly if her imagination was playing yet another trick on her. Three small figures were climbing out of a second floor window, one after the other, and shinnying down a rope made of knotted bed sheets. Anne stared incredulously at the bizarre tableau. A woman stood at the bottom of the makeshift rope, urging the others down.

"Hurry," she was calling to them. "The front desk clerk will be in the room in two minutes with the police!"

The voice seemed familiar. Anne pushed some branches aside, squinting to see. She could barely believe her eyes! The woman was Louisa Thomas, calling to her children! Standing in the midst of a small circle of suitcases, she was coaxing Violetta and her two younger brothers, Keith and Jock, down the escape route. Jock, the last and smallest of the siblings, tumbled to the street, bringing the whole string of knotted sheets along with him.

Anne had seen enough. She crashed forward, out of the brush, carpet bag in hand.

"Mrs. Thomas! Dear Mrs. Thomas," she shouted out, overjoyed.

Louisa spun around, searching for the voice that threatened to raise public alarm. In a panic, she yanked Jock to his feet. As fast as she could, Louisa picked up her bags and began to run, her children trailing behind her. She prayed no one would stop them. They headed straight into the cover of the very forest that had engulfed Anne. She glanced this way and that, searching for the mysterious voice, as Anne rushed through the foliage to greet them.

"Violetta! Mrs. Thomas! It's me, Anne!"

Louisa nearly dropped her suitcases when Anne exploded into view, her clothing disheveled and twigs in her hair.

"Oh, good Lord, Anne Shirley! What in heaven's name are you doing here?"

Although Anne herself was overcome with relief, the Thomas family, each one carrying what they could of their luggage, kept running right past her. Anne followed, struggling to keep up.

"Fate has brought us together. Jock, Keith, wait!! You look entirely like thieves running away in the night."

Louisa was mortified. She glanced back up the hill through the thin screen of branches. An angry maid leaned out the hotel window, shouting and pointing at the knotted sheets. In another moment, staff would pour out of the doors in pursuit.

"That's putting it mildly," Louisa cried, starting to run again. "Hurry! Just hurry! I'm not sure what you're doing here, Anne. We can't possibly take on a runaway when we're running away ourselves!"

This was not at all the reception Anne would have imagined coming from her mother's dear friend. Her smile was quickly replaced by fear as Louisa hustled her three children along the riverbed and into the isolation of the ravine. Anne scurried along trying to keep up, truly worried she was going to be left behind once more.

"Won't you help me? Please, Mrs. Thomas, I beg of you!"

Louisa was too busy running to argue. Despite angry looks from Violetta, Anne clung to the little band until the four of them finally emerged from the woods along a railway track. Hot and weary, they trudged toward a small whistlestop station in the middle of nowhere. Only then did Louisa feel she could slow down. She was at her wit's end. Yet here was Anne, and it was clear the girl had no intention of being tossed aside again. Louisa watched as Anne patted wisps of her hair from her sweaty face and straightened her uniform and pinafore, trying to look as acceptable as her new companions. In her mind, she was devising a way to shake off the stigma of her father, which she thought must surely be weighing on Louisa's mind.

"I know how to be resourceful. I've even thought of changing my name so no one would ever recognize me again. I'd love to be called something elegant, like Cordelia."

"That's a horrible name," scoffed Keith.

Keith was the middle child, a stocky boy with tousled hair, a flat tweed cap and little imagination. He dragged his share of the family luggage along stoically.

"What about Geraldine Fitzgerald?"

Jock chortled and Violetta was indignant. It was clear that Anne Shirley was trying to elbow her way into her family again.

"Who cares what you're called!" Violetta's voice was completely dismissive. "You can't stay with us and that's final."

Anne desperately tried to ingratiate herself to Louisa. She looked up at her with an earnest expression.

"Since you and my mother were best of friends, that almost makes us kin," she said soulfully, trying to validate her claim to Louisa's family.

Jock, for his part, didn't feel in the least related.

"Didn't you hear our mother? We're in too much trouble as it is. No thanks to you."

"Stop it, Jock," ordered Louisa curtly.

They had reached the tiny station, which consisted of a simple wooden building and an elevated water tank to fill up the steam engines when they stopped. In a weary row, all five runaways sank down on the benches to wait, goodness knew how long, for a means of transportation. Anne sat next to Louisa.

"There is a poetic irony that we are all of us fugitives. Is that the kind of trouble you mean, Mrs. Thomas?"

Despite the events of the afternoon, Louisa managed to look neat and pretty in her brown suit and tight, feathered hat that tilted, ever so saucily, over her brow. She moaned, finally explaining why the Thomas family had so little room for even the daughter of her good friend.

"Dear lord, Anne. Things have gone from bad to worse. After your father vanished, so did the funds from the parish roof box. The town accused my husband, even though he insisted it was your father."

Anne could hardly believe her ears. Her father, accused of stealing the money donated to fix the church roof! Consternation struck her dumb under Violetta's contemptuous gaze.

"Your father is just trash, Anne," the girl hurled at her bitingly.

Louisa stared into her lap as she continued her story.

"We were forced out of our house by the landlord. So we've been getting by on charity and living in the Halfway Hotel under house arrest for nine months, awaiting an inquest . . . because . . . my husband was found killed . . . by a train."

Dropping her head, Louisa covered her face with her hands. Keith, sitting on the other side, put his arm around her protectively. Violetta merely glared at Anne, every fibre in her blaming Walter Shirley for all their troubles. Violetta's resentment only made Anne feel the family's tragedy that much deeper.

"Do you think he was . . . oh, my. . . ." Anne stopped herself. She wondered if Dr. Thomas had been drunk and had fallen under a train, or even worse. She'd learned all too well in the poorhouse what angry people were capable of.

"I am in the depths of despair. I can barely swallow," she added with the utmost sincerity.

"Being a doctor's wife has been a life of bitter disappointment," Louisa said with shame, holding inside the recollection of a hundred humiliations.

Violetta's lip trembled watching her mother. "It's just too much for Mother to be cross-examined again and to have to go back over it all at an inquest," Violetta sermonized, looking protectively at Louisa and trying to control her own fears. She countered by lifting her head proudly. "Our grandmother is very rich and she wants us to live with her."

Anne's heart went out to Louisa. She patted her arm softly. "Is there anything I can do to help?"

"Leave us alone!" Violetta shrieked over the sudden whistle of a train quickly approaching the little station.

No matter how much grief Walter Shirley had caused her, Louisa could not bring herself to totally abandon this child in the middle of nowhere. "When we get to St. John, I'm sure we can find you someplace safe." Anne looked down at her toes; another institution looming on the horizon, no doubt. The local train came chuffing along the line and the entire party leaped up, hoisting their luggage as the engine steamed past the platform. Once in the carriage, they sat in silence until they arrived at the main station in St. John. No one wanted a careless word to tip off any of the other passengers that they were all runaways.

When they disembarked at the St. John station, Anne gazed around in awe. She had never seen a railway terminal with so many people bustling about, or so many tracks and trains loading and disgorging passengers. The high ceiling and tall windows, sending down great shafts of light, seemed wonderfully grand. There were pictures of Queen Victoria and schedules written up in chalk, and so many people—either sitting, waiting, or milling about—that a person could hardly move. She could barely take it all in as she waited for Louisa to consult a schedule and buy tickets for the final leg of a journey that would bring the Thomas family to their new home in Marysville. Then Anne heard Louisa consulting the ticket agent.

"Apparently there's an orphans' home in Fredericton, just outside of Marysville, isn't there?"

"Yes," the ticket agent replied. "That would be St. Agatha's Asylum, ma'am."

Louisa turned around to face the children, tickets in hand. Anne's face dropped at seeing the woman's sorry expression.

"I'm sorry, Anne. We have to find a place for you there."

She thanked the agent for his directions and immediately set off for the train platforms.

"Hurry along, everyone. Our train leaves in five minutes!"

Louisa took the boys' hands and gave two tickets to Violetta. Although Anne's hope of staying with the Thomas family had evaporated, she decided to face the prospect of another institution with courage. She wasn't going to let anyone know of the panic she felt. She could try to ingratiate herself once again. After all, there was still a chance to change Louisa's mind. Nothing was ever firm until it actually happened.

"I've made up my mind to simply enjoy this train ride," she announced brightly. "Train rides are so thrilling."

"For pity sake, it's only a train." Violetta retorted.

Violetta knew a lot more about trains than Anne, and wheels were turning rapidly inside her head. She fully recognized the charm Anne was trying to exude in order to survive, and had little faith that her mother would actually force Anne into an orphanage; even if this so-called St. Agatha's Asylum could take her. It was far more likely that Louisa would cave in at the last moment before Anne's soulful, sappy gaze and take her with them to Marysville. Then they would really be stuck. Violetta had no intention of letting this happen. As soon as they stepped out onto the crowded platform, with so many trains coming and going, Violetta saw an opportunity raise its nasty head, right in front of her. She held Anne back, making sure she looked after their tickets until her mother and brothers were some distance ahead.

"Here. You look after your own ticket. It's your responsibility."

Violetta shoved the elaborate voucher into Anne's hand then stalled in front of a flower stand overflowing with bright blossoms.

"We really need to buy some flowers for grandmother. Mother has some change. You choose the colours, alright?"

Violetta could not have hit upon a better distraction. Anne loved flowers and had seen so few in the dismal past year that she was at once transported by the vivid blooms spread out before her like a sea of colour. She set about selecting just the right kind of a bouquet for a rich lady about to take in her grandchildren and perhaps an orphan. Pink would be entirely perfect. She clapped her hands over a bucket at the front of the stand.

"Oh, what spectacular wild roses! Looking so happy to be roses. I wish roses could talk."

"They'd surely have hopeful thoughts." The vendor smiled indulgently as she spoke.

The woman's beaming face might have had possibilities as a kindred spirit if Anne had had the time to make her acquaintance. As it was, she barely had time to take the fragrant bouquet into her hand, before Violetta reappeared with money. She shoved the coins into the vendor's hand and boldly yanked Anne along the platform by the arm.

"This way, you," she bossed. "Hurry up! Mother is already sitting in the coach. She told me we had to get a move on. Train schedules won't tolerate latecomers. It'll leave without us."

Luggage trolleys, hurrying people, and wooden crates waiting to be put into the baggage cars all added to the confusion on the platform. Before Anne had a chance to look around for the rest of the family, Violetta hustled her up into a car that was just loading. Still enthralled by the perfume of her exquisite pink roses, Anne climbed on without question.

"I hope your grandmother likes pink," said Anne, inhaling the sweet scent once more. "Isn't it the most fetching colour? I love it, but I can't wear it. Red-headed people can never wear pink."

Violetta led Anne deeper into the bustling coach to a spot where there were empty seats. Anne was still thinking about her braided hair, which had mercifully grown long enough over the winter to hide all evidence of the matron's hacking.

"Did you ever know anybody whose hair was red when they were young, but changed colour when they grew up?"

"No, I don't know as I ever did," Violetta replied anxiously. "Put your bag up there."

As Anne struggled to arrange herself, Violetta called out, "We're this way, mother!"

Trying in vain to get her carpet bag upon the high luggage rack, Anne was too distracted to notice the ploy.

"Would you help me, sir?" she asked a nearby passenger.

An obliging gentleman stood up and lifted her carpet bag into the rack above the seats. Just as Anne turned around, Violetta had disappeared. A jerk beneath her feet told Anne the train was starting to pull away. Where were the other Thomases?

Through the window, she saw Louisa and the boys lined up on the platform, about to ascend the train on the opposite track. Anne pounded on the glass and shouted as loud as she could.

"Mrs. Thomas! Mrs. Thomas!! You're getting on the wrong train!"

Louisa whipped round to see Anne, her little face pressed against the windowpane. She pulled her boys out of the line and began to run along the platform beside the now moving train.

"Anne, whatever are you doing?"

Anne ran from window to window.

"Mrs. Thomas, you're on the wrong train."

"No, Anne! *You're* on the wrong train. And where is Violetta?"

"Last call for passengers for Marysville, Fredericton, Perth, Dark River. All aboard," called the conductor of Louisa's train. Suddenly, Anne saw Violetta running to join her mother. Louisa was gesturing frantically.

"Anne, get off!"

Anne ran to the end of the coach for the exit door, but stopped in her tracks when she realized she had forgotten her carpet bag. Struggling back, she tried to tug it off the rack, only freeing it when the gentleman seated below helped her again. Anne raced through the carriage as the train gained momentum. She arrived at the exit to find the stairs were speeding along just above the edge of the platform. Louisa held out her hand.

"Jump, Anne, jump!" Louisa shouted. "It's now or never!"

Anne gulped, then tossed her carpet bag into Louisa's arms and took a flying leap down to the platform, barely able to prevent herself from crashing onto the cobblestones as she landed. Louisa tossed the carpet bag back to Anne as she and her brood began to run toward the train bound for Fredericton, which had begun to build up steam for departure.

Their luggage stood piled up just where Louisa had left it, and the children gathered their things. Then Louisa screeched to a halt.

"My purse. Oh, I've lost my purse! I left it right here beside the valise!"

The purse, containing all of Louisa's money, was nowhere to be seen. Even worse, their time was up. Louisa saw that their engine had started to pull away in a cloud of steam. Everyone grabbed their suitcases and made a run for the train, but the caboose passed by even as they struggled nearer. The five were left standing on the platform as the train chugged out of sight, growing smaller and smaller on its way down the track.

"It's the only train to Marysville until tomorrow," Louisa lamented. "Grandmother will be waiting at the other end and she'll burst a blood vessel!"

Four pairs of eyes looked at her in alarm, and Anne suffered a surge of guilt, feeling that her heedless mistake had instigated this entire calamity. Violetta's accusatory frown drove through Anne's heart like a blade.

Composing herself for the children's sake, Louisa calmly picked up their luggage and headed toward some long benches on the platform. With no money, there was nothing to be done but to settle down and wait through the night until the morning train came along.

Violetta's dastardly plan had gone all wrong, and now she busied herself with shooting angry looks at Anne, who had set her suitcase down and sunk into the bench. The boys did their best not to whine and generally succeeded in entertaining themselves, watching all the station activity around them. Louisa tried not to openly show how anxious she was about losing her purse. When dusk fell and the stream of passengers thinned to a trickle, Keith and Jock fell asleep on the bench. Violetta pretended to be sleeping but inwardly, she was still fuming.

Anne's guilt had not diminished by nightfall when she felt the need to unburden her conscience.

"I blame myself entirely, Mrs. Thomas," said Anne miserably. "Violetta was following me. If I hadn't lost myself in the beauty of those colourful blossoms! It's only that I've had so little colour in my life lately. Insult has been added to injury, now that we are all obliged to sleep in a common railway station."

Louisa had spent the time mulling over the potential effect of this mishap on her rich and fearsome mother-in-law. Trying hard not to become emotional, she patted Anne's arm, her own troubles mellowing at the sight of the defenseless child beside her. "I'm just cross at *myself* for losing my purse . . . and all my money. My mother-in-law will be entirely unimpressed."

"Feel free to blame this entire mess on a hapless orphan who wasn't given the brains God gave geese, Mrs. Thomas," declared Anne, readily sacrificing herself to make amends.

Her earnestness softened Louisa and she slipped an arm around the child. She remembered how kind Bertha had been to her.

"You must call me Louisa." She beamed at Anne. "You know your mother was really quite brilliant. I discovered that when she would often help me with my Sunday school. She knew how to foster intellect. A wonderful teacher she was, who knew ever so many lovely poems off by heart. Walter Scott's "The Lady of the Lake" and "The Seasons" by James Thomson. She cultivated me. If you're half as bright, you'll make a fine teacher one day, too."

Anne's lip trembled. She had heard those same poems read frequently by her mother and she had never ceased to become spellbound.

"You have given me hope, Mrs. Tho . . . ah . . . Louisa." Anne tried out the name and was encouraged by Louisa's nod. "I'd hate to part ways on bad terms, especially when I was trying so hard to imagine you'd keep me . . . forever."

The appeal in these last words would have moved the most callous heart. A response caught in Louisa's throat. She glanced a bit awkwardly at Anne.

"I have a confession to make, Anne. I kept some of the money from the sale of your mother's things. Not a lot, but I was short at the time. My husband wasn't very dependable and I was so cross at your father." Warmth spread across Louisa's face. "I see now that we were destined to be great friends and I give you my word that I won't desert you again either."

Hope instantly revived in Anne's soul. She dared to lay her head upon Louisa's shoulder and was rewarded by Louisa's gentle arms around her, pulling her close. Violetta squinted at the scene in the dark and immediately decided that a new plot was needed—something that would rid them of this intruder for good.

Spending a night on a railway platform turned out to be chilly, uncomfortable, and very boring. The little party received odd looks from the last vacating passengers and passing pity from the station employees who finally shut down the building for the night. Jock and Keith complained about the stiffness of the benches while Violetta huddled against her brothers for warmth. Anne did her best to imagine that they all had silken coverlets spread over them and a downy mattress under their aching thighs.

Despite the usual reliability of her imagination, Anne did not have a lot of success in creating this illusion. Her conscience was still a burden. The air was cold and she could see her breath. If it was truly her fault for getting them into this situation, she was determined to find a way to rescue her little party!

Seven

Anne was the first to rouse from a fitful sleep, just as dawn was gilding the walls of the station. She had been startled by a clatter of wheels and clop of hooves close by. Rubbing her eyes, Anne saw the freight wagon backing up along the platform. The side of this colossal wagon read Royal Mail Post, accompanied by a handsome provincial crest. The wagon was driven by a woman in well-worn men's clothing, which included a long overcoat and a broad-brimmed hat now silhouetted against the sun. As Anne watched with curiosity, this able woman began unloading bags into the mail carriage of a train parked on the platform. She then proceeded to load the heavy mail bags, which had been sitting on the platform, up onto her wagon. This, Anne figured, was the mail left for distribution by the previous train.

Ever enterprising, Anne ran over and started shifting mailbags too, trying to help her way into another situation. The mailwoman smiled at the child and let her carry on.

"I'll help you all morning if you'll give us a ride," Anne offered halfway through the job.

The mailwoman's name was Nellie Parkhurst. As she regarded the small, eager volunteer, a trace of curiosity showed on a face well worn by life. "If you want a ride, you better tell me your name," she said as she continued to check off the cargo on her list.

"My name . . . my name is Cordelia Shirley. We walked all

the way from Bolingbroke and missed our train," said Anne, determined to shed her previous identity. As a poorhouse runaway, she knew she'd better be careful.

Nellie stopped writing and tilted her head at Anne.

"You don't know a Walter Shirley from Bolingbroke, do ya? Accused of doing his wife in as I recall?"

Anne swallowed the hard lump in her throat. Was there anyone in this entire province who hadn't heard about her father and blamed him for her mother's death?

"No, ma'am," Anne replied stoutly. "I've never heard of such a man."

"He'd just got the contract for the mail route up to Grand Falls, 'fore I took it over."

Anne was concerned that this woman was too close in proximity to the world of her father. However, she resolved not to let it show for even a second.

"My father was called Jedediah." She chirped back happily. "Even though it's rather a woeful name, don't you think?"

Nellie went back to her list, casting a sideways glance at Anne. The morning sun caught in the little girl's hair and gave it a vivid golden sheen. The child looked like an angel, who could easily be trusted. Nellie found it peculiar that such a little thing would be left all alone in a large station.

"An odd name, to be sure. What did Jedediah Shirley do?"

"Oh...," Anne scrambled for an answer and her imagination did not fail her. "Both my parents were teachers at the Bolingbroke Primary School. They each died of a fever when I was only three months. They were just a pair of babies themselves. I've had the good fortune to be rescued from an asylum by friends. We're all going to live in Marysville. They're members of the affluent Thomas family."

That name caught Nellie's full attention.

"Thomases you say? And you never met old Mrs. T?"

Anne shook her head and pointed to Louisa, who was still asleep on a bench with her children around her.

"But young Mrs. Thomas over there is as benevolent as she is loyal."

Something like delight fluttered across Nellie's face.

"Get your bags, then. Anyone knows the Thomas place, if they know Marysville."

Anne could barely contain herself as she hoisted her carpet bag up onto the wagon and raced to rouse the family. She had redeemed herself by finding them a ride.

"Do wake up, Louisa! Violetta . . . boys! The sun is shining on us this morning. The chaos I've caused is over!"

Anne was brimming over with pleasure at her success on finding transportation in a mail wagon. Louisa straightened up, rubbing her eyes. Violetta yawned. It would be hours yet before their train came. Best to take the mail wagon, no matter how undignified.

With the mail and all the Thomases' luggage loaded, there wasn't much room for the passengers. The two boys plopped down among the mailbags, while Louisa and Violetta sat on the tailgate with their feet hanging over. Anne sat up front with Nellie. The team of lively black horses soon took them out of town and onto a lumber road where tall spruce and fir trees towered above. The scent of evergreen needles, sawdust, and brilliant morning sunshine filled Anne with joy. Life was so much more hopeful on a sunny morning, even when Violetta still criticized her.

"I can't believe we had to spend the night in that train station. Thanks to you, Anne!"

Anne attempted to mend fences, while Nellie glanced sideways at the curious child who'd said her name was Cordelia.

"I'm sorry I vexed you, Violetta, but it gives me great satisfaction to know that the inequity has been righted. I feel just like a heroine in a novel right now."

Violetta rolled her eyes. She would not allow herself to be impressed in the least. A ride in a freight wagon hardly made up for any of the real trouble Anne had caused. Violetta knew her grandmother was going to be apoplectic when they showed up with a stray child, especially one connected to someone like Walter Shirley. Her mother was going to have to depend heavily on her grandmother's charity from now on, and the senior Mrs. Thomas was a domineering woman of strong opinion. Violetta knew that trying to foist an orphan into her household would put Louisa on shifting ground with her irascible mother-in-law.

"You talk too much!" Violetta called over her shoulder to Anne. "Don't be so certain our grandmother won't toss you out on your ear."

"Be nice to her," admonished Louisa, trying to hush Violetta in front of Nellie Parkhurst. "She's a really interesting little thing."

Violetta shook her mother's hand from her arm, trying to startle some sense into her. "It'd be more to the point if she was useful. Grandmother will toss all of us out on our ear if she has to listen to her nonsense."

Up in the front seat, Anne refused to be crushed. The best way to stave off fear for the future was by seizing on the beauty of the moment. All around was a majestic forest that soared over her like the arches of a great cathedral.

"Well, I won't worry about asylums for a little longer. I'm going to imagine this is all part of a beautiful mirage. I feel as if I am in a sacred place and I shall thank God for it two and three times a minute."

Anne held her head high, gazing at the great white shafts of light falling through the green branches onto the wagon and dappling the road ahead. Nellie could not help but smile curiously at such pluck.

Eventually, the wagon trundled into Marysville—the lumber, cider, and cotton mills each emblazoned with the Thomas name. Marysville was a company town, laid out by the Thomases right down to the very bricks and mortar. Numerous townsfolk greeted Nellie with a wave or the nod of a hat as she drove past. Children ran through the streets past vegetable, fish, and fruit stands while their mothers went into the shops. The place had an air of vibrant activity. People were dressed predominantly in work clothes, since the town was almost entirely populated by mill workers. As Nellie's wagon clattered along, men and women made their way down the main street toward their work places.

"We're right proud of this place," Nellie whispered to Anne, who was trying her hardest to take everything in. She had never been to a mill town before. "Marysville was named by old Mr. Thomas who built the mill, on account of it's always been so *merry*."

Nellie's grin expanded widely at her own joke.

The wagon veered away from the smokey mills across a wooden covered bridge then through the countryside to a small hamlet outside the main thoroughfare. There they passed a white clapboard church, and the town hall, complete with a park and a large gazebo for outdoor picnics in the summer. Eventually, Nellie turned the mail wagon down a long drive that wound through a grassy park with wonderful shady trees and a pond beyond, gleaming in the sun. At the end of the lane stood a mansion of cream-coloured brick. It had a great, Italianate tower rising up at the forefront and a covered portico above the front door. The gardens they passed through beyond the lane were very stately, and Anne felt engulfed in flowers. She let out an audible gasp of admiration.

"Christopher Columbus! I must be dreaming!"

She had read about this kind of grandeur in several books, but had never expected to actually see it. To Anne, this was a residence worthy of any earl and she began to wonder if perhaps her musing about being a heroine in a novel was about to materialize.

"You certainly are!" snarled Violetta. Anne was unquestionably dreaming if she thought she'd be staying there.

"No need to be nasty, Violetta," Louisa reproved, wanting her children on their best behaviour.

Nellie's freight wagon certainly wasn't the kind of vehicle meant to drive under such a graceful portico. Nonetheless, the mailwoman pulled right up to the front door and reined in her burly team. The moment the wagon stopped, a tall grey-haired woman came tearing out of the house, followed by two uniformed maids.

"God's nightgown!" she exploded as Louisa and her brood climbed down. "We wondered what in heaven's name happened to you. And now Mrs. Thomas has gone all the way to St. John looking for you!"

Louisa froze in dismay. She knew full well that Mrs. Thomas was not a woman to ever be inconvenienced.

"Hepzibah, no! Please don't ..."

"If she has a coronary on the way, you'll never hear the end of it!" Hepzibah snapped.

This wizened and scrappy family retainer had been Mrs. Thomas' housekeeper for ever. She was infuriated for the trouble her employer had been put to and her eyes blazed as she took in the little group. Several white-capped maids filed out of the house behind her and began to gather up the luggage that the boys and Violetta had pulled out from among the mailbags.

Then Hepzibah caught sight of Anne, still sitting uncertainly in the wagon seat beside Nellie. She gawked at both the mailwoman and the child, who was still wearing poorhouse clothing and whose face that hadn't been properly washed in days.

"Louisa Thomas! What is that?"

Anne might as well have been a large, revolting slug perched on the wagon seat. Louisa tried her best to calm Hepzibah down.

"It's a heartrending story, Hepzibah. Please keep my mother-in-law calm until I have a chance to get her used to the idea."

Hepzibah's head jerked back.

"You don't mean to think I'd take in a street urchin like that!" Hepzibah cried. "You don't march in here with a stray cur, thinking she'll be of any use to me."

Hepzibah hurried back toward the house with Louisa following close behind. "She's such a bright little creature! And her mother was my good friend," Louisa tossed in, gamely defending Anne. "I have promised the little thing she could stay and I don't mean to break my promise. Why can't she do house chores?"

"She doesn't cross the threshold of this household."

As their voices faded inside the long hallway of Mrs. Thomas' mansion, Anne sat frozen in the wagon seat, trying not to let her face crumple. She imagined herself reaching a castle gate after an exhausting crusade only to find the drawbridge pulled high, leaving her stranded on the other side of a moat. Violetta tossed her head as she passed, happily accompanied by maids carrying all of the family's luggage.

"Good day, Anne!" quipped Violetta. She might as well have said goodbye and good riddance.

Anne's lip quivered. Nellie watched the drama play out with raised eyebrows, reins still firmly in hand. Despite the dire circumstances, she decided her help would not be required just now.

"Off you go. You can't just sit here. Once you're off you'll be forced to stay." Nellie jerked her head toward the house, listening to Hepzibah's final diatribe on the matter. It sounded like Louisa had achieved some success over the issue of Anne's accommodation.

"I been waitin' to settle a score with that one for awhile." Nellie rolled her eyes at Hepzibah's squawking. "You have any trouble with her, you just ask around for "Nellie the Whip," she instructed Anne with a conspiratorial wink.

The girl climbed down across the big front wheel and gratefully took the carpet bag from the woman's able hand.

"Thank you," she said politely. "I am very grateful for all your help."

Nellie clucked to the team and the wagon started down the drive. A small figure standing alone in front of the stately country house, Anne watched her drive off. She turned to see Louisa emerge from her confrontation with Hepzibah, Violetta in tow. She imparted her news with a sigh.

"Hepzibah won't let you do house chores, but she's agreed that you can help in the stable. Violetta will show you the barn out back."

Anne had learned to appreciate any kind of shelter, even if she had never yet been relegated to a stable.

"Please tell her I'm very good at washing dishes," Anne offered, trying to keep the idea of a position in the main house open for herself. Violetta seized her arm and began to drag her off toward the stables. "But I am resigned to fit into a household however I can," Anne called over her shoulder.

Violetta, for her part, was beside herself. As expected, her mother had given in and figured out a way for the girl to stay. With great impatience, she marched her companion across the lavish grounds toward the path that led to the large barn and sundry outbuildings.

"The stables are this way," she growled as they approached a dainty footbridge that arched across a winding stream of running water, sparkling and dancing in the sun. The lush lawns expanded on either side of the little rivulet under lovely old shade trees.

"Goodness, a brook!" Anne ran ahead and leaned over the rail to look down into the glimmering depths. For a few moments, she forgot her situation. "Brooks are such cheerful things, aren't they? Always laughing; even in winter under the ice. Your grandmother has her very own brook to listen to whenever she feels in need of cheering up. Don't the pebbles look like a fairy spilled a basket of gold nuggets in the sunshine?"

Violetta could not bear Anne's fanciful talk.

"Can't you ever quit being so phony?" she seethed. "Trashcan Anne! That's what I'm going to call you, because you're garbage."

Anne set her jaw as Violetta laughed at her own wit. Even a destitute orphan about to be consigned to the stables could be provoked only so far. Her volatile temper flared as her red head flew back haughtily in the air.

"I wouldn't give myself such airs in the presence of a true aristocrat." Anne spoke in a haughty tone. "Myself being the progeny of royal Irish blood."

Violetta couldn't believe her ears. This was beyond endurance.

"The only royal blood you'll ever have is with my fist on the end of your nose. You're a *con* just like your father."

This insult cut to the quick.

"You're so queenly," Anne threw back sardonically. "The test of a true noble is having such a high instep a stream of water could run right underneath it!"

"I don't believe anyone has that! Least of all you," scoffed Violetta, trying to move Anne toward the stables.

Anne promptly walked down to the stream, took off one black boot and a worn black stocking and arched her foot so delicately over the stream that a rivulet of water did indeed run under it. She then recited her pedigree.

"My family is descended from the warrior monarch Queen Maeve, who led the Celts into battle, riding bareback by moonlight."

Anne was pleased at having come up with such a notion so quickly. She had pilfered it from a chapter in *Collier's British History*, a text used by her mother at Bolingbroke School. Bertha too, had loved to dramatize stories. The red hair she and Anne shared naturally pointed to the Celts as their fiery ancestors, she had once exclaimed.

"Queen Maeve sounds more like a witch than a queen," Violetta countered dismissively. "Anyway, you couldn't ride by moonlight let alone even mount a horse."

Violetta turned on her heel and started down the path again. Hot outrage shot through Anne's veins. There was only one thing to be done. Without another word, Anne tore past Violetta, one foot bare and wet. She barely paused to pull her boot on again, hopping across the stable yard before dashing straight into the stables.

"You just watch. I have a way with equines."

"Who do you think you are?" cried Violetta, scurrying after Anne.

The stable was a long building with a loft above to store feed for the winter. A pair of double doors stood open in the sunshine. One of the grooms was busy unsaddling a large bay after having taken it out for some solid exercise. The horse was standing in the doorway with its head lowered, basking in the sun after an extensive canter. Its bridle was still on but its back was bare. As the groom turned away to set the saddle on a wooden bar in the tack room, the drowsy horse paid no attention to the pint-sized redhead who managed to climb the steps beside it and wriggle right onto its broad back.

The horse startled out of its catnap with a snort as Violetta made her way into the barn, frightened now at what she had driven Anne to do.

"This is foolish, Anne. Stop! If you kill yourself, you can't blame me!"

Anne only straightened up, assuming the pose of a Celtic princess.

"I shall prove you a liar or perish!" she announced, tossing up her chin dauntlessly.

Before Violetta or the groom could stop her, Anne gave the bay a mighty kick with her heels. It bolted off at a fierce gallop, across the brook and up onto the lush green lawns of the Thomas property.

"Anne, Anne, stop!" shouted Violetta in terror as the uncontrollable animal galloped past.

As the horse gathered speed, Anne forgot all about her illustrious ancestor, Queen Maeve. She clung to its mane and reins with all her might and begged for it to stop. The more she shrieked the faster the horse ran, thoroughly spooked by the featherweight bouncing to and fro across its back. The animal circled the formal garden, throwing up chunks of sod with its hooves and trampling the rose parterre.

Running and screeching in its wake, Violetta was able to accomplish nothing in trying to halt or calm the frightened steed. Two horrified grooms were now also tearing across the grass.

"Mother," shrieked Violetta, panting past the front portico. "She's completely out of control!"

Louisa sped out the door then stopped and stared at the mayhem proceeding across her mother-in-law's property.

"Hepzibah!" Louisa cried. "It's Anne!"

As Hepzibah dashed out the front entrance, her mouth fell open in disbelief. The horse crashed through the manicured shrubbery and hurtled down the driveway straight toward a gleaming, ebony carriage pulled by a high-strung but elegant team barrelling through the property gates. The startled coachman hauled on the reins to avoid any collision, but the carriage and team swerved so sharply onto the lawns that the graceful coach was very nearly tipped on its side. Anne's horse reared up at the obstacle, swerved and bolted in the opposite direction. Anne's pinafore and braids were flying behind her. Trying in vain to find a grip, she worked her legs and arms frantically. When the anxious horse finally skidded onto the muddy bank of the millpond and slid down an embankment, it tossed Anne headlong into the water.

The carriage that Anne had nearly sideswiped moments before now careened among the trees as the driver struggled to gain control. The aristocratic occupant of the carriage alternately clutched at the straps inside to steady herself and shouted at the driver to stop.

"What the devil is going on? Charles, don't you have any

control? Who was that? Where are the grooms? Where is the stable boy, for pity's sake!"

The driver, Charles, was far too preoccupied to answer. Only by much skill did he pilot the rocking vehicle up the grassy slope without losing a wheel against one of the trees. Inside, the impatient passenger was still demanding that he stop.

"Whose horse is that? Stop this carriage at once! Charles, please stop! I'm going to lose my lunch!"

Finally, the carriage stopped, askew on the lawn in front of the Thomas portico, the team still stamping and snorting. Louisa dashed across the lawn, followed by her children and Hepzibah. She halted abruptly as the carriage door banged open. The very picture of shaken, offended majesty emerged, pushing away the coachman's help in irritation.

"You *oaf!*" the beleaguered passenger hollered at Charles, who had done his very best.

Amelia Thomas was an elegant woman who still retained her youthful slenderness. Dressed in heavily embroidered brocade, relieved only by a square gold brooch at the throat, she was a true matriarch from head to toe. Her thick hair, drawn up in a knot at the top of her head, had been auburn in its heyday but still held its rich colour under pale streaks of grey. She strode across her lawn toward Louisa in a fury, jerking her shawl about her shoulders with long, fine fingers and waving a fashionable hat.

"Louisa! If this is your manner of showing appreciation for my munificence, you can pack your bags and go."

Louisa paled at the words and her three children shrank around her. Amelia Thomas was the sort of woman who expected her decrees to be kept, no matter how inconvenient. She was quite capable of changing her mind, and Louisa was now prepared for the worst.

"Now don't excite yourself, Mrs. Thomas!" Louisa pleaded, trying to induce harmony.

Amelia's eyes sparkled with outrage. No one was going to tell her to compose herself after the trouble she had just encountered! Her pace did not slow as she approached, forcing Louisa and the children to scramble backward to keep from being physically run down. "Of course I'm going excite myself! How long can a day go on, searching hither and yon for relatives as giddy as cats out of a bag! Then to encounter this ... this *mania* in my own yard! Horses tearing up my garden and," she added heatedly, "*you* driving my only son to drink with the same kind of upheaval, I'm sure!"

"I'm so sorry, please ... Mrs. Thomas!" Louisa begged in desperation.

With a great flourish, Amelia turned and headed for her house. Suddenly, she reversed direction to take another strip off Louisa. The children hugged their mother, eyes wide and frightened, fearing the worst. For a moment, Amelia just stared silently at the little cluster in front of her then erupted in another spate of emotion.

"Don't think the gang of you can worm your way in here like I am a doormat, to take advantage of a mother's broken heart."

She shook her gloved finger at them before sailing indignantly toward the front door. In her haste, she failed to notice the dripping figure who had staggered from the slime of the millpond and squelched up the bank, just in time to hear this final harsh exchange. All at once, Amelia was halted in her tracks by something clutching the bottom of her skirt. She twisted around to see a child, a girl, soaking wet on her knees in the driveway gravel.

"Mrs. Thomas, Mrs. Thomas! Please don't think I'm lacking

in sympathy, but Louisa is neither a worm, nor you a doormat!"

It took Amelia a heartbeat to find her tongue.

"What! Are you rumpled in the head, girl?"

"I may be rumpled in spirit but not in the head, Mrs. Thomas! Louisa and her children came here grieving for a husband and a father. The least you can do is offer some pity. They've nowhere to go either."

With that, Anne burst into tears so vehemently that even Amelia was taken aback. "Who are you?" Amelia demanded in amazement.

Anne clasped her hands before her and looked up with large, glistening eyes.

"Anne Shirley, ma'am. I should know better for speaking out, but they are in as much anguish as you."

Amelia glanced at her grandchildren, huddled together with dread on their faces. She twitched her skirts out of Anne's grip.

"All right, all right. No need for you to put yourself in a state on our account," she told Anne scratchily.

But Amelia's words made no impression. Anne's imagination was already off and running. All of the refugees were about to end up homeless, herself included. Here was another disaster—and she was the cause. Her eyes grew even larger and more pathetic.

"Oh, but there is need! Imagine you were an orphan with nowhere to go. And you'd come to a place like this hoping an important person like yourself might grant you a chance."

On bent knee, Anne fervently kissed the hem of Amelia's dress. Pond water dripped onto the brocade and Anne's damp hands crushed the fine fabric. Amelia snatched her skirt away from the impudent girl again and stepped back.

"I know tomfoolery when I see it. Stand up, for goodness sake, and stop this begging business."

Amelia took Anne by the arm and hoisted her bodily to her feet. Pond weeds clung to the girl's clothes and wet strands of red hair were plastered across her cheeks. The matriarch gave the pint-sized supplicant a very annoyed look, but softened her tone. "And there is no need to cast my prominence up at me either. It's been an extremely difficult day and I have a right to say what is on my mind. Of course Louisa can stay."

Everyone was relieved and emotional, now.

. "'Thank you, Mrs. Thomas," cried Anne, looking at Louisa and her family with a broad smile lighting up her face. She was so overcome with relief that she dropped to her knees again.

"'I withhold not my heart from any joy,'" Anne whispered. "Ecclesiastes, chapter two, verse ten.'"

Applying biblical scholarship may have proven a mistake in judgment. Amelia waved Anne away, even as she motioned everyone else back to the house.

"Yes, I know." Amelia flapped her hand at Anne. "Stand up, dear. And stop with the biblical authority. Any child that behaves like a pagan one minute and quotes Old Testament just turns my stomach. This is such a dissolute age, don't you think, Louisa?"

Having finished with Anne and Lousia, Amelia Thomas decided to take out the remainder of her irritation on another ready and easy target.

"Hepzibah, come here," She spoke at her housekeeper, who had been standing on the outer edge of the little group, taking in the usual events of the morning." Why haven't you got my grandchildren settled in! Don't ogle me like that. I find it offensive for a housekeeper to be so incompetent. I don't know how I tolerate you. You're a disaster. You're never prepared for anything. I have to do everything myself."

Amelia tossed her shawl and hat at Hepzibah as she turned on her heel to disappear up the stone steps and through the ornate glass front door. Hepzibah knew when a bark was bigger than a bite, but she stammered and mumbled nonetheless. She was in complete servitude to Mrs. Thomas and had been for almost forty years.

As the two old women vanished, Louisa released an enormous sigh of relief. She sent Violetta into the house behind her grandmother and shooed Keith and Jock off to do their part, too.

"You were always wonderful at keeping her amused boys. Now go!"

Alone with Anne, Louisa brushed the girl's wet hair back from her face affectionately.

"Anne . . . thank you," she smiled.

Anne was feeling quite proud of herself as well, and was already rerunning the scene in her mind. "I could have made it more flowery if I'd had time to think it through. I wish she wasn't so inhospitable."

Louisa winced to imagine just how much more florid Anne's utterances might have become had the girl found a few extra moments to elaborate. No doubt Amelia already thought the child was slightly touched in the head. Anne was too young to understand Amelia's imperious manner. Louisa had had considerably more experience dealing with the doughty woman. She understood that her mother-in-law was on edge over the loss of her only son, and this partly accounted for the burst of hysteria. For all her money and influence, Amelia was alone in that big house with only her servants for company. Louisa sighed.

"Well, she needs us as much we need a place to stay."

"I hope someone will always need me," Anne replied wistfully.

Struggling to craft a response to that particular comment. Louisa became aware of water dripping onto her shoes and the distinct odour of pond mud emanating from Anne. She put her hands on the child's shoulders and turned her toward the path leading behind the house.

"You'll need a bath if we are ever going to persuade Hepzibah to give you a place indoors."

A word out the back door produced Hepzibah and two sturdy maids in succession, rolling up their sleeves. "You're the disaster," Hepzibah growled at Anne as she ordered her troops into action. "I've had enough of your caterwauling and your shenanigans. Get her in there. You know what to do, ladies."

The two maids hustled Anne into an outdoor shower stall surrounded by only enough wooden panelling to ensure modesty. Before Anne knew what was happening, her wet clothes were peeled from her and she was thrust under a cold shower that descended from a bucket above. The water was so freezing that Anne's determination to cooperate vanished.

"No, no!" Anne gulped in protest as the torrent poured over her shivering body. "It's freezing!"

"You just behave yourself," commanded Hepzibah, not caring how loudly the girl howled. Grinning at Anne's discomfort, a sureptitious Violetta hurried back into the house to be at her mother's side and to report Anne's degradation.

Hepzibah watched the two maids scrub down every bit of Anne and every article of her clothing. When her ordeal was complete, Anne sat wrapped in a towel while her rough poorhouse garments dried out on the clothesline for all to see. Once again, she had no idea what would happen to her next.

INSIDE THE BIG HOUSE, Louisa and Violetta had been summoned into the parlour by Amelia. The room, with large, elaborately paned glass windows facing the gardens, was lavishly appointed. Paintings in great gold frames covered the walls. Rich, multicoloured Oriental carpets smothered the floors. Heavy dark furniture sat gleaming while a tall pot of palms and ferns graced the presence of a carved marble bust of some classical beauty.

Violetta and her mother stood anxiously waiting for a comment from Amelia, who stood staring out the wide windows. Amelia held her beloved cat in her arms. It was a lilac point Siamese with piercing blue eyes, a pale body, and a face masked in a shade that matched the colour of smoke. This exotic aristocratic breed entirely suited its owner.

Louisa had been doing her best to argue a position for Anne in the Thomas household, but she did not feel she was making a lot of progress.

"Louisa, you have some queer ideas," Amelia was saying skeptically as she stroked the cat and turned back from the window.

While Violetta looked on, wanting no part in the undertaking, Louisa forged ahead, feeling miserable about her best friend Bertha and her promise to Anne that she would not desert her. Her only hope was to find some useful role for Anne in the main house, as all other suggestions had been swiftly rejected.

"Her poor mother was such a gifted teacher, and the child's unbelievably bright. At one point I thought she might even help the children with their studies, seeing as they've missed so much school this year. What do you think?"

Slowly, Amelia settled into a delicately carved armchair. Only then did Louisa and Violetta dare to sit on the grand silk sofa opposite Amelia.

"You are so irresponsible, Louisa," She sighed, still upset at the chaos she convinced herself Louisa had caused in her life.

Violetta barely heard her grandmother's words.

"I refuse to be taught by a stray!" Violetta interjected vehemently.

Louisa cast her daughter a very aggravated glance, silently willing her to hold her tongue.

"I've always felt some level of responsibility to her mother, since she died." Louisa countered. "Anne's so well read and she really has a heart of gold that you will see in time, Mrs. Thomas."

No annoyed glance was going to keep Violetta quiet on this subject, lest her grandmother soften too. "She's quite odd, if you ask me."

Louisa gave Violetta another biting look, but she needn't have bothered. Amelia was little interested in Violetta's opinion on anything. She continued stroking her cat, which continued to stare at the two on the sofa, not once blinking its unsettling azure eyes.

"I just don't have it in me to send her to another asylum," Louisa finally confessed, her voice filled with genuine emotion.

"You've got as soft a heart and a head as my son," Amelia told her, preparing to make an imperious decision. "I intend to see if any local family needs help."

It wasn't the outcome Louisa had hoped for, but at least it wasn't an orphanage.

"I can tutor the boys then, grandmother." Violetta exclaimed, pleased that Anne would be gone from the house. It would leave a perfect opening for Violetta to rule over her brothers and direct her own lessons. Amelia raised her elegant eyebrows and looked Violetta up and down, as though assessing exactly where the improvements needed to be made.

"Your life is to be elevated above that of your parents," Amelia informed her. "A girl's education starts with a proper governess. I've engaged someone to start right away, who can provide a firm hand. It will make all the difference in the world, dear."

Before Violetta could open her mouth against the idea of a firm hand, Louisa managed to pinch her to keep her quiet. The sooner Violetta learned the limits of her grandmother's tolerance, the more confident they would all be in the house.

"Now I've had enough," Amelia told them, rising with an effort that suggested complete and utter exhaustion. "Good night."

Louisa and Violetta rose obediently, curtsied respectfully, and vacated the room. When they were gone, Amelia sat down again and pulled the Siamese cat closer in her lap. A portrait of her deceased but raffish son gazed at her from a frame on her desk.

"My life will never be the same again," she murmured sadly to him.

A low meow from the cat seemed to echo in agreement. Softly, Amelia caressed the animal as though it were the only individual in the world she could trust.

Eight

Still relegated to stable chores, Anne willingly headed to work the next morning. She was clean top to toe, and her hair was neatly braided—a relief after months of dirt and grime. One of the grooms, Mr. MacAdams, finally recaptured the bay that Anne had almost driven to insanity the day before. He had quickly gotten over his anger when he caught the runaway horse unharmed, however. In fact, he thought the whole incident so hilarious that he gave Anne a gift of one of his peaked tweed caps, so that she could look like a proper groom herself. The two were well on their way to becoming friends.

The stable door once again stood wide open, letting in the afternoon sun and fresh air. Anne was helping Mr. MacAdams fork hay for the carriage team when she noticed a plump woman marching purposefully toward the portico of the house. Anne's natural curiosity, coupled with constant anxiety about her own fate, made her exceedingly interested in everyone who came and went from the house. Quickly, she hit upon an excuse to investigate.

"Someone's left a pitcher of lemonade for the hired help. Want some?" she asked the groom.

"Sure," he nodded, always ready for a treat. "Go get me some."

Anne leaned her pitchfork against the wall and hurried across the grass to the summer kitchen, where the glass pitcher filled with lemonade sat on a sideboard. All the better homes had a summer kitchen. Most of the cooking would be done here during the hottest months, in order to keep the main house cool while the wood or coal burning stoves were in use. At the Thomas mansion, the summer kitchen was a long room at the back of the house with plenty of windows to light the worktables.

As Anne carefully poured a tall glass, she peered around the doorjamb to see the strange woman now seated on a bench in the main kitchen. Middle aged and very respectably dressed, the woman was not sitting placidly, as most visitors would. Instead, her eyes darted from left to right and back again, as if trying to take in and remember every detail while she had the chance.

All at once, the woman's gaze stopped at an open cupboard on the wall—home to all the house and grounds keys, carefully arranged so that they could be guarded by Hepzibah. The house keys were the housekeeper's domain. No one else dared touch them without her permission. Everyone who worked at the Thomas mansion knew that she was completely in charge of everything to do with running the house, except the stables, which were run by the head groom. On Hepzibah's orders, the doors of the key cupboard stood open during the day for easy access, but they were carefully locked each and every night. Slowly, the woman got to her feet, walked over to the keys, and scrutinized each of their labels. Her hand appeared to reach out for one when she suddenly noticed Anne watching her while pouring lemonade. Quickly, the woman sat back down again, her hands folded neatly in her lap—but not before Anne thought she had seen a decidedly guilty look on the woman's face.

A moment later, Hepzibah appeared.

"Mrs. Thomas will see you now," she told the waiting woman.

Just as Hezpibah was about to escort the visitor into the parlour, she noticed Anne.

"What are you doing here!" she demanded.

"Uh...," Anne sought to concoct some excuse for loitering there with a full glass of lemonade. "I was...just enjoying those crows up there."

As she spoke, Anne pointed at the two stuffed crows high atop a pantry cupboard, surveying the kitchen with their beady, black looks. If Hepzibah had had a broom in her hand, she would have swept Anne, like some flea-bitten stable cat, right out the door.

"You come back in here again and those crows will pick your eyes out! Now get out of here!"

Balancing the glass of lemonade, Anne scurried back the way she had come, wondering who on Earth the woman was and why she was so interested in the house keys.

SHE LEARNED THE ANSWER to her first question soon enough. The stranger was a governess by the name of Ruth Bridgewater, whom Amelia had engaged to teach not only Violetta but also the boys. It did Anne no good to look up longingly at the study window where the three Thomas children were set to work, catching up on their studies. They had missed an awful lot of schoolwork due to all the dislocations caused by the death of their father and their sojourn in the Halfway Hotel. In wealthy families, a governess tutored, disciplined, and generally took over the education of the children, producing polished students in the end—a feat that village schools could not hope to match. In the privilege of the Thomas house, Violetta, Keith, and Jock would have the luxury of continuing their studies while Anne, though brighter by far than the lot of them, was relegated to menial labour in the stable. Louisa was still making efforts to persuade Amelia that Anne would be an asset to her children's education, but to no avail. Her mother-in-law simply thought Louisa was addle-headed and she flatly refused.

Competent as she was, Ruth Bridgewater seemed to have something besides education on her mind.

She did make the children work hard—setting them up with history questions and arithmetic problems, and making them learn about the geography of the vast and imperial British Empire—but as she walked up and down between their desks while they worked, her eyes darted here and there, taking in things that should have been of no importance to her. A week after Ruth began teaching, as the noon hour approached, she decided it was time for a rest. All three children had been struggling to determine how far a train would travel in three hours if it had to go at two different speeds and stop at a siding for fifteen minutes, and it seemed a logical opportunity for a break.

"All right, close your notebooks. You can break now. Your grandmother has asked me to send all three of you outside for lunch with her on the verandah while I mark your notebooks." Violetta, Keith, and Jock were only too pleased to scamper off, arguing about the train as they went.

"I feel dumb. That last question was too hard to even understand," complained Keith.

Violetta agreed with him for once, as they trotted down the hall eager for their lunch.

"Guess what, I couldn't get it either. I think Bridgewater's just trying make us look stupid."

Sums, fractions, long division, and erratic trains were not Violetta's taste at all, but she had stumbled upon a grain of truth in her assessment of their new governess.

As soon as the children were gone, Ruth put the notebooks down on the table, slipped out into the corridor, and began looking into various drawers, nooks, and crannies. Finding nothing of consequence, she looked furtively both ways then climbed the set of back stairs that led to the attic. She extracted a key from her pocket and unlocked the door. Quick as she could, she dodged into a room full of drawers and cabinets, used to store all manner of books and papers no longer needed downstairs. With practised hands, she began to open drawers and rummage through the contents, systematically searching for what she assessed to be the private secrets of the Thomas empire.

THOUGH SHE DESPERATELY missed being able to do schoolwork, Anne did not mind her stable chores. Mr. MacAdams was cheerful company and did not give Anne any task beyond her ability. He even got her fixed up with trousers and a work smock so her legs would be protected from the prickly hay. She got on wonderfully with all the horses, which were glad to see her whenever she had a bucket of feed in her hand. After all the work was finished, the tack in order, and the stalls cleaned, Mr. MacAdams and Anne would go outside and Anne would wait while he locked the stable door. It was a rule that the outbuildings be locked when no one was using them. One day, after completing this ritual, the groom handed Anne the well-worn ring of keys.

"You go and put these keys back in the cupboard in the kitchen. Then come back and help us over at the pond well," he instructed.

It was an honour Anne had not been accorded before. Feeling very important and responsible, she obediently jogged up to the house, entered the summer kitchen, and slipped the keys onto the carefully labelled hook. She had just walked away when Hepzibah came around the corner, catching only a glimpse of Anne's red braids. Checking suspiciously, Hepzibah saw that the one marked "Upstairs Hall" was missing. She had given no one permission to touch such a key!

She quickly and thoroughly searched her own pockets and asked all the maids if one of them had the key. Within twenty minutes, the situation seemed perfectly clear. Hepzibah was certain where the key had gone. She marched over to the stables, calling on Louisa to witness the inquisition. Hepzibah confronted Anne directly. "It is missing as sure as the day is long. And I caught her loitering in the summer kitchen."

Hepzibah's thin lips were pressed together in accusation and she fixed Anne with flinty eyes.

"Anne, did you notice a key lying anywhere?" Louisa asked carefully, praying it was all just some silly mix-up.

The girl was already pierced with the pang of fear. Her all-too-recent experience in the poorhouse had taught her that when adults accused her of wrongdoing, nothing could convince them she wasn't guilty.

"Yes," she admitted. "I put away the stable keys in the cupboard not an hour ago."

"What business of it was yours?" Hepzibah demanded. "You don't meddle with my keys."

"I did exactly as Mr. MacAdams told me, when we locked the barn door," she said, invoking her legitimate reason for entering the summer kitchen after Hepzibah had warned her not to. "He said to put *his* keys in the cupboard then come and help him over at the pond, which I did dutifully. Only . . ."

The words died away on Anne's lips as she suddenly remembered who else had been near the keys. She looked down at the ground.

"Only what, Anne?" urged Louisa, seeing the child's hesitation.

Anne refused to speak, sure that she would bring on only more trouble for herself. For Hepzibah, Anne's hesitancy was simply more evidence of the child's negligence or just plain criminal tendencies.

"Only she likely mixed the stable keys with the missing key and can't remember where she put them! Or worse, she stole them!" Fast as a snake, Hepzibah flashed out her hand and gave Anne's ear a vicious twist. "Didn't you steal them, you little sneak?"

Anne let out a screech of pain.

"Stop it, Hepzibah!" Louisa snapped as she pulled Anne out of the housekeeper's grasp. "Anne, did you touch any other key?"

Anne tried hard not to burst into tears.

"Believe me ... if I was being led to the block for it, although I'm not certain what a block is, I never touched any other key. Only the stable keys that were Mr. MacAdams's responsibility."

Anne might as well have confessed to murdering the cat on the front doorstep for all the credibility she had with the housekeeper. Hepzibah summed up Anne's response as pure insolence. She might not get away with twisting Anne's ears in Louisa's presence, but she could still strike back.

"I will not allow that child to sleep in here until she finds the upstairs key. She stays in the barn until she rots or hands back the key."

Hepzibah stomped back to the house, shaking with anger. Louisa lingered, knowing that Anne still had more to say.

"There's something else, Anne? What is it?"

Anne had little faith that anyone would believe her and knew she couldn't risk alienating Louisa too. She only shook her head dolefully.

"Nothing," she said. She tried to hold her head high as she turned and walked away into the dark of the stable.

Before the incident with the key, Anne had been permitted a tiny cot near the mop closet, but now she was banished even from that bit of shelter in the house. When night fell, she made herself a nest in the hay as best she could, and lay down to sleep. The hay was prickly whenever she moved and her only cover was an old horse blanket with a strong animal smell. By day, the barn might have seemed a friendly comfortable place. But by night, in the creeping gloom, the building changed its character completely. It was full of frightening dark spaces where gleaming eyes glared at Anne, seemingly ready to pounce. The horses stamped their hooves in the stalls and the barn itself creaked and groaned in the rising wind. Anne had not realized that the rafters were home to bats and owls until the creatures began to fly out, wings flapping loudly in the air as they passed. She pulled her head under the blanket, like a turtle, fearing that some swooping creature would end up tangled and clawing in her hair. She also tried not to think about rats creeping toward her toes, or barn spiders crawling unseen down the neck of her clothing.

An imagination can prove to be an enormous liability in the dark. It was well into the early hours of morning, while an owl occasionally hooted like some lost soul, before a very nervous barn girl managed to fall asleep.

AS DIFFICULT AS HER NEW nighttime arrangements were, they were not Anne's only torment. In the days that followed, Hepzibah embarked on a campaign to wring the truth from this urchin foisted upon her household. She set Anne tasks far beyond a child's strength. Anne had to struggle in and out with great armloads of wood for the kitchen stove and carry heavy pails of water, two at a time, on a yoke that nearly crushed her neck. She bailed hay with the farmhands and was sent to the fields to help with the second cutting. She was able to endure the heat and hard work only because the other labourers were good to her. No one could understand why this child had been assigned such physical tasks. Some workers complained and eventually Mr. MacAdams brought Anne back to the barn under his supervision. Hepzibah refused to let up. She pushed Anne personally at every opportunity she could find. One day, when Anne nearly fell down as she staggered under a load of water, Hepzibah stepped in front of her. "Ready to tell me what happened to the missing key?"

Anne dropped the pails and the yoke to the ground. She nodded wearily, her neck simply aching. She could take no more of this punishment. She described to Hepzibah what she had seen in the summer kitchen the day Ruth Bridgewater had arrived.

"She fully planned to take the keys off the hook, but when she saw me, she froze and went and sat down."

Just as Anne had feared, the very idea that anyone other than her might be guilty sent Hepzibah into a tirade. The house-keeper marched Anne straight into the house and called not only Louisa but also Amelia and Ruth to witness the girl's testimony. Anne retold her tale, just as she had seen it happen. She varied not one iota from the truth.

"That's preposterous, Mrs. Thomas." Ruth Bridgewater swelled up with righteous indignation. "I'm to be accused by a mischievous child who's never had an upbringing?"

"Well, she's getting one now!" gritted Hepzibah, addressing her employer. "This goes beyond a mere scolding, ma'am."

Amelia weighed the situation. She could not believe that the respectable governess she herself had chosen could be capable of such petty theft. It was obvious—it simply had to be the child's fault. Everyone waited while she scrutinized Anne critically. Finally, she marched across the room and leaned over to her daughter-in-law.

"Louisa, the child is a liar," she whispered.

Louisa did not know what to say—or what to believe—but Anne didn't wait for Louisa's support. She set her small jaw and confronted Amelia head-on.

"Mrs. Thomas! I speak the truth because to be unjustly accused is an assault on my good name," she burst out vehemently. "My heart may be broken, but my one consolation is that someday you'll feel remorse for having crushed it."

Impervious to this dramatic hurricane, Amelia made up her mind faster.

"I'm setting my hand to the plow, Louisa. The child is going straight to that home in Fredericton."

The injustice drove Anne right over the edge. In her hurt and anger, she chose exactly the wrong thing to say.

"You're a heartless woman," Anne spoke with utter fury, fighting back tears. "I'm sure your own poor son was driven to drink by your pushing him away."

Amelia considered this for a fraction of a second before nodding her head in Louisa's direction.

"No," she said coolly. "She did that!" She turned curtly and marched out of the room. From halfway down the hall, she shouted back at Hepzibah. "Pack the child's bag, Hepzibah, and get her off our premises!"

Louisa spent nearly an hour pleading on Anne's behalf. It amounted to very little, other than that Amelia agreed to send the child to work in her lumberyard, instead of to St. Agatha's Asylum. She gave in primarily because she was exhausted by Louisa's whining. In her heart, however, she felt that someone in that difficult environment would probably take the child under their wing, like a stray cat or dog. At the very least, it would save her the trouble of finding a local family. Eventually, the saucy girl would simply disappear, maybe even from the face of the Earth, for all she cared.

HER CARPET BAG AGAIN BY HER SIDE, Anne was helped into a Thomas Lumber wagon by Louisa that very afternoon. The wagon had made a detour from the road to stop by the door of the mansion, the white-haired driver stolidly waiting until Anne was loaded. Picking up an undesirable orphan was just one more task in his long day.

"I did my best, dear," Louisa told Anne, patting her arm. "Working at the lumberyard will be much better than a foundling home."

After hearing Anne's recent tales of life in the Bolingbroke County Poorhouse, Louisa had determined to do everything she could to keep the child out of another such institution. She had no idea what it would be like for a young girl to work in a lumberyard but she firmly believed she had won a concession from her mother-in-law.

Anne took Louisa's hand in hers as she sat down on the wagon seat. Violetta and the boys were noticeably absent from the farewell, on Amelia's instructions.

"Goodbye, dear friend. I don't believe God himself could do any better in the face of such an obstinate person."

With a sad backward glance over her shoulder, Anne was driven away. As the wagon rounded the corner and disappeared from sight Louisa was left wondering at how fate had played havoc with both their lives. She felt a inkling that her life was tied to Anne's in a way she could not fathom.

Nine

In the upstairs hallway of Green Gables, Anne took a copy of a book of short stories entitled *Avonlea Chronicles* from the box of old books she had found at the back of the cupboard under the stairs. It was inscribed "To Matthew and Marilla Cuthbert for their unfailing support, and for Gilbert, who inspired me in the first place." She remembered the thrill of tearing open that brown paper package on receiving the proofs of her first publication the afternoon that Marilla brought the mail into her room. She had been sitting on the bed, ridden with anxiety after hearing the news that Gilbert had caught scarlet fever. She remembered what a tonic the glow on Marilla's face had been for her, as she read the dedication.

"You do beat all, Anne," Marilla said, looking embarrassed, proud, and all mixed up inside. Anne also remembered the confidence Gilbert had given her to write her first short story.

The moment was fleeting. Anne put the book down, her imagination once again fast at work. She desperately needed that kind of confidence at that moment. She was on to a brand new idea for her play. She had massaged and reworked it in her mind all day and felt that perhaps she had begun to foster the beginning of a really interesting scenario—something she could put down on paper. It was a story she knew all too well, by heart, in fact. But her overheated brain was exhausted. Anne had set up a table and her typewriter in Marilla's old room, hoping the setting would offer some inspiration. The view out the window showcased the fields and an inlet of the ocean just beyond. The purple twilight had begun its descent across the cloudy sky. As Anne opened the window to enjoy the breeze, the air filled with the scent of lilies in the garden below, and she noticed that the apple trees were still covered in a cloud of blooms.

Satisfied with both the new concept and the headway she had made in her mind, Anne spread out her original manuscript, covered with notes from Gene, as a kind of guide. It would show her how not to go wrong. Beside her on the floor lay Gabriel's carpet bag. It was the oldest memento of her childhood, and she had retrieved it from a broken chest in that same forgotten cupboard under the stairs. As a little girl she had carried it from place to place—a talisman of hope that her prospects could change at any minute. The bag was made of frayed corduroy and was in such a delicate state that Anne was concerned it had deteriorated beyond saving. Nonetheless, the bag had greeted her like a long-absent friend. Several of the tattered, leatherbound books that Gabriel had bequeathed her still lay inside, their titles speaking out with grandeur as she'd lifted them out, one by precious one. Tennyson's *Morte d'Arthur*, Shakespeare's *Compleat Histories, Comedies, and Tragedies*, and Cervantes' *Don Quixote*.

These books were now arranged in a neat row across Marilla's bedroom writing table as Anne sat down to begin, her workplace set for enchantment. The sky deepened in colour. She rolled a sheet of paper into the typewriter and let her mind drift in and out of the past as she typed without interruption into the small hours of the morning.

ANNE WOKE UP SUDDENLY. It took a moment to realize where she was. After turning out page after page of work, she had fallen asleep with her head down on the table next to the typewriter. Ideas had come to her in such a swarm the previous evening that her fingers had hardly been able to stay on top of the keys. She had been pacing outside Green Gables nearly all day, thinking and jotting down notes and dialogue until she had conjured up an entirely new version of her play. The story had practically flooded into her mind that night, it was so vivid, until at last she fell asleep over her work. She must have at least taken the time to change her clothes, she realized, because she was now wearing her nightgown and a woolly cardigan. Her red hair hung loose in a whirl about her face, making her look years younger.

The banging and clanging of pots in the kitchen below caused her to sit up with a start. The lamp by the bed was still on, even though bright morning light filled the room.

"Helloooo?" she called out, wondering who had wandered in. On Prince Edward Island, it never occurred to anybody to lock doors. "Who's there?" she called again, with no response. Then she looked at her desk and realized her manuscript had vanished.

She hurried down the stairs to find Gene at the kitchen table, a brown teapot and a cup of freshly brewed tea beside him. He drew long and deep on the cigarette in his hand as he silently digested each of the pages Anne had just written.

"You might have at least woken me, instead of breaking in." Anne leaned shyly against the door jamb, stifling a yawn. Gene did not even look up. He took a sip of tea and flipped over another page.

"The local real estate agent in Avonlea was running around town telling people she caught you talking to yourself in the yard."

"Real estate agents," replied Anne wryly, "have absolutely no diplomacy."

Avonlea townsfolk had considered her eccentric since the day she first arrived at Green Gables, she thought to herself. Why not continue the tradition?

"I figured it was a good sign . . . I knew you must have decided to make some serious revisions," said Gene, looking pleased. "You've got something here. Finish the draft by next week and I'll have time do a cast read-through."

Anne smiled, partly out of embarrassment, and partly out of relief. She was getting used to Gene. The demanding man had little time for fools and if he approved of her new scenario at this early stage, she was at least on the right track. Perhaps this elusive play she had unaccountably desired to write might materialize onstage after all.

Gene turned the last page, stood up, and headed out the screen door without a further comment. Anne followed him anxiously, hoping for another word of either praise or criticism, but he offered none. Halfway down the lane, he turned and looked back.

"What turned the light bulb on again?"

Anne's mind flashed with the thrill of reconsidering so many dramatic ideas—ideas that had emerged from a place deep inside.

"A letter. From my father. It made me rethink things, so I tried to take the story in a different direction."

"From your father? I always thought you were a stray mutt."

All Gene received in response was an enigmatic smile. He stopped, realizing that he was still holding Anne's tea cup in his hand. He walked back up the path and handed it to her. Anne nodded in appreciation. The cup was one of Marilla's prized Blue Willow set. It reminded Anne of how much she still treasured all of the things that were a part of that old house and her past with the Cuthberts.

As Gene set out again in the direction of the lane, he noticed the For Sale sign lying on top of the woodpile by the barn.

"You'd never get what the place is worth anyway," he grunted, heading out through the picket gate and down the lane toward Stanhope Beach and the hotel. Anne watched him go, pleased that she had won at least some of his tough approval.

ANNE COULDN'T RECALL the exact moment she had decided not to sell Green Gables. Perhaps it had to do with walking through all the old familiar rooms and feeling the stories they had to tell. Now that the Wright family had moved out, the empty house seemed to belong to her again and it had simply cried out to be occupied. She thought constantly of Matthew and Marilla. She longed to hear Gil's voice. But they were all gone forever; nothing more than fleeting memories. Then she remembered that perhaps her father was out there somewhere, and the thought of him pulled at her core. He had broken her heart more times than he could ever have imagined, and yet her mother had loved him passionately. The letter had emerged and now it seemed like an olive branch she might have decided to accept once, had she been given the chance. Forgiveness stirred at the bottom of her soul. She longed to meet this ancient stranger who spoke to her from the shadows of the past; if he were still alive. As she mulled over her options, trying to decide what to do, Anne realized that Green Gables was the perfect place—the only place—to make her decision. It was the only real home she had ever known; Matthew and Marilla her only real parents. She needed the well-being of this place if she was ever going to make any sense of her life. After so many years of pretending her past had never existed, Anne wondered how she was ever going to delve into it all over again.

Gathering her strength, Anne returned to the writing table upstairs, and took out a piece of paper. She hesitated for just a moment before putting the pen firmly on its surface.

"Forty years may have passed," she wrote, "but your long-lost letter finally arrived in my hand a week ago. I am hoping your return address is still valid. I have no idea if you've ever come across any of my work, but I am a well-published author and recently an aspiring playwright. I still publish under my maiden name, Anne Shirley, even though I am a widow. I have two wonderful daughters who are all grown up with families of their own and an adopted son who is still overseas. It's never been easy for me to put into words my feelings about you. My memory of you has been somewhat rekindled in a play that I have been working on. I hope we can arrange to finally meet and that this letter actually gets to you. I suppose it's up to fate again. Your loving Anne."

Anne's hand shook just a little as she wrote the address on the envelope before she sealed it: "Walter Shirley, 78 Old Fort Lane, Fredericton, New Brunswick." After this many years, he had most likely moved away or perhaps passed on, she mused. Still, it was worth writing such a letter if there was even a chance he was alive and might receive it.

Anne dressed and walked into Avonlea, for the sake of appearance looking like a striding, confident woman. No one would ever have guessed that she'd been unable to eat a bite of breakfast before heading to the post office.

The town had changed since Anne's childhood. There were paved streets now, and cars parked where horses and buggies had once lined up, but people still waved, doffed their hats, and called to Anne as if she belonged to them. Word had gotten round that she was back at Green Gables, a fact that added fuel to the town's ever-busy rumour mill. The intense interest in the comings and goings of all of its residents was the one aspect of Avonlea life that hadn't changed.

Her story as the troublesome red-headed, orphan taken in by old Matthew and Marilla Cuthbert remained a treasured part of Avonlea folklore. So a letter from Anne Shirley to a man with the same last name was certain to stir up all kinds of speculation.

In the post office, Anne bought stamps and lingered over the letter with its conspicuous addressee. She knew the postmistress was watching her with increasing curiosity, but there was no point delaying the inevitable. The talk would start soon enough. She handed the letter across the counter, closed the door behind her, and walked back toward Green Gables. Her reliable typewriter sat upstairs waiting for her.

Ten

Looking out of Marilla's window into the orchard below, Anne prepared for another journey into memory. She was compelled to stumble through Marysville again in search of bits and pieces for the play.

Once again, she was a child, sweeping the floors of the bustling mill and trying to keep out from under the feet of the rough men who came and went, never sparing a glance for the little figure behind the broom. She passed the hours in silence, figuring that the Thomases had forgotten about her completely. Her fears about being sent to another orphanage were quickly replaced by the hardship of trying to survive among people who could not have cared less about her.

The lumber mill was a busy, dangerous place, where a small girl could easily get stepped on by horses, run over by heavy wagons, or even mangled in the terrifying machinery. All day long Anne worked beside giant saw blades that were taller than her. They whined and screeched; their myriad teeth cutting log after log into lumber that the mill workers then stacked out in the yard for shipment.

Anne battled to keep sawdust from creeping into every part of her. She ran errands, took drinks to the sweating men, and even learned to tag lumber according to cut and quality. No one spoke to her—save to toss an order or tell her to get out of the way—or bothered to notice her when *they* talked. Particularly since the talk among the men was filled with grumbling complaints and dissatisfaction. To Anne's surprise, she discovered that the magnificent Amelia Thomas, who owned all of the town's lumber, cider, and cotton mills, was universally feared and disliked. Although too young to understand the friction over proper labour practices, she knew the workplaces were off-balance. Mrs. Thomas, it seemed, was stubbornly resisting what the workers felt needed to be done. They worked so hard and wanted wages that at least kept up with the times. Most had families to feed, and they risked their necks every day with dangerous, antiquated machinery. Nevertheless, Mrs. Thomas didn't seem to care in the least about making improvements.

Jeremiah Land was manager of all the Thomas enterprises and Amelia's right-hand man. He was often booed when he came to inspect any of the mills. His bowler hat and good suit set him apart from the workers in their dusty caps, braces, and work pants. While Anne wearily swept, the foreman walked past her to meet Mr. Land at the door.

"I can't fill my orders because they're working too slow. A lot of bickering among the men. There's an uproar brewing. They're threatening to go on strike over unsafe conditions!"

Anne listened quietly, not daring to say a word. She knew better than to mention her connection to the Thomases in these surroundings.

That night, Anne tried to sleep in a hay nook on an upper floor of the mill, completely exhausted by her day's work. She didn't hear a thing when several masked figures snuck onto the mill property through the darkness to tamper with the log chute just outside. Nor did she see the team of horses that was being put in place beneath the chute, or the thick rope run around the bottom of one of the supports. Lying on a pile of hay and an old bit of ticking, her head resting on her carpet bag, Anne was restless and entirely consumed with despair. She glanced at her own reflection in a window pane beside her.

"Katie . . . I miss you," she whispered. "I don't believe I'm long for this world. I pray you'll find me in the next."

Her sad reverie was shattered by a burst of thundering water and a loud rumble outside the mill. Someone had opened the gates at the top of the log chute and the water from the upper millpond flooded in.

Logs reached the mill by river, floating down in the spring by way of log drives. Men like Walter Shirley spent the winter cutting trees with big crosscut blades and hauling them onto the river ice. When the ice melted, thousands of logs were pushed by a stiff current down to the mills. At the mill, they were trapped within a circle of logs or by a boom across the river, where they waited. During the day, water flowed through long chutes that carried the logs down to the huge whirling blades, which cut them into planks. At night, the water was shut off and the chutes sat empty until morning. Yet here it was past midnight and water was filling the chute—and with the water, hundreds of logs.

Anne raced to peer out a window just in time to see a team of horses plunge forward in the darkness. There was a tremendous crack followed by an ear-splitting roar as the team pulled away the struts that held the chute in place. Braces, beams, and supports ripped apart, and everything tumbled down together in a tangled heap. Water gushed from the broken end of the two-storey-high chute, spitting logs into a jagged pile in the yard below.

Instantly, workmen began to run toward the collapsed structure as the foreman shook his fist in anger.

"You people think you can terrorize management," he yelled at the three saboteurs, who managed to escape.

"Turn off the sluice! Shut the gate!" someone else called.

From the window high up in the mill where she slept, Anne stared down at the horrific scene below. She climbed down a ladder to the yard below, only to slam right into the foreman.

"What's the matter?" she cried.

"Buncha damn troublemakers!" he was sputtering, so red-faced and furious he barely noticed it was the little girl he'd collided with. "Tryin' to tamper with the chutes, claiming they aren't safe to work around. The bloody thing collapsed alright and we think the guilty ruffians are caught under it."

The attempted sabotage had certainly backfired. Anne watched as the mill workers started pulling away at the logs. The first person they found was a mere youth, limp and blood-stained. A hush fell over the men as he was carried out. He would never get up again.

A groaning from deep beneath the chute told the crowd there was someone else in there, still alive. Hastily, the men laid the dead lad on the ground and went back to the rescue effort with double the speed. They were interrupted by a round of jeers as the foreman and Jeremiah Land hurried past.

"Boo!" went up the cry. "This is all management's fault!"

Moving anything in the heaps of logs piled up under the cascading water was tricky work, and the men were soon forced to stop. In the gloom, and confusion of the dark night, no one could determine which logs needed to be lifted. Pulling indiscriminately at the heap might fatally injure whoever was caught in there and the spaces between the crumpled supports were simply too small to admit any of the rescuers.

"Hey kid!" With a start, Anne realized that one of the men was calling to her. He pushed at the chute supports, trying to create a bigger hole. "We need you to climb in here. This guy's still movin'. You're little. Come on!"

Big hands seized Anne from behind, lifted her, and shoved her into a small space between the logs and the broken flume. Terrified, she had no choice but to crawl ahead, praying the pile would not shift and crush her as well. Soon she had squeezed down right beside the man who was pinned underneath. He wore a scarf to mask his face and he was moaning in pain.

"Hurry up," bellowed Anne's accomplice up above—a powerful fellow with an old hat crammed low over his eyes. "Can you reach him? Hold on, buddy. Lift that beam, girl!"

The man's whole body was quivering from shock as one splintered strut held him down by his arm.

"I can't even budge it!" cried Anne in exasperation. Through sheer force of will, however, she managed to lift the beam about a foot.

At once, strong arms strained and heaved above until the beam shifted, creating enough space for the others to climb in a little ways and start pulling the victim out.

"Good job, kid," said the worker who had sent Anne into the hole. She crawled out at the same time the injured man was finally hauled free. As he reached the surface, the scarf he had been wearing slid away from his agonized face.

For a moment Anne struggled to catch her breath. The man was her father, Walter Shirley!

Walter was barely conscious and in far too much pain to notice his daughter. The men cheered when his body emerged and was hurried onto a makeshift stretcher. Anne barely had time to take this all in before the stretcher was passed to other men and a seriously injured Walter vanished into the darkness. Before Anne could utter a sound or the foreman was able to even pursue any of the troublemakers, a deafening explosion rent the air.

Anne recoiled as the windows blew out of a nearby warehouse and the roof flew upward in pieces in a grand burst of flames. Jeremiah and the foreman wheeled and ran off in the direction of the explosion, too shaken to notice two more masked figures running away from the fire in the opposite direction.

The workmen deserted the fallen log chute and raced off toward the explosion in the warehouse. Anne was left all alone in a state of shock, watching the orange conflagration as it roared across the night sky. She did not hear the hoofbeats barrelling toward her until a strong arm slipped around her waist and hoisted her onto the back of a stocky white horse. A dark figure sat in front of her, riding with enormous power.

"Come on," urged a female voice. "Get out of there."

It was Nellie Parkhurst, the driver of the mail wagon who had given Anne and the Thomases a ride from the railway station. Terrified and confused, Anne hung on for dear life as they galloped down the Marysville road, entertaining thoughts of what it would have been like to ride with Queen Maeve by moonlight.

"That was Walter Shirley, girl! " Nellie told Anne when they'd slowed a bit amid the solitude of the forest. When Anne didn't reply, Nellie supposed the girl didn't know who she was talking about. "The one you rescued!" she explained. "I saw his arm was badly mangled, but he's safe. Our men got him away."

"I know," Anne finally uttered in a very small voice.

"I'm taking you to the workers' cottage down by the cider mill," Nellie told Anne as the horse turned in before a simple group of clapboard dwellings next to a cider press. "You'll be safe there."

Anne was quickly bundled inside. No one spoke to her and she didn't dare ask questions. Other female hands took her into a room where children were sleeping and tucked her in beside them where it was warm and clean. She lay still in the dim light, until exhaustion overcame her and she fell asleep.

SOMETIME CLOSE TO DAWN, Anne awoke with a start. Faint grey light crept into the room as Anne tried hard to remember where she was. Soon enough, the bruises on her knees and the strange bed caused the incidents of the hours before to enter her mind. Low voices could be heard through the open bedroom door.

"What about the kid?" someone asked. "We can't afford to have her go to the police."

Anne's eavesdropping was interrupted by low moans coming from nearby. Someone else was in the room.

Wiping sleep from her eyes, Anne slid softly to the floor and tiptoed across to look. She saw, through a low arch, that men were sitting in subdued silence around a lantern while the woman of the house, the one who had taken Anne in, stood with her arms crossed, looking very worried. Anne was filled with dread as she approached the prostrate figure lying on a cot in a corner. Bloodstains slashed across a heavily bandaged arm. The face was drained and ashen, the eyes closed. Yet every few moments, the pathetic figure emitted another ragged cry. The man in the bed was her father!

Anne wanted to call out to him, but couldn't. Instead, she took his good hand in hers. His small groans sounded like some delirious effort at speech.

"I . . . don't understand." she whispered. "I can't make out what you're saying."

Walter stirred restlessly, but he was too far gone to know Anne was there. Anne felt awkward confronting this man, her father, here in such a public place. She wished, so very much, that she could have her family back again. Through the open door, the figures at the table watched silently as she dozed off sitting on a stool beside the bed.

When Anne awoke again, her father was gone. Someone had carried her back to her bed again and it was now full daylight.

The moment with her father seemed like a mirage.

"You were fools to bring in union organizers to help you," the woman who had taken Anne in was saying.

"What about the girl? We don't know what she knows or who she's talking to...."

"That's enough," the woman responded firmly.

Sitting up on the bed, now empty of the other children, Anne looked across the room. The other cot stood empty too, covered with a grey blanket, but there were bloodstains still on the mattress.

All at once, the woman was beside her, with a hand on Anne's shoulder. Anne threw back the covers and put her feet on the floor. She longed to ask a hundred questions, but fear kept her silent. If she seemed too curious, she would be immediately connected to Walter Shirley or, perhaps even worse, Amelia Thomas. Anne took a good look at this woman who had helped her. She had a kind, homey sort of face and accepted Anne's presence in a matter-of-fact way.

"Want some breakfast?" she asked. "What's your name?"

Suppressing a twinge of panic, Anne resorted to the pseudonym she'd thought up after escaping the poorhouse—the same one she'd used when she first met Nellie.

"Cordelia."

The woman patted Anne reassuringly and pointed out the carpet bag sitting neatly on a blanket box at the end of the bed. Someone must have rescued it from the mill and brought it there in the night.

Gently, the woman shepherded Anne into a humble kitchen with a plank table and two benches drawn up. The children Anne had been sleeping with turned out to be four girls whose ages ranged from ten to thirteen. They all sat at the table eating porridge from stoneware bowls. Though they regarded Anne with curious eyes, none dared comment. A cast-iron stove stood in the corner and the walls were of plain, unpainted boards with a frying pan hung up on a nail over a few sturdy shelves. To all appearances, it was a simple, cozy family home. No one mentioned that a wounded man and furtive groups of mill workers had used the cottage as a refuge in the dark of night, or that a mill chute had been destroyed, a saboteur killed, and a warehouse gone up in flames.

"Come and sit down. Don't be shy, dear." The woman was already doling out a generous bowl of oatmeal for Anne. "You can stay with us and pick apples. We're here until September then we move back to Maine. Penny a bushel. Lotsa other kids here to help, too. All right?"

"Yes, ma'am," Anne agreed meekly.

From outside came the fading sound of men's voices.

"Let's go," they were saying. "Nellie Parkhurst says we're to look after that one."

Anne had found a new haven, at least for the time being. Her father, however, had disappeared from her life as quickly as he'd appeared, and Anne concluded that he hadn't even been aware of her presence. She had no reason to think she would ever see him again.

Eleven

Apple season was just getting started so there was plenty of work for everyone, including the children. No one questioned the presence of another little girl joining in the work. The family with whom Anne was lodged was made up of migrant workers who travelled from crop to crop as harvest times came and went over the summer. Nobody ever bothered to count how many little ones they brought along. They were a cheerful lot and treated Anne kindly, especially when they saw how willingly she worked. Not one of them inquired as to who she really was or where she'd come from.

The job was outdoors in the fresh air and the children could eat all the apples they wanted. For Anne, it was ever so much better than being trapped in the lumber mill with its rough men, shrieking saws, and constant danger. The orchards were laden with rosy fruit, filling the air with the heady scent of apples. Anne thought this to be one of nature's most wonderful perfumes and it set her mind wandering. The days passed with a pleasing rhythm. Bushel after bushel accumulated under the trees to be picked up by the teams and wagons drawing the apples to the cider press. Anne was nimble at getting the very highest apples. When no one was watching, she could slip into the centre of a big old tree, surrounded by a green, rustling shield of leaves, and imagine she was a tree dryad claiming her leafy throne.

It was only at night, when she had time to think about things, that she gazed anxiously out the small window at the stars and the lonely moon. She worried about what would happen when the apples were all picked, and the group of families moved on to Maine. Would she go with them and adapt to the life of a migrant worker, forever leaving everything she knew behind? Or would Nellie come back for her so she could stay in Marysville?

The suspense weighed heavily on Anne's mind as the last of the russets were plucked from the branches. Burying her thoughts in the leafy wonderland of the tree branches, Anne tried to imagine what it would be like to ride on a train for days to a place where she wouldn't recognize a thing.

"Anne! Anne!"

Anne peered out through the tree branches and, to her amazement, saw Violetta running through the orchard toward her with a lanky boy at her heels. The boy was pointing to Anne. Violetta stopped, gasping for breath, under the very tree where Anne had been so absorbed in her work. "I wondered if we'd ever find you after all these weeks, Anne!" cried Violetta, her face burning red and her blond hair completely disheveled. "This is my friend Peter, from the smithy." Peter, not quite as out of breath as Violetta, nodded politely in silent greeting. Violetta gabbed on in a rush.

"Mother was so concerned when you disappeared. Peter told me he knew all about a girl who'd been working at the lumber mill and was now working here. I knew it had to be you! Please come back. We're desperate for you to help!"

Violetta had never before asked for anything from Anne, much less her help. "What's wrong, Violetta?" She climbed down the ladder. But Violetta didn't answer. She simply grabbed Anne's hand and pulled her away. The other apple pickers paused in their work but did not interfere. Anne hesitated for a moment. Did she really want to return to the family that had sent her to that horrible mill? She carried on a little ways beside her, leaving Peter to make his own way home.

Violetta never once let go of Anne's hand as she hauled her through the orchard and out onto a main road. She veered into the Marysville woods, explaining to Anne that it was the shortest way home. Finally, Violetta slowed from a run to a swift walk.

"That stupid cat attacked Bridgewater," she said, explaining her predicament at last.

Violetta told Anne how Bridgewater had been up in the attic, where she had no business being. Amelia's Siamese cat, a breed once used to guard temples in Siam, did not take kindly to this invasion into its private territory. From the top of a tall cupboard, it launched itself with a blood-curdling yowl straight at Bridgewater's head. Startled out of her wits, Bridgewater jumped so high that she hit her head on the low, slanting ceiling, screeching as she tried to pry off the cat. Before long, both cat and governess had toppled down the attic stairs, making an extreme racket. Of course, everyone with in earshot came running, and they caught Bridgewater with papers and books in her satchel that belonged not to her but to Mrs. Thomas.

"We knew she was up to something in the attic, going through old papers," Violetta continued, describing the shifty, guilty look that had come over the woman when she saw the whole household staring at her. "Claimed she was working on a history of the county, but no one believed her. Grandmother fired her on the spot."

Unsatisfied with this punishment, the Siamese cat was still in battle mode, hissing and snarling at everyone. They had to throw a blanket over him to catch him without getting scratched or bitten. Violetta had carried the squirming creature downstairs and tossed him, blanket and all, out the door onto the lawn. The cat had not taken kindly to the action. It set out across the grass in high dudgeon, and disappeared into the woods.

"Hepzibah told me to put the vile animal outside for a few minutes to cool it off. Now Grandmother is near hysterical over her 'Old Blue Eyes,' as she calls it. The cat's been gone now for two days. Mother's terrified we'll be thrown out forever just because we lost that contemptible thing!"

As Violetta finished her tale, Anne felt a leap of vindication. Here at last was proof that she hadn't stolen the key.

"That woman took the key because she came for something," Anne said with conviction.

"Mother insisted to Grandmother that you were unjustly accused," Violetta responded. "She says you weren't lying and that your suspicions about Bridgewater were true! Grandmother says you can come back and speak your mind, if you like."

With a sinking heart, Anne remembered her last furious words to the intimidating Amelia Thomas. She was certain she had burned all of her bridges spectacularly that day.

"Why would she believe anything I had to say?" Anne wondered out loud.

"She will now that a governess has been found quite suspiciously upstairs in her own attic. Come on. This way."

The pair walked quickly over a carpet of spruce needles in a light fog. Looking around, Anne realized just how far into the woods they had wandered. The trees were so tall and the branches above so dense that very little sunlight could reach the ground. Almost nothing grew below, making the vistas through the tree trunks eerie and inhospitable. Flaps and shrieks from some large, angry-sounding bird made both girls startle. Anne balked at going any further.

"No, I don't think so. Violetta, let's go back. I know this is the wrong way."

"Oh, come on!"

Violetta was in too much of a hurry to worry about Anne's fears. She knew this was a shortcut that avoided the town road and she meant to make the most of it. Stubbornly, she gripped Anne's hand tighter and pulled her forward. The light was beginning to fade, and the dimmer it got, the more the spruce trees appeared to loom menacingly over the girls. Anne pressed close to Violetta, looking about anxiously

"I feel as if there are faces watching us . . . white things behind those trees. . . ." She shuddered with cold and fear.

Now Violetta, too, was beginning to have second thoughts. Behind and before them stood a wall of trunks with nothing visible beyond but more trees. Violetta looked around, not wanting to admit she, too, was considering the possibility of white faces among the branches.

"It's only your imagination, Anne. Hepzibah goes on and on about the phantoms that kidnap children no one cares about."

"And I'd be the first to qualify." At any second Anne fully expected to be picked up by the neck and carried away.

"I'm absolutely positive it's this way." Violetta ran ahead, determined to get through the woods. "I recognize this road. Come on, Anne!"

But Anne hung back, still afraid. Her instincts warned her not to move.

"No," she called as Violetta ran out into the open road. "Stop!"

If there was anything other than phantoms at work, it was Violetta—who triggered a trap that had been impossible to see on the path. In an instant, a net flew up from the leaves, caught

Violetta, and whipped her up so that she hung in mid-air, tangled in the web, screeching at the top of her lungs.

"Get me out! Get me out!" she howled as Anne stood petrified with shock. Anne had no hope of reaching either the net or the rope itself.

Violetta clawed and squirmed and squealed so much that Anne did not even hear the sound of hoofbeats behind her. Suddenly, Nellie was galloping past. She grabbed Anne by the arm and swung her deftly up onto the white horse—the same animal she'd ridden the night of the mill sabotage.

"Nellie! Help us!" said Anne when she realized who it was.

But Nellie just kept galloping away from Violetta, with not even a backward glance.

"That trap's set so the police don't get too close to our meetin' place," She eventually explained. "My friends will get the girl loose."

The last Anne saw before the trees obscured Violetta from view was a man riding up and skidding to a halt before the hanging net. Anne prayed he could get Violetta down easily, if only she would refrain from such hysterics!

Nellie galloped up to an abandoned grist mill and helped Anne off her horse.

"Come on in. This is where we meet." She pushed the pine door open with a bang. "This old grist mill has been abandoned for years. No one really knows I live here."

Nellie was wearing a long red and black tartan skirt and a man's tan jacket. She took off her old felt hat as soon as she entered the door. Anne followed Nellie into the main floor of the old mill. It had tall ceilings and equipment hung on the wall. A large grist stone turned on the floor below, creating a gentle, rhythmical grinding sound that seemed quite hospitable. The place was shadowy in the dim late-afternoon light, but Anne could see where Nellie had fixed up a simple kitchen. They turned a corner and came through a short door between the walls. Anne caught a glimpse not only of some mill workers but also, of all people, Ruth Bridgewater! She was seated across the table from an important-looking man in a business suit. Startled, Anne stepped back from the door, being careful not to enter, or be seen.

Nellie, meanwhile, had crossed the open room and proceeded directly to a wicker basket sitting on a bench at a desk. She promptly lifted up the lid. Amazingly, she extracted Old Blue Eyes!

"The Thomas' imperial kitty got caught in the trap too! This is the feline what yer lookin' for?"

Gratefully, Anne held out her arms and clutched the animal close. She couldn't resist a quick glance sideways. All at once, Ruth turned her head and noticed Anne.

"What's *she* doing here!"

Nellie abruptly pulled Anne away and pushed her toward the door. "Take the cat home. But don't dally at the Thomases'! Promise me you'll go back to the workers' cottage by the cider mill. You'll be plenty safe there! I left specific instructions with them."

Nellie did not explain more; she simply watched as Anne raced out the door, awkwardly clutching the cat, her red braids flying behind her. Only when Anne was out of earshot did Nellie mutter under her breath.

"Worse things in store for the Thomases than missing cats."

She turned back to the important business going on behind her, signalling with her hand that Anne was gone and that there was nothing to be concerned about. The well-dressed visitor was a lawyer for the bank, a man by the name of Phillip Granger. He had allowed himself to be taken to the abandoned mill on the promise of important information. He couldn't have looked more out of place in his formal attire, but it didn't seem to bother him in the least.

Granger had been poring over certain papers Ruth had managed to pilfer from the Thomases' attic and she had laid them out in front of him while the others looked on excitedly. The former Thomas family governess was positively bursting with self-satisfaction as she handed him yet another important sheet.

"This correspondence was in the old lady's files. Her husband knew full well he was lumbering on Crown land for decades without any deed ... or timber rights. Somebody ought a put a stop to the whole operation."

"Or ... have another company just take over the business for the bank completely," Mr. Granger added smugly.

"The town would be better off if she sold out," Ruth concurred.

She was voicing the deep dissatisfaction that now permeated every corner of Marysville—a town that had its fortunes totally tied to the lumber, cider, and cotton mills that had brought about its very existence. Marysville had always prospered or suffered according to the health of those mills. With Mrs. Thomas refusing to make any equipment upgrades, pay better wages, or improve the working conditions, some feared the entire operation was becoming more unsafe by the day. There was talk of the businesses being run into the ground; not like when old Jameson Thomas had overseen things. Times were tough since he'd passed on. Amelia, his widow, struggled to keep things going and to maintain the lifestyle to which she'd grown accustomed. The workers, meanwhile, were being driven to desperate measures by the concerns of the Abbey Bank—an enterprise that believed the mills needed a big new infusion of cash. They were prepared to endorse such an infusion, but only under the leadership of someone who would not frustrate the workers at every turn.

Mr. Granger stood up and slid the revealing pile of papers into his briefcase. His journey through the woods had certainly yielded a profit—even better than what he'd expected when he recommended Ruth Bridgewater to Amelia Thomas for the position of governess. To cut timber on Crown land without permits was a very significant oversight on the part of the Thomas companies, and Mr. Granger intended to turn this oversight into a windfall for the Abbey Bank.

"Thank you, Mrs. Bridgewater," Mr. Granger's tone indicated that Ruth had done a real service for the workers—something well worth losing her job over. Her snooping had bolstered the Abbey Bank's position. Armed with the knowledge of the Thomases' illegal activities, the bank could now move forward with its search for another company to run these profitable mills to the bank's advantage. In the meantime, they would need to deal with Mrs. Amelia Thomas.

AT THAT VERY MOMENT, Jeremiah Land was following Amelia through the front door of her beautifully appointed home. Hat in hand, he had come to convey to his employer the increasing gravity of the situation at the mills. Discontent seemed to erupt in some form almost every day now.

"The workers' attacks have been quelled by the police, but a young man was killed and another seriously injured, ma'am."

Amelia flung up her hands in frustration as she glided into the parlour, Mr. Land in her wake. She could not understand what was making the workers—who had been obedient and co-operative for so many years—now appear to work against their own interests.

"Why would they go to such lengths to hurt our business? Marysville was built on the bricks and mortar of my husband's good will."

The set of Amelia's handsome head indicated only too clearly her impression that the workers were being unforgivably ungrateful for all that the Thomas family had done over the past for thirty-five years. Mr. Land answered her carefully.

"Some here feel it isn't a woman's place to operate so many businesses."

After her husband's death, Amelia had skillfully kept the entire Thomas enterprise afloat. She refused to even think about the disappointment her own son had turned out to be; interested only his medical practice and losing even that, as well as his own life, through his weakness for liquor. Amelia turned round to face her company manager. Her eyes flashed in the wake of his worry and concern.

"That's what I pay you for," she told him evenly. "And to be effective too, Jeremiah."

Despite the manager's best efforts, he was keenly aware of trouble in the Thomas businesses. He forged on.

"The cotton mill is struggling. I don't need to catalogue those causes."

Old machinery, and a drastic drop in the markets had combined to make the mill less than viable.

"But lumber and cider are very strong," Louisa countered firmly, as though she made it so by force of will alone.

"But the death of that boy will be difficult to reverse in the workers' minds."

Amelia leaned across a table toward Land, her chin thrust out.

"We will not be unionized, Jeremiah!"

Both knew exactly what the workers were really trying to achieve with their staged disasters and explosions. They wished to create the allusion Amelia was no longer in control of the safety of her businesses and if they ever succeeded, Amelia knew she would have to knuckle under to all kinds of demands—demands she was not prepared to grant, as long as she was alive.

Jeremiah could see that the mere mention of any accommodation was beyond Amelia's forbearance.

"Please." Amelia held out her hand to indicate the door and walked around the table toward the foyer. The audience was done. Mr. Land felt stuck. He knew the trouble at the mills was only beginning to rumble and he was earnest in his desire to give the best he could to the Thomas companies. He had done that for his entire career. He nodded in agreement, but inside, felt there had to be another way of looking at the situation. He was about to speak again, but decided to hold his tongue. Before Mr. Land turned away, Amelia came close and looked him the eye.

"Come back to me with more solutions than problems," she ordered.

Mr. Land nodded wearily as he went out the front door. Only when he was gone did Amelia let out a sigh, all the worries she had hidden from him now crowding her mind.

At that very moment she was saved from contemplating the mills' many afflictions. She caught sight of Anne Shirley running across the lawn, precious Old Blue Eyes cradled in her arms. Amelia's face instantly lit up as she hurried outside.

Amelia slipped out of the conservatory door in time to see Louisa, Violetta and the boys also running across the great lawn to greet Anne. Violetta was mightily relieved. She had just arrived home to tell her mother the fantastic tale of how she'd got caught in a mantrap. Although Louisa had been frozen with alarm, Violetta's story now seemed just silly with Anne and the cat there in front of them.

"Anne, you're back," cried Louisa, running up and throwing her arms around the girl.

"Anne, we thought you'd been roasted on a spit by bandits!" Violetta blurted out, for she had been certain Anne had been murdered or had disappeared in some hideous manner. "Who was that who picked you up?"

"I'm fine," Anne told them airily, wanting to smooth over the whole incident. "They were only vagrants who live in the forest."

At the sight of Amelia bearing down on her, Anne stopped in her tracks. Amelia did not seem predisposed to give her a tongue-lashing fortunately.

"I never expected to extend such a note of gratitude to such a saucy girl as you," said Amelia amiably, much to Anne's astonishment. Amelia nodded to Louisa and the children. "They want you to stay." Then, to the cat, which she scooped into her arms, "Come here, my darling."

Happiness leaped inside Anne as Louisa put an arm around her waist and walked with her amid her children.

"I am pleased to have returned your dear Old Blue Eyes, Mrs. Thomas," Anne declared with heartfelt sincerity.

Amelia nestled the errant cat close, stroking its smokey grey head and taking comfort from its lean body. The cat emitted a grating Siamese yowl in response. It was clearly happy to be back where food was plentiful and it had the run of a mansion.

"Violetta told us you were taken hostage by armed riders!" interjected Louisa as Hepzibah came marching up, not at all pleased to see Anne. Anne slowed to a stop.

"Not exactly . . . I did see something there. I saw Bridgewater at a meeting place with an unruly gang."

That name got Amelia's full attention. Her eyes narrowed.

"What were they doing?" she demanded intently.

"I couldn't tell," Anne hesitated, "but they looked like they were discussing some papers."

Amelia's eyes narrowed even more.

"Who took you there?"

"Nellie Parkhurst," Anne answered ingenuously. "She found us after she'd found the cat."

Hepzibah glanced at her employer significantly.

"What a strange coincidence!" she exclaimed, eyeing Anne with the same suspicion as before. Hepzibah still thought Anne an untruthful little sneak and no number of rescued cats was going to change her mind.

Worry filled Amelia's face. She turned so that Louisa and the children couldn't see her. Clutching Old Blue Eyes, she headed back inside the conservatory.

"If Bridgewater's taken anything," she said softly to Hepzibah, "we'll just have to tighten the reins in the future."

Amelia and Hepzibah disappeared, leaving Anne, who had caught the clandestine remark, quite confused.

"Did a horse run away or something?" she asked Louisa.

"Grandmother sacked Bridgewater for nosing around in the attic. She's now admitted you were right, Anne."

"But she seems terribly rattled," Anne insisted, still puzzled.

Violetta, who had despised the idea of a governess from the outset, felt she knew the source of Ruth's treachery.

"Bridgewater came here with a purpose. And all because Grandmother hired her, based on a recommendation from a bank! A bank that had ulterior motives, no doubt."

Violetta had seen correspondence from the bank arrive at the house from time to time, and she knew that it always put her grandmother in a testy mood.

"Don't be so dramatic, Violetta." Louisa protested briskly, trying to nip her daughter's gossip in the bud. "I'm sure very little will come of it." Louisa seemed to be on edge with respect to the hooligans who were connected to Ruth. Anne looked at her suspiciously, wondering if Louisa knew what was behind the governess's spying. Whatever it was, it fell far beyond Anne's and Violetta's comprehension of the matter.

Twelve

Anne knew very little about banks, and even less about what they had to do with Amelia Thomas's mills. She only knew that she'd been admitted into a kind of heaven. No more sweeping up around thundering mill machinery, no more picking apples until she was too weary to climb the ladder, and no more sleeping in the barn and mucking out the stalls. She was able to have a bath—this time in a warm indoor tub—and she received a proper dress instead of worn work clothes. Her things were even put into a lovely bedroom she was to share with Violetta. It was only when darkness fell and Anne lay alone in her soft new bed that she had time to think about the array of predicaments that had befallen her. For the first time in a long time, she thought about Gabriel, and how he'd told her she was a kindred spirit. She remembered him slipping away in the night and how it had felt when the life drifted out of his hand. Almost without knowing it, she began to cry—partly out of sadness, partly out of joy. In the other bed, Violetta lifted her head.

So many strange feelings were swirling around inside Anne's heart that she couldn't distinguish one from the other. She had been falsely accused, cast out, sent to hard labour, seen her own father badly hurt, then had him disappear without even knowing she'd been near. The memory of her mother filled her heart as well—that wonderful feeling of being gathered up into tender arms. Being in Amelia's house, accepted for once, was the closest Anne had ever come to the safe feeling of being enfolded into her mother's bosom.

"I'm just so elated. To have your mother stick up for me, so I can stay." Anne stifled another sob.

Violetta didn't know what to make of this. An elated person did not generally have tears running down her face. Getting out of bed, she tiptoed over and sat down on the edge of Anne's bed. She remembered how mean she'd been when Anne had had nowhere else to go.

"I take back the things I said about you," she whispered, trying to see what reaction this might elicit from her new roommate. To Violetta's relief, Anne turned to her and smiled. It was exactly the reaction she'd been hoping for. A few things had been eating at her and she felt comfortable enough now to test more reactions from Anne. "Mother says even your father's turned out to be a prince. He's written to her on several occasions, wanting to know how you are."

Anne froze, trying hard to keep her thoughts hidden. This was the first news she'd had of her father since he'd been spirited from the mill worker's cottage after the accident. It meant that he must be all right, and that no one had arrested him for helping to dismantle the logging chute. Anne couldn't help but turn away. She did it so obviously that Violetta peered at her with suspicion.

"Have you not heard from him?"

Anne's mind raced. If her father was all right, why would he not have sent word? If he knew Nellie, he must have had some idea how frightened she'd been, alone at the cider mill. It was not in Nellie's nature to reveal much about anything and she hadn't ever mentioned Walter Shirley again to Anne. Ever since her mother's death, Anne had difficulty reconciling any of her father's actions. In her heart, it had been easier to just forget about ever seeing him again. With Violetta confronting her, however, she simply couldn't let on that her own father would write to Louisa but not to her.

"Certainly," she breathed. "And I pray all the time we'll be together again someday."

Violetta watched Anne carefully. She knew Anne was making up a response, but she had no idea how to pursue it further. Grateful for Violetta's momentary silence, Anne shut her eyes. Soon enough, Violetta made her way back into her own bed.

AS AUTUMN UNFOLDED, Anne lived in the full splendour of the Thomas household, and was accorded the same privileges as Amelia's own grandchildren. In the absence of Ruth Bridgewater, Amelia even pressed the girl into service to supervise the children's lessons, as Louisa had originally proposed Anne set herself up properly in the bright study full of windows, with Gabriel's tattered, precious books lined up on the teacher's desk in front of her.

One day, she had set up an exercise in penmanship for the group. Violetta, Keith, and Jock were to copy out one of Anne's favourite poems, "Bingen on the Rhine." To Anne, it was a heartrending romantic saga: the last oration of a dying soldier as he lay after battle in a distant land. He spoke words of courage and comfort for his family and his loved one—not a sister—who waited earnestly for him, at home in Bingen, a tiny village on the Rhine River in Germany. It didn't appeal in the least to schoolboys, who couldn't have cared less about some village girl the soldier would never see again.

"This is sooo dull," Jock complained. He squirmed in his chair as his brother heartily agreed.

"Don't you have anything better to copy than books that are a hundred years old?" Keith chimed in. He wanted to read about fighting, not the sappy fluff about some soldier's undying love.

Anne just couldn't understand why the other three weren't all as carried away as she was with the touching beauty of such a tender epic, conjured up before their eyes.

"This poem is sheer romance," Anne asserted firmly. "I never tire of reading it. It breaks my heart. Everyone needs to have a good cry once in awhile. Don't you think so, Violetta?"

If Anne hoped to find an ally in Violetta, whom she expected to endorse the thrilling ring of the author's noble words, she was completely mistaken. Violetta firmly resented being preached at by someone younger than herself. She felt her grandmother should have bestowed the responsibility on her. Her recent truce with Anne did not include keeping her opinions to herself.

"It's ridiculous. You get away with making everyone think you're smarter than we are, just because you have a knack with fifty-cent words." Violetta fired the first shot across Anne's bow.

Anne lifted her straight little nose into the air.

"I plan to teach one day and I regard you three as my personal experiment."

Anne's patronizing retort made Violetta's blood boil. She crumpled up a piece of paper from her notebook and lobbed it at Anne. Jock and Keith quickly followed suit, howling and giggling as they chucked crumpled missiles at their fledgling teacher.

"Settle down," Anne hotly ordered after being hit in the face more than once. "This is outrageous! Wait till I tell your grandmother!"

It was an open revolt. The gleeful bombardment drove Anne to grab up the paper missiles and fire them back. Unfortunately, she was seriously outnumbered and was soon pummelled to a truce. The warfare succeeded in providing Anne with an ingenious notion. She determined she would show her unimpressed peers what the poem was really about, and force them to enjoy it for their own good.

"Fine! If you want to fight about it, I have a better idea."

Soon, the entire group was on a search for props. Jock and Keith were happy to scrounge an old colander for a helmet, topped with worn-out scrub brushes to look like a plume. With sticks for weapons, they marched down to the river where they found a section of old wooden dock lying on the bank. It was just a few boards nailed together, but it was the very thing to carry a dead warrior down the Rhine to his birthplace. Fixed up with a homemade sail, it made a perfectly ingenious funeral raft. The pole and bit of old sheet the boys fastened together were inspired in Anne's opinion and she offered her compliments.

"It looks like something right out of a storybook. What a wonderful job, boys! Now let's begin. On you go, Jock! "Anne ordered.

Violetta snorted at the idea. She considered herself far above such infantile capers. The whole exercise was stupid and she refused to participate. She stood back skeptically as Anne helped young Jock crawl onto the rickety raft, now bobbing unsteadily in the water. Anne let him lie on his back on an old grey blanket to play the dying soldier. He had the colander on his head and two sticks, signifying his spear and his rifle, crossed over his chest. She proceeded to lay two hemlock boughs across the sticks as a funeral wreath.

"What's the point of this silliness, Anne?" groused Violetta, her voice dull with boredom. "A soldier died and somebody wrote a poem about it. You make such a to-do over nothing."

Anne was determined to succeed as a teacher, even if meant sailing her whole class down the Rhine toward Bingen.

"The only way you'll ever understand romantic verse is to live and breathe it. "Bingen on the Rhine" is an illustrious piece of writing you need to relish. It's the kind of masterpiece that just gives a person a crinkly feeling up and down their back."

Jock had been enjoying himself somewhat in the make-believe raft until he had to lay prone on the rickety old wood with the river water slapping in his ears. The crinkly feeling down *his* back was not very thrilling at all. Keith, though, thought Jock was the funniest thing he had seen since they'd left Bolingbroke.

"You look really good . . . dead, Jock!" Keith laughed at his own humour.

Instead of gasping in his death throes, as Anne had intended, Jock began to feel sillier by the minute. The water below seemed even closer as the raft continued to bob. In fact, it had begun to soak his rear end and the back of his legs. He sat up on his deathbed.

"I get all three of your desserts tonight for doing this!"

Anne concurred, but dying soldiers were not supposed to be thinking about their stomachs!

"Of course you will. Just lie down, for pity sake!" She ordered. "You're supposed to be on your last breath!"

Jock lay down again, the water lapping in his ears. Violetta sighed.

"Now, everyone," said Anne enthusiastically, "push him off. Away he goes!"

The three of them shoved the makeshift raft out into the water. Much to Anne's glee and surprise, it immediately picked up the wind and sailed along the river. Startled by the immediate velocity of the raft, Jock decided to avoid tipping it by lying perfectly still.

Anne began a funereal march along the river bank, beside the dying soldier who lounged beneath the melancholy flap of the sail. Holding her head high with imperial dignity, she walked along the bank, quickening her pace as she struggled to keep up to the raft, which by now was being moved nicely along by the current. She began to recite the poem, putting such dramatic gravity into her voice that she shivered from top to bottom. The re-enactment was a brilliant inspiration, she decided. An image such as this would not fail to reduce any disdainer to tears!

She chose the most pathetic lines to call out across the waves in the fresh autumn air: "A soldier of the legion, lay dying in Algiers. The dying soldier faltered, as he took his comrade's hand. 'I shall never more see my native soil; send me back to my native land. Take a message to some distant friends of mine, for I was born at Bingen—at Bingen on the Rhine."

Out on the river, the raft caught in an eddy and began to twist as the current carried it even further from the shore. Jock felt his clothes become sopping wet. Against Anne's orders and his own convictions, he sat up and surveyed the scene around him in rising alarm. The raft was disintegrating and Anne, Violetta, and Keith, hurrying along the riverbank, were receding quite quickly. Totally caught up in the drama Anne truly did not realize that Jock's raft had gotten out of control. She continued her recitation, mesmerized by the glamour of her own theatricality.

"He saw the blue Rhine sweep along; and even dreamed to hear the German songs he used to sing in chorus sweet and clear..."

Anne was transported all alone to another land. Keith was busy trying to skip pebbles in the water and Violetta glared at Anne's affected performance in utter disapproval. By the time

Violetta realized what was happening to Jock, the raft was sinking in the distance, one corner washed completely over by the current. Violetta ran down to the water's edge.

"That blessed raft has a mind of its own, Anne! Jock! Are you alright?"

With a thump, the sail collapsed in a sopping heap. Jock crawled to his knees, his colander helmet swivelling this way and that as he tried to figure out the best means of rescue. The entire raft was being spun into the rapid current of the main channel.

"Help," Jock began to holler. "Help!"

Violetta was now shouting all the louder for Jock to come back, as if the miniature soldier had any control over his situation. True panic had grabbed hold of him, but in his anxiety he knocked some of the boards loose from the rotten underpinnings. As Jock stood up on one side to balance the raft from going under, the entire creation fell apart, unceremoniously dumping Jock straight into the water.

Jock bobbed and spit, gasping to stay afloat. Bits of timber scattered, leaving the boy floundering in the deep, cold river. Anne looked on in frozen horror. Violetta screamed and shook Anne. Jock was disappearing below the surface! Suddenly Anne came to her senses.

"Come on," she shouted and raced toward the nearby mill. Two of the mill workers were loading a wagon outside the planing shed. They looked up in surprise as three children came tearing at them, waving their arms and yelling.

"My brother was on a raft and he's fallen into the river," panted Violetta. "Help us! Please. He's drowning!"

Without a second thought, the two men dropped what they were doing and ran after the children down to the riverbank. All that could be seen of Jock was his arm. It was clawing at the air while his head slipped under, the colander bobbing on the surface. One of the workers, a powerful young fellow of about twenty, threw off his coat. He dove in, boots and all, without hesitation. Neither Anne nor Violetta made another sound as the man forced himself out into the current.

"Hold on! I'll be there. I've almost got ya!" he called encouragingly to Jock, who was trying desperately not to sink. In no more than a few seconds, the mill worker had pulled the little boy up so he could gulp in a lungful of air. He pushed his way back to shore against the potentially deadly current, holding Jock's head above water with one arm. Violetta thumped Jock vigorously on the back as her brother was literally tossed onto the shore, coughing up river water. Anne felt her knees turn to pudding with relief. She was responsible for nearly bringing an unspeakable disaster upon the family that had given her a home!

Word had already been dispatched to the Thomas mansion. Jock was wrapped in an old brown blanket and taken into the mill when Amelia's carriage drove up, disgorging her and a near-hysterical Louisa. The workers had cheered when Jock was carried in, badly shaken but enjoying all the attention. In Amelia's presence, however, they suddenly fell still and stood watching silently as a tearful Louisa hugged her little boy and wept for joy. Amelia shook hands with the young man who had saved Jock from a watery fate.

"My grandson owes you his life," Amelia said sincerity warming her voice. "The Thomases are saved from extinction, young fellow."

"So I guess the name stays up over the door, Mrs. Thomas!" the rescuer answered, anxious at being the centre of Amelia's attention. The young man hadn't intended his remark to sound saucy, but he'd let his tongue get the better of him. He and many of his colleagues worried that the mill was in danger of closing. A glimmer of steel replaced the warmth in Amelia's voice.

"It'd take more than a mere accident—or a few disgruntled workers—to remove our name," she quipped pointedly and abruptly turned to leave. "Good day, men."

A low murmur ran through the crowd of workers as their discontent became almost palpable. The men folded their dusty arms and scowled as Amelia strode past.

Louisa, who was so thankful Jock had been saved, hastily shook hands with the still-dripping young rescuer.

"Words cannot express our gratitude. We are greatly indebted. Come children."

Anne, Keith, and Jock also shook the mill worker's hand. He had a freckled, pleasant face and his hair had gone all curly from the water. Anne gazed up at him with such fervent appeal that he couldn't help a smile.

"Forgive us—forgive me—for causing such a disaster! An angel must have been watching over all of us." She could not even apply her imagination to what might have happened had this young man not been such a strong swimmer.

"Thanks, mister," added Jock and Keith on their way past.

The children and Louisa had to hurry out of the mill to catch up with Amelia, whose nose was still severely out of joint. Louisa had seen the dark looks and felt the hostility among the men. She'd been in Marysville long enough to sense how strong the undercurrents of discontent were among most of the Thomas employees. She was also privy to other information— from sources of which Amelia had no notion—through letters from Walter Shirley. She stopped Amelia just as she was getting back into her carriage.

"It would be more prudent to listen to their concerns from time to time than just the sound of your own voice." Louisa spoke decisively. The shock of discovering that her son had almost drowned had made Louisa rash and bold. Once seated in the darkly upholstered interior of the carriage, Amelia paused before closing the door on her daughter-in-law.

"The day I heed your advice, Louisa," she blinked at her condescendingly, "is the day you'll not need mine!"

Louisa watched the carriage spirit her away, and her face mirrored the same dissatisfaction as the workers.

ON RETURNING FROM THE RIVER, Anne made an elaborate, heartfelt apology to Amelia, insisting she would rather "drown in depths dark as Hades," or "expire thirsting in blood-stained desert sands," like the soldier in the poem, rather than knowingly put any of Mrs. Thomas's family members into peril. Amelia managed to look stern for only a minute before bursting into laughter. Thankfully, the incident quickly faded from everyone's minds, replaced by the routine of everyday life in the large house. Promising no more life threatening re-enactments, Anne was even allowed to continue tutoring the Thomas children. They worked hard every day, catching up on practically all the school lessons they had missed the year before.

Amelia was amused by Anne's bright, imaginative chatter. As the days passed, she quietly began to develop a real affection for the child's creativity and liveliness. Anne was so happy to be part of the household that she rushed willingly to help wherever she could. She was always ready to carry Amelia's umbrella or recite with enthusiasm some article from the newspaper that she thought would interest the old woman. Whatever recitation she undertook, Anne worked extra hard to pour her heart into the words to see if she could prevent Amelia from laughing in all the wrong places.

No one mentioned a word about her father. Anne did her best to put him out of her mind. She kept herself busy with tasks, and even found favour with Old Blue Eyes. The only person in the entire Thomas household who still harboured suspicion of Anne was Hepzibah. The more Amelia took to the child, the more the housekeeper became convinced her employer was being cleverly duped.

It was true what Louisa had told Anne about her mother-in-law needing them as much as they needed her. Louisa and the children were all that was left of Amelia's family, and now that she had got used to having children around the house, Amelia began to join in their activities, seemingly enjoying herself immensely.

Autumn passed and then winter set in, bringing its own delights. The carriage was put away and the big shiny sleigh brought out. "Skating party!" was a favourite call through the house, bringing the children running to pull on their tams and mufflers. On brilliant winter days, Amelia would crowd the family into several cutters and drive across town to the frozen river. She'd stand by the cheery bonfire, dressed in her splendid fur hat and coat, and watch the children tobogganing or skimming about on the ice with their cheeks glowing in the cold and their bright coloured scarves flying behind them. She seemed to be making an extra effort with the townspeople as well. She never gave any indication that she noticed the awkward stiffness and unhappy glances from the mill workers' wives and children.

Louisa may not have noticed the whispers and looks either, for she had concerns of her own. She was only too aware that the position and privilege her little family had gained by living in that grand house depended entirely on Amelia's whim. Mrs. Thomas was renowned for having her way, no matter what the discomfort to others. She could change her mind in a flash and become entirely antagonistic. Louisa tried to patiently bear the brunt of Amelia's impatience for her children's sakes, but she could not help but see that Anne had fast become Amelia's favourite. The girl seemed capable of ameliorating any tense domestic situation that might arise.

One day Amelia chose Anne to go for a pleasure spin with her in the cutter. The two-passenger sleigh was fast and Amelia was rakishly fond of driving it. Her skill with a single horse, as opposed to a team, was one of her solitary pleasures.

"Here," Amelia told Anne, handing her a warm driving rug for her knees. "Tuck yourself in. The mare is good for ten miles today."

With a mutual shriek of glee, they set off smartly down the road, leaving Louisa behind, concern clouding her face. A small worm of fear and worry for the position of her own children had entered her heart.

That worry grew when Amelia made sure it was Anne sitting beside her when they all went to Fredericton for a symphony concert; something totally outside Anne's experience. In the balcony of St. Andrews Presbyterian Church, the Thomas clan had a front-row view of the orchestra during this leg of their Maritime Symphony Tour. The concert transported Anne into a fairytale, which was enhanced by the crisp, new satin dress she'd been given, complete with lace that rustled most satisfactorily when she moved. Below her onstage, musicians in formal attire played waltzes and symphonies captivating enough to make Anne feel as if she was soaring right off her seat and over the balcony itself.

Whenever Anne glanced over in sincere gratitude at Amelia for this wonderful opportunity, she got a smile and a wink. Even though Louisa had to keep prodding her bored boys to stop their horseplay, she was acutely aware that Amelia spent more time watching the pleasure on Anne's face than listening to the music. When Amelia wasn't watching Anne, she was deep in thought—miles away from the concert.

Anne chattered about the exhilaration of hearing such brilliant musicians the entire way home. Happily exhausted, she and Violetta climbed into their beds. Finally feeling secure in her new home, Violetta radiated benevolence.

"Hasn't grandmother become a splendid creature these days!" she declared, pulling back her downy comforter. "She's even allowed mother to study for a teacher's degree by mail."

Anne was equally content. She climbed into bed and lay back luxuriously on her feather pillow, reminding herself just how different it was from the heap of hay and sawdust she'd slept on in the mill or the hard, lumpy tick at the poorhouse.

"I feel this marks an epoch in my life, Violetta. Four months ago I was wishing I'd never been born; now I wouldn't change places with an angel!"

Snuggling under the covers, Anne did not see that Amelia had paused by their door. From the hallway outside, she eavesdropped on the cheerful young voices coming from the room.

"The best of all is being allowed to stay here," she heard Anne comment. "I'm just so happy your grandmother finally understands I'm a human being."

A soft smile crept across Amelia's face; a smile touched with tenderness. Silently, she continued along the hall, leaving Anne to close her eyes—safe and secure at last in the world that had so cruelly beleaguered her.

Thirteen

Anne opened her eyes abruptly. She was sitting in the empty ballroom of the White Sands, in near darkness. Around her stood turned-up tables and chairs that would soon be overturned and set for hotel guests to enjoy Gene's season of dinner theatre. The only light came from the stage, where the actors, in their everyday clothes, were working on a preliminary read-through of Anne's latest draft, delivered just the day before. Gene sat beside Anne, one elbow on the table, smoking as he listened to every word with total concentration, and trying to observe the ever-evolving expressions on Anne's countenance.

"I'm just glad your grandmother finally understands I'm a human being," the male lead read out, echoing words that had once passed Anne's own lips.

A young actress stood with her arms stretched out toward her colleague.

"I'm just so happy. There is no darkness anymore, only light." Her voice was filled with wonder, hope, and a healthy dose of melodrama.

Clasping hands, the two ran off stage—completing the first attempted "performance" of this brand-new work.

Unable to move, Anne waited in silence for Gene's verdict. The remaining actors hovered on stage, also looking for some form of acknowledgement from the seasoned impresario. There was a moment of utter silence, utter suspense. Then

Gene stuck his cigarette into his mouth and began to clap, slowly at first, then heartily. The rest of the cast dashed back out onto the stage and bowed, and Anne closed her eyes in relief. She had worked so hard to simply get all of her thoughts and feelings into a cohesive scenario! She was relieved it was not a complete disaster.

"Thank you, everyone," Gene tossed out to the cast. "Take fifteen minutes and then we'll start the rehearsal for *Arsenic and Old Lace*."

He walked past Anne, and whispered rather tersely.

"It's all right. Dialogue needs quite a bit of cutting. Get back to work." He touched her gently on the shoulder for encouragement as he walked off toward the stage.

She smiled to herself, not in the least fooled by his manner. It was high praise indeed from a man who had no time or patience for anything less than brilliance. One word from him was enough to send her back to the drawing board. She had details to work out—details she now understood very clearly after watching the actors wade through the jungle of a first draft. Anne raced back to Green Gables and began typing with renewed energy.

Day after day, page after page, she cut and pasted and rewrote and polished. Her only caller was Gene, who dropped by once in a while to check on her progress. He would content himself with looking over her shoulder before eventually realizing he needed to disappear. The last thing he wanted to do was interrupt.

When Anne needed to get a scene straight or work out a knotty piece of dialogue, she resorted to the barnyard, the orchard, or the fields beyond. She paced through the grass, speaking the words out loud and gesturing dramatically, looking like a crazy person to anyone who didn't know what she was doing.

Every once in a while, she would stop, whip out the pencil she kept stuck through her knot of auburn hair, and write down ideas in a little notebook she carried in her hand. Only when a plot or dialogue problem was solved was she able to hurry back to Marilla's writing table to type the changes firmly into her manuscript.

She was in the orchard one day, playing out several parts in the final act of the play, when she saw the postman bouncing along the road on his bicycle, his mailbag over the handlebars. Instead of riding on past as he usually did, he waved to her and called her by her married name, "Mrs. Blythe." Anne's heart skipped a beat. It was an appellation reserved for the locals who had known her since she was a girl, and its use startled her. She waved back instinctively then raced along the picket fence. In that instant she could think of nothing else but a letter from her father!

"Hello, Mack!" she called out breathlessly, pointing to the letter he was drawing out of his mailbag. "Anything from New Brunswick?"

Mack looked at the envelope and shook his head. "Paris, France!"

The postman jounced off, leaving Anne to rip open the envelope and devour the words written in her son's familiar hand. Her smile grew wider as she skimmed the page. She flipped over the notepaper and uttered an enormous yelp of sheer joy. The next minute, she was pelting through the gate, across the yard, and into Green Gables.

GENE APPROVED THE LAST DRAFT of the script on the verandah at the White Sands. As he finished the last lines of dialogue he looked over at Anne, who was trying her hand at golf on the small putting green behind the hotel. She was struggling to get the ball into the cup because she'd needed some sort of diversion to keep her mind off her play for a couple of hours. Golf meant she wouldn't have to stand over Gene's shoulder, scrutinizing his every reaction. The play was done and not a moment too soon. She'd given it everything she was able to muster, but now she would be able to focus on Dominic and his news.

Gene closed the manuscript and marched across the lawn over to where Anne was lining up a shot at the edge of the green. He took the golf club from her hand, swung at the ball, and placed it in the cup in one easy stroke. Anne looked at him, astounded. He smiled broadly. "It's a hole in one—best dramatic piece I've read in five years."

From that moment on, Gene's troupe was turned upside down with rehearsals. He rearranged the cast and opted to take certain players out of the next few White Sands shows in order to be able to assemble a small cast that could travel off the Island to test the play in New Jersey before critics and an upscale audience. Gene felt confident that he had an important new work on his hands. So in between directing, he spent a good deal of time on the telephone, negotiating and making arrangements to open the play at a prominent New Jersey playhouse that was black for several weeks. It was a bit risky, but it would give him just enough time to open and close this show within a specific time period on the chance he could get exposure to solid reviews from the New York press. After that he would consider whether it was worth trying to mount the play on Broadway.

Although Anne was initially disappointed that this personal work—about which she was now quite emotional—would not premiere on the Island, Gene was firm on his strategic decision. He was very confident that the show would positively galvanize an audience. He was so enthusiastic that he was prepared to risk the last two shows in the season at the White Sands—and a small fortune from his own bank account—to turn Anne's play into a reality. In the end, Anne respected Gene too much to argue. Once the Jersey Playhouse was firm, Gene sank his heart and soul into marketing and publicity, not to mention literally wringing brilliant performances from his tight little cast. Anne stood by in awe, mesmerized at what he'd created from her script.

On the morning everyone was to leave for New Jersey, Anne wasn't thinking at all about her play. She was on the telephone breaking the news to friends and family that Dominic would be coming to Green Gables within the month, bringing with him a fiancée! The girl's name was Brigitte and Dominic had met her through cousins he'd contacted in Normandy. Anne was beside herself with the idea of wedding plans. She hoped to persuade the couple to be married at Green Gables, as she and Gilbert had done nearly thirty years ago to the month. She immediately began making arrangements with Frannie and Rilla to help her prepare for a real down-home wedding—if only Dominic would agree! She was now anxiously awaiting his response, very much aware that all of her prayers had been answered. Dominic was coming home, and before long she would hold him in her arms again! Just that morning, Anne had finally been able to get in touch with Diana in Bermuda. It felt as if they were young girls again, sharing their most intimate secrets, even though Anne had trouble hearing her old friend on the trunk line that connected them over thousands of miles.

"I'm begging you to come, Diana!" Anne entreated, shouting over the din in the hotel lobby. Behind her, actors were carrying their bags out as Gene herded them into the bus that would take them to a ferry. From the mainland they'd sail on to

Atlantic City. "Hurry up, for Pete's sake, Anne!" Gene was saying impatiently. "The boat won't wait. Let's go!"

Anne shouted into the receiver, waving Dominic's letter in her hand.

"I'm still shaking, that's why," she replied excitedly to Diana's questions. "I have Dominic's letter in my hand right here! Both my girls are helping me plan the wedding. Oh, please, darling, promise me you'll come and bring everyone. John and Elsie have been wonderful. They two of them have been helping me fix up the grounds and anything else that needs doing around the farm."

Anne paused again to listen to Diana's banter and ongoing apologies over the state of Green Gables.

"Oh, don't fret, dear. I enjoy being exhausted ... It's all so exhilarating now that Gene's previewing the play in New Jersey. If it's any success at all, I'm going to use the royalties to completely renovate Green Gables."

Gene put his foot down and threatened to arm wrestle the receiver out of her hand. Anne knew he meant business.

"I love you too, Diana. Please come." Diana wouldn't stop talking though.

"Oh, honey, I have to go. Sure, I'll try to call you when we get there. Goodbye."

For a moment, Anne closed her eyes, overwhelmed. She rushed out and flung herself into one of the crowded buses with the rest of the entourage.

A FLUTTER OF PRIDE and nerves overwhelmed Anne when they finally arrived at the Jersey playhouse and she saw the theatre marquee with her name on it: "The Interloper, A New Play by Anne Shirley."

Somehow, she had gone back to all those early memories, back to the real story of her childhood. However, she had fashioned and moulded them into a new narrative, emotionally rooted in her own beginnings, but peopled now with fictional characters, which were set to play out their lives in a completely original scenario. Anne was unable to remember anymore where the truth began and fiction ended, but she was relieved and proud at what she had created. Now that the tickets were sold and the crowd was streaming in, Anne didn't know what to expect. She allowed herself to be consumed by self-doubt. If her first play flopped, it would likely be her last. As the curtain opened and the actors began, Anne paced back and forth at the rear of the auditorium, holding onto every line of dialogue and trying to gauge the audience's reaction. The performances were superb and, as the action progressed, she found herself drawn into the story. Gene's staging and lighting effects, the scenery, and even the costumes transported her into another world.

As the finale approached, Gene appeared and quietly took her arm. Anne was distraught, thinking that he was being kind, preparing to save her from any embarrassment. The play had started to drag in the third act and she sensed the audience moving around in their seats. A hush had fallen over the entire theatre. Without a word, Gene slipped Anne along the exit corridor and through the backstage doors. She'd initially planned to wait in the Green Room for the cast, but now Gene insisted she wait in the wings.

As Gene disappeared again into the dark behind the flats, Anne found herself hovering inconspicuously among the offstage props and set decoration. She sighed in relief as the curtain finally came down. She heard the audience applaud and she watched the wall of green velvet lift quickly. The actors all came forward in a row to take their bows. Nothing out of the ordinary registered in Anne's disoriented brain until she saw Gene running across the open stage right in front of the cast. As they took their second bow, he grabbed her arm, indicating that she should come out and take a bow as well. Anne hotly resisted. She was dressed in pants and tennis shoes, and terrified of standing in footlights before a packed audience. Gene simply grinned with excitement and pride, refusing to let her retreat.

"Come on, Anne," He said, pushing her in front of the cast. "They're calling for you. You absolutely need to do this! You can't back out now"

All at once, Anne found herself at centre stage, standing before a backdrop painted with a white picket fence and green fields, surrounded by an adoring cast who had enjoyed performing every moment of the drama she'd created. Anne bowed modestly, as the applause grew into a loud roar at the sight of the playwright. The cast stepped aside, leaving the stage to Anne. When the audience rose to its feet in a standing ovation, Anne was barely able to believe what she was experiencing. She felt a large lump in her throat. Her humble story had moved this crowd so deeply they were now overwhelming her with deafening waves of appreciation. She stood still, simply trying to take it all in. Then in the glare of the hot, blinding stage lights, she stepped forward to perform a sweeping bow of grateful acknowledgement.

Anne travelled back to Prince Edward Island the next day, aglow with feelings of relief and elation. The closer she got to home, the more her mind turned to Dominic's arrival and the peculiar lack of a response from her father. The minute she stepped into the yard at Green Gables, she dropped her suitcase on the ground and picked up the stack of mail that had accumulated in the box at the gate. She shuffled through the envelopes one by one. Her father *had* replied; by the way of a short note from his housekeeper merely acknowledging her earlier correspondence. Dominic had also written that he would be arriving in three weeks and that he would be looking forward to having a small ceremony in the orchard at the farm but that he was in his mother's and sisters' hands for whatever kind of party they would like to arrange. Anne was beside herself with joy at that news.

Up in Marilla's room, she sat in the window seat and decided to take up her pen once more to address the peculiar response from her father.

"Dearest father, I received the note your housekeeper sent a couple of weeks ago saying she had read you my letter and that a reply from you would be forthcoming. I am still waiting. I am anxious to meet. Your loving daughter, Anne."

Anne could not fathom the reason as to why her father had not written himself—a least a single line, if his hands had grown shaky with age. If he were too frail to answer, surely the housekeeper would have said so. A very old pain rose up inside Anne. She was beginning to feel the way she had as a small girl—alone among strangers, wondering why her father wouldn't ever come for her.

NOW THAT HER PLAY was finished and would perhaps have a life of its own beyond her typewriter, Anne felt emancipated. She walked along Stanhope Beach, watching the gulls soar against the rolling clouds and listening to the waves tumble endlessly at her feet. With her mind now free from worry about plot points and characterizations, Anne's imagination wandered into darker territory. She began to worry that her play might have been a one-night wonder. Critics could be harsh even if an audience showed appreciation—she had certainly discovered that with reviews of several of her books. And poor Gene! He had put his lifeblood into making the two-week preview work. The play had seemed popular, but Anne found herself falling into turmoil at the hundred-and-one worries that plagued her. What if Gene were to lose money? What if Dominic changed his mind and decided to elope? It was still four weeks before he would arrive, and he seemed so in love and ready to marry. Her father had responded to her last note, but once again through his housekeeper. Anne grew concerned. Everything was wound up in one big bundle of worry that gnawed at her. She was snapped out of this trance by Gene himself, waving and hurrying toward her across the dunes. Anne ran to meet him. He was smiling from ear to ear.

"Anne! Anne!! The Jersey box office exceeded everybody's expectations. And the reviews . . . Well, I'll let them speak for themselves. Congratulations!"

Anne let out an exuberant cry as she flipped through the *New York Times* and *The New Jersey Daily News*. She wanted more than anything to jump into Gene's arms but managed to contain herself. She stood there in the sand, grinning at her friend just as widely as he was grinning at her. It was Anne who broke the silence, thinking out loud about how she planned to restore Green Gables to its glory days, exactly as it had looked when she lived under the care of Matthew and Marilla. As they walked back to the hotel together, Anne voiced a tempting thought.

"Does this mean you really get a shot at Broadway again?" Gene laughed and stuck his hands into his pockets.

"Who needs Broadway? Be happy we got it to New Jersey. No, I have my feet firmly planted here. I wouldn't desert summer theatre, even if you paid me," he replied genially, looking as though he really meant it. "Come on. I'll walk you home." he whispered, changing the subject. Anne knew exactly what this short burst of success meant to Gene, who had suffered through a dry spell for many years.

Arm in arm, they headed for Green Gables at a very companionable stroll. Before long they were on the old wooden bridge crossing Barry's Pond. Mist was rising off the water and the wind shuffled the leaves in the aspen trees. Anne had grown quieter as they got closer to the farm. On the bridge, she stopped to lean on the weathered railing and lost herself in her reflection in the water rippling below.

"What is it?" Gene queried, sensing that something was not quite right.

"I don't know." Anne shrugged. "Everything is in its right place. Dominic is getting married. I've finally managed to create a serious drama onstage. But I feel so ... empty."

"Why?"

Through a long silence, Gene waited for Anne to speak. Anne had confided in him when they returned about her father's note, and Gene had an idea of what was up.

"He won't respond to me directly. It's as if he doesn't exist," she admitted at last, her face transformed by anxiety and confusion. "I've written him back several times but the response is always from his housekeeper ..."

She stared into the watery depths. Her reflection reminded her of Katie. She knew that until she heard from her father himself, she would not be able to rest.

Gene leaned in close enough to give Anne a penetrating look. Their reflections rippled in the water like two shapes searching for their proper form.

"What happened with your father," Gene asked softly, "that you're so reluctant to talk about?"

Anne just shook her head. The end of the story pertaining to her father was the most difficult to rationalize.

Fourteen

I t was a warm, windless spring day at the Thomas mansion. Warm enough that the children, as a special treat, had been permitted by Amelia to do their lessons in the garden at the wrought-iron table under the trees. Jock, Keith, and Violetta had all their workbooks spread out and were labouring over their lessons while Anne supervised. Louisa sat nearby in a lounge chair, reading a book, and keeping an eye on the proceedings, a light rug thrown across her knees.

Anne carried out her tutorial duties conscientiously, but she caught herself daydreaming for a moment as she gazed up at the lush green buds on the trees. She wondered what they really had to say to the orioles that had newly arrived in Marysville from their long migration north. Orioles were such colourful birds, they would be right at home in a tropical forest.

Jock pulled her out of her reverie, holding out his notebook. "You're supposed to check my spelling."

"Of course I will." Anne quickly came back to earth and leaned over to inspect his work. "Jock, *you're supposed* to write the words out three times each."

"Sorry. It's just so much more boring than even algebra."

Jock was saved from more excuses by the appearance of his grandmother, heading toward the table followed by a retinue of maids. The maids carried plates and cutlery, which meant lunch was going to be served outdoors—a special event. Jock and Keith brightened immediately.

"Time for a break, children!" Amelia called across the lawn. "I'm so pleased at the progress these children are making in their studies, Louisa. You're to be commended, Anne."

"Thank you, Mrs. Thomas," cried Anne, gratified that her teaching skills were now producing recognizable results. "We could be even more model children if we were allowed to dine outdoors every day."

Amelia laughed and patted Anne on the back as she arrived at the table.

"And to think, I thought Louisa was a nitwit for arriving on my doorstep with a stray child. Well, I was wrong."

"We're all grateful for your hospitality, Mrs. Thomas," Louisa offered with a small, tight smile. She was growing tired of always making sure she said the right thing. It was wearying to constantly think about how to please her demanding mother-in-law. Amelia had just started supervising the lunch layout when Jeremiah Land interrupted.

"Excuse me, Mrs. Thomas," he said, making his way across the lawn. "I need to speak to you!"

A shadow passed over Amelia's face. She excused herself and went to meet him.

"Speak!" Amelia replied, almost as brusquely as they disappeared into the house. The maids continued to set plates and food on the table. Louisa watched the children close up notebooks and clear their papers off the table.

"Violetta, will you help Hepzibah put the chicken salad on the plates so it doesn't spoil before your grandmother comes back."

Obediently, but with a scowl, Violetta stood up.

"Why do I have to do everything? The boys never have to do anything."

Louisa remedied this at once. She couldn't afford any arguments.

"Boys, help clear up the table. Your sister does more than her share. And be careful. No arguing!"

With mock groans, Keith and Jock slid out of their chairs and followed Violetta toward the summer kitchen. When all the children were gone, Louisa beckoned Anne to sit beside her, very close, on the edge of the wicker lounge chair. Anne was uneasy as she noticed Louisa looking about furtively to make sure they were truly alone. Louisa opened the book she had been reading and handed a note to Anne.

"Your father's written to me, Anne. He wanted me to pass this along to you."

Anne swallowed hard as she opened the single sheet of coarse paper.

"I am safe and doing so much better," it read. "Nellie Parkhurst is helping me get organized to come back to Marysville. I want you to do everything she asks. It won't be long before I can come back for you, too."

Anne felt as though someone had suddenly turned out all the bright lights in her room. She was alone in the darkness.

"How...?" she asked in a wavering voice.

"Last fall in St. John, I went to write the teacher's board exam. He was just out of the hospital. He saw me on the street and called to me. We've corresponded ever since."

Louisa was smiling to herself, her face soft at the memory of their chance meeting that past fall. Walter Shirley had considerable charm, she'd discovered. However, all Anne could think of was how furious Louisa had been with her father for stealing the parish roof money and letting the blame fall on Dr. Thomas. In the end, her husband had been killed! Louisa's reaction made absolutely no sense to Anne.

"But you vowed never to have anything more to do with him!"

Louisa positively leaped to defend Walter.

"I misjudged him, Anne. Your father is a good man. You must understand that he is much reformed. Come along—we only have a short time."

Walter had obviously convinced Louisa that he was not the one who'd stolen the money from the roof box. Louisa had finally come to the conclusion that perhaps her own husband had been guilty; yet more evidence of how low the doctor had fallen. Now, she was intent on blaming her mother-in-law for her husband's upbringing and all of their suffering. With a glance toward the house, Louisa leaned even closer to Anne.

"Your father's involved with a lumber company called New Hampshire Timber and Plank, which is willing to help Grandmother. And your father's going to help all the workers keep their jobs or find new jobs if the mills are sold."

"Does Mrs. Thomas know?" Anne was trying hard to digest this new and confusing information.

"No. You see, the banks are behind it. They *want* her to sell."

Anne had no idea what Louisa meant, and she didn't understand anything to do with business or money. She only knew she didn't like the way Louisa had lowered her voice to a whisper. In response, she resorted to one of her fifty-cent words.

"It . . . sounds so insidious."

For a moment, Louisa's face lost its pleasant expression. She became cold and distant as she looked toward the Thomas mansion.

"Grandmother's never cared much for anybody but herself. She only values people when they are of service to her or amuse her."

She smiled again entreatingly. "Your enthusiasm is a tonic. *You* can influence her."

Anne was stumped as to how she could possibly influence the important Amelia Thomas.

"To do what?" she asked.

"Sell, *retire,* and leave Marysville."

The notion of such a task took Anne's breath away. She had no idea at all of how to move Amelia. Her head was spinning with thoughts of her father, and now Louisa was looking at her as if everyone involved in this plot was depending on her to sway the balance.

Anne was completely flummoxed. Her generally carefree mood had been severely upset by the cryptic message from her father. Was he planning to take her away from this happy place? That was the last thing she wanted to happen! And what of Louisa? It seemed she was a traitor who had no intention of staying in the Thomas household any longer than she needed to. Anne was happy for once in her short life and completely resigned to living under Mrs. Thomas's benevolence. She did not have it in her to upset her own apple cart for the benefit of a father who had long ago deserted her.

AS ANNE SPOKE WITH LOUISA, Amelia watched them distractedly from the parlour window. Her back was to Mr. Land, straight and unmoving as he recited a long string of business reports, all of them depressing.

"That price drop put an end to shipping to the States," Mr. Land was saying. "The cotton mill will simply drag the other mills under. If you don't shut it down in several weeks, we won't be able to pay the mortgage to the Abbey Bank on all the other mills."

He continued pacing up and down in front of the satin striped settee. "I'm concerned about the bank," added Mr. Land. "They are pushing you to sell out."

He had no need to explain to Amelia just how deeply the whole endeavour was in debt. She'd realized weeks ago that she was going to have to take action—drastic action. She knew full well what had fomented all this union-organizing activity. Yet she stood there before her manager as if she believed the best course was to completely ignore the situation. She wanted him to plead with her. She needed to push him right to the edge as well as to gain his absolute loyalty.

Taking a quick look at Mr. Land's face, Amelia knew she had reached that point. She marched over to her desk. With an impatient gesture, she reached for the papers in his hand, slapped them down, and dipped her pen in the inkwell, signing every document decisively. Mr. Land stood back without another word as Amelia turned away from him again. She stared out of her parlour window, looking out across the expanse of green grass and brilliant spring blossoms. The manager slipped out of her parlour and left silently while Amelia remained deep in troubled thought. Then a sudden idea illuminated her face. Lifting her chin, she swept grandly back out into the garden, ready to make her next move against the forces trying to topple her little kingdom.

Outside, the maids had cleared away all traces of the snacks the children had been allowed while they studied. Now the table, clad in a snowy white cloth, was laid for an outdoor lunch, complete with good china and silver. Anne and Louisa were already standing behind their chairs, awaiting her arrival. Amelia crossed the lawn toward them, and while they waited, Louisa redoubled her appeal to Anne.

"We have to help her make the right decision for everyone, including us, if we're ever going to leave this place. You have the ability to convince her to retire."

For the first time, Anne saw the desperation behind Louisa's fears. The younger Mrs. Thomas felt trapped by her mother-in-law's power and was prepared to do whatever she could to gain her independence.

Violetta and the boys came running along in Amelia's wake. They all stood waiting for her to sit down so they, too, could sink into wicker chairs around the lunch-laden table. Amelia appeared carefree and benign as she made her announcement.

"Everyone, I have come to a very important decision. I've decided to host a picnic next week, for the town and some important visitors!" she declared optimistically.

Violetta, Keith, and Jock exchanged delighted glances as they helped themselves to lunch. Louisa shot a meaningful look at Anne, and nudged her under the table. The girl felt all of Louisa's expectations pressing down on her. Louisa pushed her foot again and Anne exploded like a nervous chatterbox.

"A picnic! Oh, this can't be real. I'm so excited I could faint! I'd love to be able to really faint. It sounds so romantic."

She talked so fast and so nervously that Amelia simply held her fork in mid-air, staring at Anne with astonishment. "Violetta, will you wear that new dress with elbow sleeves to the picnic? Are you sure the weather will be good for a picnic next week, Mrs. Thomas? If anything ever happened it would be a lifelong sorrow for everyone! The entire town would be beside itself if they are half as fluttered as me."

Now Violetta was also staring at Anne, while Louisa simply compressed her mouth in pained dismay. This was not what she'd had in mind when she asked Anne to work her magic on Amelia! Anne, who barely knew what retirement was, blundered on. Under the tablecloth, her knees were shaking.

"Someday, I'd like to . . . to retire. Looking forward to things is half the pleasure of them, though, don't you think? Will you have boats? And ice cream? Ice cream is one of those treats that sounds sublime, even though I've never truly had it."

Amelia suddenly lost her patience.

"Anne Shirley, what mental anguish has consumed you?" she cut in when Anne paused to suck in her breath. "You have prattled on for five minutes. Can you hold your tongue for at least that equal amount of time?"

Anne was only too glad to be told to clam up, though she was certain she had failed in her mission and failed Louisa. While Louisa picked at her chicken salad with stiff little movements, Amelia went back to her picnic plans. She had, at least, gleaned one good idea from Anne.

"We will serve ice cream—with lady fingers. Violetta, you and Anne will work with Hepzibah and select the luncheon menu. Boys, you'll do all the decorations—the bunting and the flags."

Amelia had been watching Louisa's reaction out of the corner of her eye.

"Louisa, I want you to see to the invitations. I have had several callers from the Abbey Bank of late that I'll need you to contact. We wouldn't want to neglect making sure at least one of their representatives is free to attend."

Louisa nodded and stared at her mother-in-law, uncertain as to whether she considered her guilty of some duplicity or not. Louisa maintained a faint smile on her lips.

"This will be a celebration the town will never forget." Amelia continued, revealing the real reason for the event. She then glared at Louisa. "And it will bolster assurance about Thomas Mills!"

FOR THE WORKERS in the Thomas Cotton Mill, however, it was too late for any assurance. By the end of that week, the pulleys slowed, the driving belts stopped turning, and the rows of mechanical looms clattered to a complete halt. The whistle blew for the very last time, and the power was switched off. Not another length of fabric would be woven.

As the dust settled inside, a subdued procession of men, women, and even several children lined up to receive their final pay envelope. Clutching their bits of money, the workers spilled out into the street and began their sad journeys home. Some of the women were in tears, many more were stone-faced. Men and women alike cast furious glances at Jeremiah Land, who waited by the factory door until the last employee had left the mill. Trying to remain oblivious to the mutters and hissing remarks he took a great iron key from his pocket, locked the door for the very last time, and walked off in the opposite direction of the workers. He knew better than any of them that there would be no replacement jobs in Marysville as long as Mrs. Thomas continued her stubborn, inflexible course of action. He only wished he had the power to change things.

Meanwhile, the Thomas house was buzzing with preparations. Louisa took advantage of all the activity to catch Anne's eye one afternoon when they were both upstairs. Anne was folding a smock in her room when Louisa approached. With a meaningful look and a small nod, she left the book she'd been reading on a table in the corridor and walked on without speaking.

Anne understood at once. With some trepidation, she waited until Louisa left before slipping over to the table. Quick as she could, Anne opened the book and removed the note from her father. Once it was in her hand, Anne could not resist sitting down at the little sewing table and scanning the words, trying to take it all in. So absorbed was she that Anne did not notice Hepzibah coming out of the shadows toward her. The housekeeper had witnessed Anne's furtive action from the end of the hall and the older woman's face was tight with suspicion as she watched the child intently reading a note hidden in a book. The girl may have weaseled her way into the Thomas household and even bamboozled the mistress, but Hepzibah had decided long ago she would not trust Anne Shirley one inch.

"Get downstairs, girl, and help with the party things," Hepzibah called out harshly. "I don't care for children who don't know how to work."

Startled and guilty, Anne jumped up. She jammed the note into the pocket of her apron and dashed for the stairs. The moment she was out of sight, Hepzibah flipped through the book Anne had been studying. There was nothing inside. Nevertheless, she guessed Anne was up to something and she meant to find out what it was; or at least whatever it was she was reading so intently.

In the kitchen below, Anne went to work polishing a silver tea service. When she was finished, she arranged it on a tray and carried it over to where several other tea services sat on the sideboard under the window. Amelia Thomas obviously meant to put on a splendid show. Beautiful china cups and saucers were lined up on the sideboard in a military row, ready to be carried outside. Violetta had just set down a tray containing a gleaming teapot, sugar bowl, and creamer.

"There," Anne said as she slid her own tray in beside the others. "That's the last of the silver to be polished."

It was the day before the big event and everyone was pitching in to prepare as much as they could. Anne and Violetta had had a tremendously good time helping to choose the menu. There had been many spirited arguments over the merits of velvet sponge cake versus lemon tartlets, mustard pickles versus pickled beets, macaroons versus ginger drops, and, most of all, what kind of ice cream should be served. The boys had been putting up great swaths of bunting all morning. Days earlier, Louisa had sent out the invitations from a long list approved by Amelia.

Violetta was in her element, humming to herself and dreaming of one day hosting such a grand event. As Anne looked about for something else to do, the parlour bell rang. All the main rooms of the house had an old-fashioned bell pull so that a servant could be summoned when needed. Anne jumped at the sound, ready to answer the call.

"I'm happy to go see what she'd like," she volunteered, grasping for any reason to get out of Hepzibah's way.

It was just the opportunity Hepzibah had been waiting for. She nodded permission for Anne to go, but before Anne could trot off, Hepzibah brought her up short.

"Wait a minute. You don't go up to her dressed like that. Take your apron off. You don't see Mrs. Thomas with an apron on."

Anne hesitated, thinking of the note in her pocket. Hepzibah, standing in front of the tall grandfather clock and flanked by her staff of housemaids, flicked her hand impatiently.

"Come on, hurry along. She's waiting for you. Hang it over the back of that chair." Hepzibah ordered. "Off you go."

Anne had no choice but to untie the apron and drape it over the kitchen chair. As soon as she ran off, Hezpibah went straight to the apron and took the note out of the pocket. As she read it, her face dropped, then hardened implacably. Every suspicion she had ever harboured about Anne was proven correct.

IN THE PARLOUR, Amelia got out of her chair and stepped over to a table near the fireplace where she began to review some papers connected to the final closing of the mill. She'd only managed to turn over one sheet when she felt a sharp pain above her stomach and below her heart. The pain shot through her arms, taking her breath away. She gasped to catch her breath and found herself completely bent over.

She was clinging to the edge of the table for support as Anne came skipping into the room. The girl stopped cold at the sight of Amelia struggling for breath, her hand pressed to her chest.

Rushing over, Anne took Amelia by the arm to steady her. The older woman was ghostly pale and nearly sank to the floor, frightening Anne even more. Gratefully, Amelia put her arm across Anne's shoulders. Her other hand pointed urgently to a cabinet containing a liquor decanter and glasses.

"Fetch me some whiskey quickly. Over there."

Amelia staggered up, regaining her balance as Anne sprinted off to do her bidding.

"Oh ... I'm having ... such a fright ..."

Amelia struggled back to her chair and sank into the cushions. None too steadily, Anne splashed the strong-smelling amber liquid into a glass and hurried a tumblerful over to Amelia.

"I'll fetch a doctor," Anne whispered, quite terrified. "Hepzibah!"

"No, no doctor. Now listen, you tell *no one* about this!"

A large swallow of the potent brew did instant wonders. Amelia got her breath back and the colour returned to her cheeks. She took hold of Anne by the sleeve.

"I want you to swear you'll tell no one!"

"It's quite wicked to swear," replied Anne dubiously.

An amused exasperation flickered through Amelia's eyes.

"It's not wicked to swear when you do it in aid of someone you care about."

Anne's eyes grew large. This was the kind of trust reserved only for family! It was a grave responsibility for one so young.

"Oh, Mrs. Thomas, I knew you liked me but ... I ... never presumed you cared about me. Oh, I do swear. I swear to never reveal this moment to a soul."

Amelia sipped her whiskey again, stunned by Anne's burst of emotion. She'd had no idea that the child had become so attached to her. Neither of them saw Hepzibah, who had followed Anne and was lurking outside the room. The housekeeper stopped when she saw Anne fall to her knees beside Amelia. She shrunk back into the velvet curtain hanging outside the door.

"On pain of death I remain your loyal confidante," Anne promised with all the fervour in her young soul, speaking as if it were an oath drawn in the halls of Camelot.

With a wry smile, Amelia patted her reassuringly.

"You go down to the kitchen now and finish up with Hepzibah."

Anne started to walk away, but Amelia suddenly caught her by the wrist and pulled her back. This little scamp had provoked a deep emotion to well up inside of her—something that bordered on complete devotion. She pulled Anne close and embraced her firmly, scrutinizing her carefully to assure herself that the sincerity she found in the child's heart was genuine.

"I feel better now," she murmured reassuringly as she hugged Anne again after looking into her eyes.

Anne was enormously relieved. Hepzibah, eyes flashing, turned into the shadows and disappeared.

IN THE KITCHEN, Hepzibah found Violetta helping with the cutlery. As the eldest grandchild and quite the young lady in her own right, Violetta was beside herself with excitement at the prospect of a position of visible prominence.

"It will be so exciting to be sitting at the head of the table and pouring tea for all the important guests. Don't you think so, Hepzibah?"

Hepzibah sniffed.

"You won't have such a high opinion of it when you've served as many as I have, nor lived as long."

"Violetta!" came Louisa's voice, requesting her from deep inside the house.

"Off you go. Your mother's calling. I'll finish up."

Out of sight, Violetta rolled her eyes at the ceiling as she passed Anne coming back into the kitchen. She would never, ever be tired of entertainments the way Hepzibah seemed to be. But then, the housekeeper was staff who always had to do most of the work. Violetta was prepared to work, but what she really wanted was to reap the glory.

"What should I do next?" asked Anne.

"I've left it all organized for you, Anne!" Violetta boasted on the way past, totally pleased with her own efficiency.

Anne despised being alone with Hepzibah In all her time in the Thomas house, she had never been able to win over the inflexible woman, despite all of her efforts to be friendly. Neither compliments about the excellent dinners nor efforts to do her best helping around the house made the least impression on her. Whenever the two looked at each other, they were more often than not remembering all the harsh words that had flown about over the affair of the upstairs keys. Anne did her best to rise to noble clemency for what had happened, but the housekeeper's aversion rankled deeply.

At that specific moment, Anne was so lost in thought about her recent intimacy with Mrs. Thomas that she didn't notice Hepzibah bearing down until the housekeeper stood right before her, rigid with fury.

"Don't fool yourself into thinking you have the missus all stitched up," the woman snarled in a voice that made Anne's neck hairs prickle.

Completely confused, Anne stared back at Hepzibah timidly. "What ... do you mean?"

"You're no better than the child of a common swindler."

This blast of pure contempt was totally unexpected. "How dare you!" Anne exploded.

From the moment Anne had arrived with Louisa, Hepzibah had been resentful of her worming her way into the household, and now she had wormed her way into Amelia's unsuspecting affections. After so many years at Amelia's beck and call, Hepzibah instinctively flew to protect her.

"How dare *you* try your wheedling ways on Mrs. Thomas! It will crush her when she discovers the truth ... that your father is a union instigator, known to police. And him, in touch with you!"

Stabbing her forefinger into Anne's breastbone, Hepzibah drove her words home with venom. In a snap of her wrist, Hepzibah pulled Walter's letter out of her cummerbund and waved it in front of Anne. The girl almost made a lunge for it, but knew she would never be able to yank it from Hepzibah's fist. Fear made Anne feel weak in the knees. Her father was now officially known as one of those working to destroy the mills, and she herself was the conduit.

Hepzibah's voice dripped with grim prophesy.

"It will get out. Things always get out in Marysville."

Anne backed away from this dire prediction, trying to catch her breath. Hepzibah shot her finger at Anne once more.

"You're just full of original sin. You aren't fit to call this house your home."

With an anguished cry, Anne crumbled completely and bolted for the door.

With Hepzibah's awful words ringing in her ears, Anne could think only of getting as far away from the house as possible. She ran blindly across the drive, through the gardens, and into the woods. She didn't even notice the thunder rumbling above her until a lightning bolt ripped across the sky and the first spatter of rain struck her face.

At first, Anne didn't know where she was going. She ran down the forest track through mist that swirled like ghostly apparitions, obscuring nearly everything around her. A strange bird screeched its outrage at the intruder in the forest, making Anne run faster. She tripped and fell on the spruce needles, barely able to scramble up again. Thunder crashed overhead and lightning leaped from cloud to cloud.

The next thing Anne knew, she found herself in the place where Violetta had been caught in the net trap. Through the trees up ahead she could see the abandoned grist mill. Without slowing, Anne ran across the mill bridge and burst through the heavy pine door in earnest, just as giant drops of rain began to hammer on the ground behind her.

Nellie was at the cookstove, just about to pour a cup of tea. She looked around, startled.

"Come in," she said, and set about calming the storm-driven bundle of misery who had just barrelled into her home.

She dried the raindrops off Anne's hair and set her down at a plank table for a restorative cup of hot tea. Anne held the cup in both hands, trying to draw in its warmth. Her breath had slowed, but now threatened to turn into violent sobs. Nellie's comforting face with its weathered skin soothed the tears. She just sat, elbows on the table, until Anne could talk.

When Anne found her tongue, she spilled out all the horrible things Hepzibah had said. Her small face burned hot as she explained what had happened. Nellie listened quietly and poured more tea. She didn't seem in the least surprised.

"She's a tartar, that Hepzibah," Nellie agreed when Anne was done.

Still shivering a little, Anne looked mournfully into her cup. "A woman born to scrub floors shouldn't take such mean advantage," she said in a ragged voice.

Nellie nodded. She had her own set of complaints about the Thomases' housekeeper.

"She got Mr. Jeremiah Land, the manager, to fire me at the mill, because she wanted to weasel her nephew into my delivery job. Didn't matter, though. I got the mail contract your dad bungled, instead—with my swift team of horses."

Anne didn't want to comment on her father. He had bungled that mail contract in the horrible accident with her mother. Anne was quick to change the subject.

"She said I was full of original sin," Anne revealed, recalling Hepzibah's condemning eyes.

Deep inside, Anne wondered if perhaps there really was something wrong with her; something so terribly wrong that it always brought on disaster, despite her best efforts at being good.

"You got a knack for trouble and it ain't easy bein' different, I'll give you that," Nellie conceded. "Look at me. Lost my baby and my husband years ago. Can't cry about it now. Ya move on."

This tragic revelation pushed Anne's own troubles right out of her mind. Her eyes opened wide and she examined Nellie's weather-beaten face from a new perspective; that it was lined with sorrow.

"Don't you miss belonging to someone?"

Nellie was in the same situation as Anne and the girl wanted to know what the woman had done about it. Nellie gave Anne a slow smile.

"I belong to the community here. The town is my family. Exceptin' Mrs. Thomas. She's a stubborn fool."

Anne knew what a tight, happy community lived in Marysville, but she thought it unfair that everyone was so against Mrs. Thomas because of her position, wealth, and rank.

"She's not half the monster people think she is," Anne defended the old woman immediately.

The smile faded from Nellie's face. Anne remembered the concert, the skating parties, and the warm embrace in the parlour. Most of all, she recalled how Mrs. Thomas had forgiven her the misunderstanding over Bridgewater and generously took her back into her home.

"People stick by each other here," Nellie averred, gently trying to persuade Anne to think differently. "It's a fine community. A union can force her to sell to someone bigger and stronger before she goes bust. A union can save everyone's jobs."

Anne knew that the Thomas family had built Marysville with sweat and risk, and that Mrs. Thomas' mills provided everyone with a job. Her best interests were their best interests, Anne reasoned. She began to fear that perhaps Nellie was going crazy if she couldn't add all this up.

"Controlling things in her way destroyed a lot of what was good here. She'd like to see the town finally fail," continued Nellie with a hardness in her voice.

"No, she wouldn't!" exclaimed Anne, appalled at the very idea. Nellie had gone too far! What did she know of the truth? "She's in dire straits," Anne continued. "The bank is forcing her to . . . to . . ."

Anne suddenly stopped, worried that perhaps she had said too much and fearful of the divided loyalties struggling inside her. She wanted to explain that Mrs. Thomas was a good person and that she had come on hard times. But she also knew Amelia had sworn her to secrecy. In the awkward pause that ensued, Nellie eyed Anne closely then shrugged.

"I don't know much about banks."

Nellie could see the worry on Anne's face. The child had been completely won over by the mill owner, which, to Nellie, was not healthy at all.

"People stick by each other here," she repeated. "This town is a good place for you to belong to. You could settle down with your pa. Live a long life here." She stared at Anne, trying to determine if her words were getting through. But Anne was intransigent. Nellie decided Anne needed to know the full truth.

"Despite all their money, the Thomases have never been very decent."

Fortunately or unfortunately, Nellie's revelation had backfired. In Anne's young mind, an attack on her benefactress was beyond the pale. She got up from her chair, paused, and, after a moment, politely offered Nellie her hand. Her manner was completely detached.

"Thank you. Please tell my father I am in kind and caring hands and not to worry about me."

Head high, Anne turned and hurried out the door. Nellie sat at her table, wondering what powerful influence Mrs. Thomas could have used on a child to turn her against her own father.

ANNE RAN BACK ALONG the forest track, now sodden from the sudden storm. The path was lined with ferns gleaming with drops of pearl. She was going home. If she had to brave the terrors of Hepzibah, then so be it. Anne was prepared to gamble on the kindness of Mrs. Thomas. Anne arrived back to learn that her disappearance had created a minor turmoil. Hepzibah cast a frozen glance, as if to say she knew Anne had run off to the union agitators. Louisa and the rest of the household were too caught up in the picnic preparations to give Anne more than a half-hearted scolding. Amelia said nothing, merely regarding the child with inquisitive, thoughtful eyes.

Finally, Anne and Violetta hurried to bed, exhausted. Violetta, dreaming of the day to come and tired from all her preparations, simply passed out. Anne tossed and turned, distressed that the two sides of her life—Amelia Thomas on the one hand, and Nellie and her father on the other—were somehow at war.

Anne was wide awake when Amelia walked quietly into the room in her dressing gown, her hair falling loose down her back. She shook Anne by the shoulder. Anne lifted her head off the pillow in surprise as Amelia sat on the edge of the mattress.

"Whatever made you run away like that? I was worried." Amelia's brow was furrowed in legitimate concern.

Anne could smell the fragrance of roses that always accompanied Amelia, and she remembered how soft her cheek had felt when she'd pulled Anne close that afternoon. It had been perfectly thrilling to find herself embraced by the dowager whom so many others feared. She was so worried about Amelia's health, she dared not reveal that she had received a letter from her father—or any of the dreadful things Hepzibah had said to her.

"I was afraid…," she improvised.

Amelia sat back in surprise, her eyes widening.

"Of me?"

Anne nodded, hitting upon a thing that Amelia would understand.

"I was frightened…maybe you'd change your mind, about me staying."

"Why?"

Amelia couldn't think of a single reason that Anne would

take such a notion into her head. In her anxiety, Anne responded by speaking aloud what she truly believed about herself.

"I'm such an unlucky girl. Always getting myself into scrapes and getting my friends—people I'd shed my life's blood for—into them too."

"You certainly said something that made Hepzibah very cross. What was it?"

Once again, Anne had to stop herself, agonizing in her sincere little heart at what she dared not tell the woman who had been so good to her. She was afraid she had already revealed too much to Nellie Parkhurst and how it might come back to haunt the woman most people in Marysville viewed as disreputable.

"I was wrong to run away, Mrs. Thomas," she said instead. "You are a true kindred spirit. "

"A what?"

Amelia had grown accustomed to Anne's fanciful language. It was one of the child's main appeals, but this was something new.

"A kindred spirit," Anne explained, taking Amelia's hand, and laying it over her heart and speaking earnestly, "is someone you can rely on right to your innermost soul."

Anne remembered what Gabriel had told her and it seemed an appropriate title for Amelia. The old woman's heart filled up. All at once, she realized just how much she truly loved this innocent child. Smiling, she tucked the covers softly about Anne. What she could not fathom was how she concocted such elaborate turns of phrase. The girl was outlandishly fanciful, but Amelia loved her intelligence and was determined to protect her at all costs.

"Go back to sleep," she whispered as she stood up.

Anne smiled back and turned over, her eyes finally closing with weariness from the long, disturbing day, and a feeling of relief that Amelia had accepted her explanation. The uncertainty about Hepzibah and what she might still do felt less intimidating as Anne drifted to sleep. Amelia stood in the doorway for several minutes, watching the red head sink into the feather pillow. In some ways, this little imp was a complete enigma, she thought to herself.

Fifteen

The next morning, no one—and certainly not Anne—had a moment to think about anything but the picnic taking place on the broad green lawns. Hepzibah and a full compliment of maids and butlers had been up since dawn, completely consumed with the hundred things that remained to be done. Mr. MacAdams and two of the gardeners had carried out wooden tables and set them where the shade was the most pleasant. The maids covered them with the whitest of linen tablecloths and set out rows of shining plates, cutlery, and teacups for the refreshments.

Anne, Violetta, Jock, and Keith dashed back and forth, running errands, carrying napkins, and counting the chairs that were scattered about for the comfort of those guests who would tire of standing. Violetta oversaw the menu she had chosen with a proprietary bossiness, directing where and how each item should be placed and served. She saw herself as heir apparent to all the prestige her grandmother commanded. Someday, she knew she would be able to render the authority required to run her own large household.

The preparations for ice cream making sent Jock and Keith into a tizzy. Ice, salt, cream, and fruit were ready to go into the churn. However, it required a tremendous amount of strength to keep the handle revolving until the ice cream formed in the centre of the churn. They knew the marvellous concoction inside would have to be eaten as soon as possible, as it would not keep frozen for very long. Both boys meant to ensure that not a single unbelievably delicious mouthful would ever have an opportunity to melt. Hepzibah found them covered in the spoils. She instructed one of her servants to take over and she sent Jock and Keith packing.

Just before the guests were to arrive, the boys were told to wash their faces and get into their best clothes for the occasion. Anne had her hair out of her everyday braids and hanging straight down her back, brushed to a ruddy glossiness and held off her face by a beautiful dark blue ribbon; another gift from Amelia. She looked like someone who had just stepped out of a bandbox dressed in a new blue, seersucker dress that made her feel so elegant she literally danced down the stairs. Even the weather co-operated with mellow sunshine, a breeze too delicate to pluck at the tablecloths, and an obliging display of nodding blooms in the flowerbeds. Amelia had invited just about all of Marysville to this grandly fabricated event—in her effort to win over their hearts—as though a picnic might be influential enough to divert them from their desire to have a union to stand up for all that they had determined they were owed. From the head of the ladies' auxiliary to the many mill workers, the people of the town streamed onto Amelia's manicured lawns. No matter how they felt about her, they were not about to turn down ice cream and cake and all the treats the poorest ones had never seen in their own homes.

Fulfilling her greatest desire, Violetta presided over the refreshment table, pouring cups of tea from the heavy, gleaming silver teapot while the maids dashed to keep it filled. Hepzibah strode about like a general in the midst of battle, eyeing the supply lines and directing maids to circulate with trays of punch and sandwiches among the hungry crowd. Everyone had worn their very finest attire, from the lacy afternoon dresses and flowery hats of the more well-to-do to the plain cotton skirts and unadorned straw boaters of the mill workers. Even Nellie Parkhurst appeared in the midst of the crowd, her dark hair neatly pinned up, wearing a pretty patterned blouse with a flowing skirt. It was a radical change from her rough, wagon-driving attire.

The crowd stood in silence, listening as Amelia stepped to the centre of the festivities to address her legion of guests.

"It is unfortunate that economic conditions have forced the closing of our prized cotton mill, but the cider and lumber mills are both resilient businesses with a bright future. I wanted to take this afternoon to thank so many of you who have been dedicated to the Thomas mills . . . and to helping me personally during this time, at filling my husband's shoes."

There was some unenthusiastic applause when Amelia was finished. Though most of the crowd tried to wear a friendly face, dour glances flitted among the listeners. Nellie folded her arms and shook her head. Undaunted, Amelia swept her hand toward the waiting tables.

"I'd be most pleased to meet each and every one of you if you'll join me for tea in the garden."

Moving past the long tables of refreshments, Amelia gathered her family and set about shaking hands vigorously, taking every opportunity to introduce her grandsons to the locals.

"Thank you for coming." She smiled over and over again as the line of guests snaked by on the way to tea tables and plates laden with delicacies. Louisa stood at her side as a staunch lieutenant, also shaking hands and greeting the people one by one.

Jeremiah Land was in attendance, dressed in a jaunty straw fedora, a light cotton suit, and a check vest. He noticed some well-dressed businessmen walking down the main driveway. He immediately interrupted Amelia and drew her away from the receiving line, leaving Louisa to continue shaking hands. Mr. Land pointed out the tight little group of men making their way through the crowd. Their arrival had caused quite a stir.

"It appears as if the bank has brought along a guest," Mr. Land whispered to Amelia. "Let's put our best foot forward." When the manager said "the bank," he really meant Phillip Granger, the invited representative of the Abbey Bank.

"Speak for yourself," Amelia retorted. In her eyes, it was presumptuous of a bank employee to bring anyone to a party without an invitation. Any such guest of the Abbey Bank must surely have his own agenda. She was also concerned about Mr. Land. Had he known about this in advance? Anne, who was standing close by enjoying the wonderful feel of her full sleeves, picked up on Amelia's concern. Suddenly, she recognized the man in the dark suit and top hat as the one who had been at the grist mill the day Violetta was caught in the trap—the same man to whom Ruth Bridgewater had been passing papers. Anne was too nervous to let on what she saw, particularly as she watched Mr. Land steel himself in preparation for the meeting.

"Mr. Land looks as if he's being led to the gallows, Mrs. Thomas," Anne whispered, tugging at Amelia's sleeve. Amelia squeezed Anne's arm in return.

"It's all in his head. He's intimidated by bankers. I don't see the use of meeting trouble halfway. I'm not here to entertain bullies."

Amelia sallied forth in a striking effort to be as gracious as she could to the powerful-looking newcomers who had not been on her guest list. The man beside the sober-looking Phillip Granger was dressed in a fine tweed suit and bowler hat. He was broad in the beam, with an expansive waistcoat, and sported a prominent gold watch and chain. His large beefy face featured a trimmed, grey-peppered beard. He looked about him with great interest, and gave the impression of being a blunt fellow, used to getting things done. Both men doffed their hats as Amelia strolled up.

"You know Mr. Granger," Mr. Land said as the man from the clandestine meeting stepped up.

"Mr. Granger," Amelia acknowledged, shaking his hand.

"Mrs. Thomas," said Mr. Granger, "this is Alan Laing from New Hampshire Timber and Plank."

To Amelia's credit, only a fleeting look of provocation passed across her face before she hospitably extended her hand to this new member of the competition.

"Thanks for having me," Alan Laing boomed. "I am pleased to see such an enthusiastic throng, Mrs. Thomas—with all the rumblings."

It was brazen to mention such a thing when he was a visitor at such an event. But neither man, it seemed, had come along merely to drink tea or even be polite. Amelia regarded them unblinkingly.

"Believe only half of what you see and none of what you hear, Mr. Laing. The Abbey Bank has a vested interest in union talk, as I perceive it," she returned, looking sharply at Mr. Granger.

A chill instantly settled over the group.

"The bank has to address financial burden head-on," Mr. Granger stated baldly. "We're concerned that your mortgage payments have lapsed."

Phillip Granger could not have said a more shocking thing at a garden party. What's more, he made it clear that he'd brought the solution with him—in the form of the corpulent Mr. Laing, a thriving timber entrepreneur ready to buy up the Thomas holdings at a moment's notice. Amelia kept her composure magnificently, though she shot a sizzling sideways glance at Mr. Land. He shifted uncomfortably, but did not lose his air of dogged determination.

Not far away, Anne was about to entertain her own drama. Leaving Amelia to talk to the men, Anne went over to Violetta's tea table, on a quest to polish her own manners. If she were going to live with Amelia, she meant to do her proud in the conduct department. She held out one of the fine china cups for Violetta to fill with amber Earl Grey tea.

"Is this the correct way to balance a cup? I'm not well versed in the rules of etiquette. I'm afraid I'll . . ."

She never finished the sentence. Violetta had stopped pouring and was now staring beyond Anne.

Anne turned around to see what had captured Violetta's attention. At first, she saw only the milling guests. Then, looking farther, she saw a man with a cane standing in the grove of aspen trees, just beyond the edge of the lawn. One sleeve of his suit was tucked neatly into his jacket pocket, signifying a missing arm. He was gazing straight through the crowd at Anne.

For an endless minute, Anne was speechless. Violetta stood with the silver teapot suspended in mid-air. She glanced at Anne suspiciously, wondering what was preventing her from moving. With a quick glance at Violetta, Anne tore across the grass toward the tall figure—determined to make Violetta believe she was nothing but ecstatic to see her dear papa.

"Father," she cried, running straight into his embrace. Walter embraced Anne awkwardly.

"Is there a quiet spot?" he asked in a low voice. With his good arm, he gently pulled her away into the perennial garden, where they sat on the edge of a low stone wall. He walked with a limp and sat stiffly.

Anne had no clue what to say. She was dazed and still half-disbelieving. In particular, she wanted to make sure she provided no evidence of anything that would give Violetta an opportunity to gossip, or to tell Hepzibah, heaven forbid. Underneath it all, Anne's heart was in her throat; she was thoroughly frightened.

Walter looked much improved from the last time Anne had seen him, lying bandaged in the cottage bed, ghastly white and delirious with pain. His skin was ruddy and healthy, and he wore his suit rather dashingly. He took Anne in from head to toe, trying to determine if she would help him.

"Louisa has told me how helpful you've been in softening up Mrs. Thomas."

Apparently Louisa had been doing more than writing, she had been talking to him, too. Proof of this occurred when Walter glanced over Anne's head. His eyes met Louisa's, where she was still shaking hands with visitors in the receiving line, and her sudden smile revealed how glad she was to see him. Her complete lack of surprise told Anne she'd known he was coming. Louisa immediately turned back to the parade of guests so as not to draw attention to herself or Walter. Nellie and a small group of workers also watched the scene with keen interest. Without any doubt, they had all been instrumental in getting Walter onto the Thomas property. Their hopes, too, were pinned on Mr. Laing, and in many ways on Anne herself, if she could offer any influence.

Though Walter had done his best to keep his left arm out of sight, Anne realized that much of it was gone. She shuddered at the thought of what had befallen him. Walter jerked his head toward Phillip Granger and the well-padded Alan Laing.

"I can't talk for long, but if this deal goes through many men can keep their jobs and the town will carry on. I plan to do very well out of it, too."

Anne felt her cheeks burning. Fear, confusion, and duty were all mixed up inside her. Her father might want to help the

mill workers, but to profit from it himself seemed mercenary.
He also had the power to harm Amelia. It was clear now that
her father had been willing to use her in the hope that she could
influence the proud Mrs. Thomas to do something she had
patently refused to do.

"Why do you have to be like this . . ."Anne's voice trailed
off. She was too caught up in her emotions to realize that Hepzibah had come to a sharp halt on the grass.

The housekeeper stood watching the two in what she
sharply assessed as deep conversation. Fury blazed across her
face as she hiked straight through the dense crowd over to
Amelia, who was by now standing alone in a foul mood herself
following her conversation with the bankers. Hepzibah pulled
the note that she had taken from Anne in the kitchen the day before from under her cummerbund. "Read this," she shot at her
employer, thrusting the creased paper into Amelia's hand. "I
found this in Anne's pocket yesterday."

Amelia quickly scanned the damning sheet of paper. Her
eyes turned stormy. Hepzibah seized the moment to point out
Anne and Walter with their heads together, half-hidden in the
shrubbery and the roses.

"And there they are."

Amelia looked at Anne talking earnestly with the beleaguered man holding the cane. Her anger made her crush the
note into a ball.

"Whatever's necessary, go ahead and just do it!"

Taking this as open season on Anne, Hepzibah sprinted
across the lawn. With a dark face, Amelia watched as Hepzibah
marched right up to the girl and grabbed her by the arm. With
her other hand, she shooed Walter away like some nasty vermin.
He stood up and moved back without protest, watching as Hepzibah dragged his daughter unceremoniously across the vast lawn.

"You're to have nothing more to do with him!" Hepzibah growled to the mortified girl.

Quickly, Amelia strode over to where Jeremiah was still conversing with Misters Granger and Laing and several other men. Excusing herself curtly, she took Jeremiah Land by the elbow and pulled him aside. Once out of earshot, Amelia lit into him.

"Of all the cunning, manipulative schemes! Using a child as a go-between and having the audacity to display it on the lawn of my own home," she raged, jabbing a finger in the direction of Anne, who was being hustled up the garden slope while Walter stood staring defiantly in Amelia's direction.

Mr. Land refused to be made guilty.

"You're being too guarded."

"Am I?" Amelia retorted. "They certainly have the inside track on all of *our* discussions. What have you been saying to them?"

Mr. Land was silent for only a heartbeat. No one knew better than he the dire situation of the Thomas businesses. He mustered a reply.

"Nothing but listening to an excellent offer for timber rights that could solve virtually all of our financial issues."

Such talk was treason in Amelia's mind. She went nose to nose with the manager, furious that he would ever dare to operate behind her back.

"Jeremiah, you've worked for me for fifteen years and we've never had a cross word. Is that correct?"

Amelia paused only long enough for him to nod before she thundered on.

"So I'll give you the benefit of the doubt. But listen to me fully. As sure as I stand here now, I will close down all of my mills myself before I sell . . . or before I toss even one morsel at those vultures. Do you understand me?"

The manager had to bite his tongue to stop himself from venting his frustration.

"I understand, ma'am."

He caught his breath and retreated from Amelia to rejoin the Granger crowd.

"Come and have some more refreshment," he invited them with open arms, trying to cover up his altercation with Mrs. Thomas. "Have you tried the buffet?"

Crestfallen, Anne was left standing alone inside the house, where Hepzibah had finally pushed her. Realizing his daughter was gone for good, Walter prudently hid himself away in the safety of the Marysville woods. Amelia returned to her guests, concealing her inner tumult behind a warm and gracious smile.

BESIDES BEING DEEPLY agitated by the encounter with her father, Anne was tormented by the idea that she had offended Amelia. She could not rest until she was able to explain to her benefactress both her feelings and everything to which she'd been privy. Anne waited until Amelia was in the parlour, writing a letter at her desk, before knocking timidly on the open door. With barely a glance, Amelia nodded for her to come in. Cautiously, Anne approached. Her hair was pulled back in braids and her party dress had been exchanged for everyday cotton with a frilled pinafore, another of Amelia's extravagances. Anne's eyes were swollen from crying, but she found her voice.

"Hepzibah explained how those people wanted to use me," Anne was able to get out in a rush. "The stars in their courses fight against me. But if you must be cross with anyone, please be cross with me."

The terrible explosion Anne had expected did not materialize. Amelia merely tilted her head and kept on writing.

"Don't fret, Anne. It will turn out all right in the end."

Anne was unable to see how. Hepzibah had told her quite flatly that the union agitators, including Anne's father, were bent on wresting everything they could from Mrs. Thomas, even if it took sabotage. Anne could not forget the terror of the night the log chute collapsed. She tried to counter in the only way she could, with deep sincerity.

"Not if you are forced to give it all away to a bank."

Amelia's imperious brows lifted a fraction.

"I've never been forced to do anything in my life. It isn't in my nature," she told Anne calmly.

Another child would have accepted the tolerable response and tiptoed back out of the room, but Anne was incapable of such logic. She was compelled to get everything off her chest.

"I'm used to having people cross with me, but Hepzibah said such merciless things that night. I ran away to Nellie's...to talk to her about everything I'd found out."

Amelia's pen stopped in its tracks. She'd never imagined that Anne was a source of information for Mr. Granger. She shook her head, regarding Anne with much irritation.

"You're just so heedless and impulsive."

Tears welled up in Anne's eyes again and spilled down her cheeks.

"I was terrified you'd throw me out if you found out about my father," she said in a quavering voice, "You have to believe me..."

"You never stop to think!" Amelia cut her off. "Whatever pops into your mind, you leap on it without a moment's reflection!"

Anne hung her head in misery. Being foolishly impulsive was one of the regular burdens in her life.

"I know I'm culpable. But imagine the horror of finding out what my father has been involved in. An iron entered my soul at that very moment. Hepzibah made me feel like a worthless traitor. I would never go against you."

The concept of this young child with an iron in her soul caused Amelia's look to soften. The twitch of a smile touched her lips.

"Come here." Amelia set down her pen and held out her hands to take Anne's. "Grown-ups can often take advantage of a child's innocent heart. Even this father of yours. You mustn't trust everyone all the time. You have a new home here. I know Louisa wants you to stay with us."

The remorseful little face was instantly transformed, hardly believing what she had just heard.

"Oh, say it again Mrs. Thomas. It's a ray of hope on a path of darkness."

Without waiting for an invitation this time, Anne flung her arms around Amelia's neck and pressed her young cheek to the old woman's. Amelia's eyes, though Anne could not see them, brimmed with unaccustomed sentiment.

"And I want you to stay, too," she whispered, wondering how she'd ever gotten on without this extraordinary child to brighten her large, troubled house.

Sixteen

Amelia's tender moment of reconciliation with Anne would have been entirely spoiled had she known that treason had entered not only her house, but also her own family. During the past several months, Louisa had developed a distinct camaraderie with Walter Shirley. She had been won over to his view that Marysville's only salvation was for Amelia to sell out to New Hampshire Timber and Plank. She also fully believed that Amelia's financial arrangements with the bank were full of loopholes. Like Walter and the other conspirators, Louisa now reasoned that the Abbey Bank was poised to gobble up Amelia by merely pulling a couple of chinks out of the wall she had constructed around herself. The more desperate the situation became, the more logical it seemed to Louisa that Amelia needed to take the most dignified way out and sell.

According to Walter, New Hampshire Timber and Plank would pump in the capital needed to refurbish the aging mills and expand the lumbering operation. With the closing of the cotton mill, town rumour had it that Amelia could barely meet the payroll every week. Soon she might not even be able to accomplish that—especially since she had to pay for her extravagant summer picnic! Like so many others, Louisa could not understand why her mother-in-law was being so pigheaded.

Louisa was so distraught over the situation that she even tried to recruit the Thomases' most fanatical supporter, Hepzibah.

Louisa approached the housekeeper in the summer kitchen one day and begged her to listen to her case. Louisa's frustration with Amelia filled her voice as she spoke.

"Amelia is reckless not to sell. This company can build a more solid community in ways she is incapable of."

If Louisa had wanted to alienate Hepzibah, she could not have chosen a better way to do it. The housekeeper knew nothing of economic matters beyond the running of a household. She also considered it none of her business to pry. She did not live in the town and her nephew had quit working at the mill three years earlier, so she saw nothing of the mill workers' hardships. As usual, she backed her employer unconditionally.

"You fault her for her determination?" Hepzibah demanded, her voice shaking at Louisa's treachery.

In her opinion, Amelia's fortitude in sticking to her chosen course of action was one of her chief attributes. The housekeeper was confident Amelia would not be swayed—either by dastardly sabotage, greedy bankers, or New Hampshire Timber and Plank sitting there like a scavenger waiting to pick at her bones.

Louisa, though, wasn't ready to give up. She frantically wanted out of the Thomas household and out from under Amelia's control over their lives, and she confidently believed Walter Shirley was the key to her exodus. She could see only one path.

"There will never be another opportunity like this," she pleaded. "Please speak to her, Hepzibah . . . to at least prolong discussions with them."

Hepzibah set down the tray of china she had been carrying then she looked Louisa derisively in the eye.

"I have a single retort for the lot of you," she flung out. "Judas Priests!"

She spat on the floor at Louisa's feet before she stalked out the room. It was almost more than Louisa could bear. With her mind spinning, she fled the summer kitchen.

Later in the day as the shadows of the afternoon lengthened, she slipped surreptitiously out the mansion's front door. Glancing about to see whether anyone had noticed her, she picked up her skirts and began to run as fast as she could across the lawn of the great property, directly toward the trees bordering the woods. She wanted to get out of sight as quickly as she could.

She might well have succeeded had Amelia not been pacing about the parlour. The quick flash of movement on the lawn caught her eye and drew her to the window. She pulled back the sheers just in time to catch a glimpse of her daughter-in-law darting for the forest. Full of her own paranoia and suspicions, Amelia immediately hurried to the back of the house in search of Anne.

She found the child hard at work in the summer kitchen, scraping carrots over a big white bowl by the window. Two other maids were also at work and Hepzibah sat at her stubby desk below the key cupboard, where she kept her accounts and wrote the grocery orders for the week. Amelia rustled past them and calmly took Anne by the hand.

"Step outside for a minute, dear."

Stunned at the sight of Amelia in the kitchen, Anne followed her outside without a word. Once they were out of the sight of the kitchen staff, Amelia bent down to look Anne in the eye.

"I need to know where those rabble-rousers you saw meet," she asked, her voice quivering.

Anne hesitated. Nellie wanted no one to know about the grist mill. Amelia shook Anne by the arm fiercely.

"Show me! Now!"

There was no denying her. Anne knew there was no choice. Slowly at first, and then picking up speed, she led Amelia straight across the lawn and over the brook, in exactly the direction Louisa had slipped away. Amelia held Anne's wrist firmly as they raced along, heedless of grass or gravel.

They scurried down a path through the forest under the towering fir trees and over a rust-coloured carpet of pine needles. A low-lying mist hung like a delicate scarf above the forest floor. Anne's wrist throbbed in Amelia's grasp. Finally, they caught sight of the old clapboard walls of the abandoned grist mill looming against the trees.

Holding Anne's hand as if for fortification, Amelia marched up to the weathered wooden door and raised her fist. At the first thump, the door swung open. A great shaft of light fell into the room, revealing Louisa sitting at a rough pine table—deep in conversation with Walter. Louisa's face clouded with guilt at the sight of her mother-in-law at the same time as Walter looked at Amelia with petulance. Louisa's culpable and awkward expression was all it took to convince Amelia that she had uncovered a conspiracy. The couple might as well have been preparing to elope!

Amelia felt as if one of the carriage horses had just kicked her in the ribs. All four people hung frozen in the moment. Amelia pulled Anne close, as though shielding her from the treachery onto which they had stumbled. With one arm around the bewildered girl's thin shoulders, Amelia walked Anne back through the woods, composed but lost in her own thoughts. Anne dared not speak. Amelia's firm embrace made her feel secure and she knew she would never waver in her loyalty to this person she considered to be a true kindred spirit.

Only when they arrived back at the house did Amelia finally relinquish her embrace. She sent Anne to the kitchen with a single hushed gesture and disappeared into the parlour. There she sat, unmoving, no one daring to approach her, waiting for Louisa.

On hearing the sound of the oak door, Amelia called out, summoning Louisa into the conservatory. As she entered, Amelia rose up in callous outrage. No questions would be asked, nor pardons requested, Amelia had concluded.

"I expect you to vacate my house immediately," said Amelia as she stood on the conservatory stairs, looming over Louisa. She pronounced the sentence in a hard, even voice that revealed nothing of the injury she felt inside.

All the way back from the grist mill, Louisa had been in a dither about what would happen on her return. This sudden, terrible decree went beyond even her worst expectations. At first, she was unable to speak. Dizziness plucked at her as her mind raced with the consequences. Amelia's set jaw and glittering eyes told her there was no point in pleading. Determined to control her overwhelming emotions, Louisa drew herself up in order to salvage her dignity.

"I didn't expect to remain," she lashed back as fiercely as she could muster. "I only hoped you'd put your stubborn pride aside and seize the opportunity. . . ."

Louisa's words made Amelia more scornful.

"You're a pathetic judge of human nature!"

Louisa knew full well that she had disastrously miscalculated her liaison with Anne's father, but in the depths of her heart she had convinced herself it was for the good of the entire family. She turned to leave but stopped just as she took hold of the doorknob. If she was going to relinquish her right to stay on, she would at least have the last word.

"I . . . I will survive. I shall get a job as a teacher and I will support *my family*," she flung out bravely. Amelia didn't flinch, so

Louisa delivered what she intended to be a final manipulative blow. "And I'm taking Anne *with us.*"

Louisa boldly closed the double doors in Amelia's face and her footsteps echoed down the tiled hallway, out of the conservatory. Although Amelia allowed herself a quiver of distress, even the potential loss of Anne could not make her change her mind.

Seventeen

The news that they had to leave, and right away, came as a great shock to Louisa's children. She called them all together to explain what had happened in the simplest of terms, clasping her hands so they wouldn't see her shaking. Although she had indeed managed to get a teaching certificate in the past year, Louisa wasn't at all confident she could find a position before her family starved, despite what she'd said to Amelia.

After the news sank in, Louisa studied the stark young faces. All of the children were wondering why she had chosen to ruin their safe, fortunate refuge. Keith and Jock were silent, but Violetta was beside herself. She loved the grandeur of the Thomas mansion. She felt it was their birthright to live there and, as such, she had no tolerance for her ridiculous mother getting involved with union agitators, let alone a cad like Anne's father. Her dream of growing up as the privileged eldest granddaughter of Amelia Thomas was completely dashed. No more pouring tea at garden parties from a silver tea set, nor maids to wait on them. They were taking to the road again and Violetta feared she knew all too well what hardships that meant.

By the end of Louisa's rationalization the most confused victim was Anne. Mrs. Thomas had promised her that this was now her home. It was beyond her comprehension that Amelia would change her mind so rashly. Anne knew instinctively that she must be exempt from Louisa's horrible news. She thought only of Amelia's sturdy embrace as they'd trudged home through the woods from the abandoned mill. In a few minutes, she reasoned, Amelia would call for her and speak to her directly.

An hour later, as everyone packed in preparation for leaving, Anne was forced to acknowledge that perhaps the woman in whom she had put her trust had let her down. Even worse, she knew it was somehow because of her father, Anne prayed that Louisa would change her mind and let her stay with Amelia once they all left. From previous experience, however, she knew this was something upon which she couldn't entirely depend.

As the afternoon wore on and no meals were even offered, let alone served, Louisa insisted that everyone get into their night shirts. Anne put on her soft white nightgown, purchased for her by Amelia, and stood at the tower window gazing out across the lawns. Her ancient carpet bag remained unopened at the foot of her bed.

"Aren't you packing, Anne?" Violetta demanded sourly. Her tone suggested she was already blaming Anne and her father entirely for this family disintegration. Anne was lost, staring at the beautiful view outside the window. The sun dappled and played through the trees, creating delightful shadows and patterns across the sweeping lawns. The fragrance of the flower beds Anne knew only too well drifted up on the breeze through the screen on the window. She would remember every detail of how lovely it had all looked, especially when the lawn had been decorated for the picnic. She and the Thomas children had played so happily under the spreading trees—snowballs in winter, tag in the spring. Sitting outside had made their lessons even more delightful. How she would yearn until the end of time for such a splendid garden so full of shady secret places to curl up in with a book. She would never find another place as grand as this. It was all to become just one more memory.

"Are you deaf, Anne? Get cracking!" shouted Violetta, trying to snap Anne out of her little reverie.

"I'm just gazing at the lawn. I shall be haunted by the fact of leaving here, forever and ever," Anne sighed in return.

Despite a disdainful look from Violetta, Anne remained motionless. All at once, a familiar figure came hurrying out of the trees and across the grass. The figure whistled at Anne, who was standing crestfallen in the tower window.

Anne immediately called Louisa as Nellie stepped cautiously out into view and took off her hat, craning her neck to see the window better above the shrubbery.

"Your pa's in a spot, Anne."

"What's wrong?" Louisa asked in alarm.

"Walter can't come," Nellie called back. "He's in serious trouble with that timber company. They claimed he was trying to double-cross the bank. They've thrown him in jail."

Anne's heart plunged. Would trouble with her father never stop? Louisa edged Anne away from the window and leaned out herself. She had spent all afternoon trying to get secret word to Walter through one of the stable hands, and he had replied that he would assist them that very evening. Louisa was stupefied at this news—at the eleventh hour when her departure depended entirely upon him!

"But he sent word he would help us leave."

"I can take you to St. John," Nellie promised.

Louisa stepped back into the room, her face wracked with worry. Anne took off down the stairs like a frightened colt, hoping to catch up to Nellie to find out more. She made it only partway down the great staircase when the sound of anxious voices coming from the parlour brought her to a dead stop. It was Jeremiah Land, talking to Mrs. Thomas. Anne could not run past the parlour without being seen. Hesitating, she sank back into the shadows on the landing. She could see right into the room. Mr. Land was holding out a letter to Amelia—a letter that Amelia regarded with utter disdain—and was trying to sound calm.

"This is a very typical type of demand, Mrs. Thomas," he said. "The foreclosure is merely a bank tactic. We can still try to close a deal with New Hampshire Timber."

Amelia remained aloof at the mention of such a solution.

"But I need to see the deeds," he continued, trying to be matter-of-fact.

Suddenly, Amelia snatched the letter from his hand and flung it down on the table.

"It isn't true what they imply here about the land rights, is it?" Mr. Land asked, a note of true alarm creeping into his voice.

Amelia's bosom gave a single heave. There was nothing to do but reveal the truth behind her long and stubborn resistance.

"We've been chopping down trees on Crown property without land rights for twenty years. There is nothing to sell, Jeremiah!"

Jeremiah stared at her in complete and utter shock. The real value of the Thomas lumber mills lay in the rights to cut timber on Crown land. Without those rights, which could be granted only by legal title through the government, the mill had no significant assets other than its outdated machinery and a lot of workers who would soon be owed back pay. The lumber mills were essentially worthless. For Mr. Land, the pieces of the puzzle began to fall into place with disturbing clarity. Phillip Granger must have had some idea of this when he'd offered Ruth Bridgewater to work as a governess inside the Thomas home. The manager's logic took yet another leap forward. If the government ever uncovered the fact that the timber cut by the Thomas crews had been hewn illegally, it would likely demand compensation. With a sigh, he realized that the Abbey Bank and

New Hampshire Timber and Plank had hoodwinked him as well. In all likelihood, it had already moved to expose the truth.

"The company has nothing," he stammered, almost at a loss for words. "It's just not possible ..."

Amelia folded her arms. She herself had learned the truth not long before. She felt as if she had inherited a pig in a poke.

"My husband was too clever for his own good."

Amelia had never before acknowledged the problems created by her husband's overreaching efforts to maximize the profits from the natural resources at his disposal. He had left his widow with a problem that was to become her downfall, not his. Amelia's eyes blazed with emotion but she repressed any sentiment. Without warning, she strode indomitably out of the room and out of the house—a fixed and fearful purpose written on her face.

From her hiding place on the landing, Anne had listened very carefully to the whole conversation. Although she understood little of how a bank could destroy someone like Mrs. Thomas, she was determined to support her in whatever manner she could. Anne snatched a sweater from the foyer rack and raced through the hallway and out the door, after Amelia.

"Mrs. Thomas! Mrs. Thomas!" she shouted as she threw open the heavy oak door, rattling the cut glass in its casements.

Amelia did not waver. She seemed to have been struck deaf. She had turned onto the drive and was walking like a spectre into the obscurity of twilight. Anne flew after her until she finally caught up to her on the lawn. With one look, Anne realized that the old woman had never had any intention of forcing her to leave. She looked so very much alone in her distress that Anne could see that she desperately needed help.

"I'm not leaving, Mrs. Thomas!" She struggled to catch her breath as she caught Amelia's arm. "I give you my word."

Amelia took Anne by the shoulders and piloted her back toward the front entrance.

"All right, my dear. Come along now," she whispered reassuringly. "You go back inside."

Anne resisted instinctively. The look on Amelia's face—an eerie combination of distress and control—filled Anne's heart with dread.

"I want to stay with you! Please let me stay!"

Amelia's grip only tightened as she propelled Anne forward.

"I know, dear, and it's all right. There is nothing to do but pray. Listen to me. Just do as I say. Pray for me."

Anne clung to Amelia and tried to prevent herself from being pushed back inside the front foyer, But Amelia was inexorable. She pushed Anne gently inside the doorway, then bent down and lifted Anne's chin, looking deep into the little girl's eyes.

"No tears, Anne. Promise," she said as she began to shut the outer glass door in Anne's face.

Anne could promise no such thing.

"I want to go with you," she insisted. "Please let me go with you. I want to be with you."

"Go on, now. It's all right." Amelia gave her a final push as she closed the big oak door between them.

Amelia resumed her walk into the dim night. Anne lingered just inside the door, bewildered and frightened as she watched the proud old woman disappear down the drive. Anne ran upstairs again after Mr. Land, forgotten in the parlour, stepped past her and jammed his hat onto his head. He raced after Amelia into the twilight, determined to stop whatever plan was formulating in Amelia's mind.

Upstairs, Louisa and Violetta were still packing. They had both moved across the hall to the boys' room where Jock and Keith sat glumly watching. Anne could think of nothing else to do but crawl into bed. Under the familiar quilt, Anne lay wide awake, running the day's events over and over in her mind. Through the partly open door, she saw Louisa folding Jock's undershirts and putting them into the same suitcases they had arrived with more than a year earlier.

An hour or so later and still full of nameless anxiety, Anne could not tell whether she had managed to doze off. The urgent clanging of a distant bell made her open eyes. She stared up at the dark ceiling, which, in her mind, reflected a strange, dancing orange glow. Hopping out of bed, Anne sped over to the window and pulled back the muslin curtain. The clanging of emergency bells was louder than ever. Immediately, Anne shouted out an alarm.

"Louisa! Louisa, come quickly!"

The panic in Anne's voice brought Louisa running across the open hall.

"What is it, dear?"

Anne pointed. Against the nightfall of an indigo sky, a twisting column of flame and cloud reared up. All the lumber mills were completely on fire.

"Oh ... my dear lord...," stammered Louisa in shock.

"She went into town while we were still packing," Anne confessed, traumatized. "She told me ... she told me just to pray for her."

Louisa exchanged a horrified glance with Anne. With a leap, she began to run down the hall, searching from room to room.

"Mrs. Thomas! Mrs. Thomas!" she shouted out, banging on doors and flinging them open.

Violetta, Keith, and Jock had run to the windows as well and now stood watching in disbelief as their mother ran through the house calling out their grandmother's name as if she had gone mad. Very shortly the whole household was thrown into chaos, but Amelia was nowhere to be found. Anne remained by the window the entire time, unable to look away from the towering inferno etched against the night sky, sending wild streams of sparks into the atmosphere. Finally, a massive explosion ripped the mill apart, shaking the mansion window-panes and tossing massive, burning beams, like fiery match-sticks, in every direction.

Eighteen

Amelia Thomas never returned. Anne imagined over a dozen scenarios as to what could have happened to her, but never spoke a single one aloud. Rumour in the town speculated that Amelia had destroyed the mill herself rather than let it go to New Hampshire Timber and Plank. Others said the fire was an accident caused when several workmen got into a fight. Wooden mills—filled with sawdust and covered with boards bleached tinder dry by the sun—could go up in flames from the smallest spark.

The chaos of that night was something Anne would never be able to forget. The Marysville fire bells clanged madly for hours while the whole town gawked at the destruction. Nothing could have been done to combat such a fire. The mill workers stood by watching helplessly as their place of employment evaporated in smoke.

Louisa had run all the way down to the mill herself, though she forbade the children to leave the house. She came back, flecked with ashes and shaken to the core. She simply slumped on a chair, unable to speak. All the packing had stopped. There was no question now of leaving the house for St. John the next day. As the morning light filled the mansion's rooms, several local officials tramped in and out. Hepzibah was in such a state that she was beyond seeing to breakfast. None of the maids, who lived in the town, showed up for work.

No one seemed too concerned about finding out why the fire had started. With the mill gone and all Thomas payments stopped, the bank simply moved in and took possession of everything it could get its hands on.

"I'm very sorry, Mrs. Thomas," Phillip Granger said to Louisa, his voice filled with the gravity of the situation, "but without timber rights there is no point in rebuilding. The holding is worthless to any prospective buyer. It also remains burdened with a heavy mortgage that, as Amelia Thomas's heir, you bear."

Louisa could not believe the nightmare into which she had become entangled. As Amelia's only living adult relation, Louisa was heir to her entire estate—as well as to the stupendous debt that encumbered it. If she tried for three lifetimes, she could never hope to pay it off. As one sheaf of papers after another was put in front of her, she found herself completely over-whelmed by the amount Amelia actually owed. The Thomas mills had all been hanging on by the merest thread.

Now the bank owned everything: the house, the furniture, the carriage horses, and even the pots and pans in the kitchen. Everyone on the estate lost his or her job, for there was no more money to pay wages. The news was particularly hard on Hep-zibah, who had been with Amelia almost since Mrs. Thomas had come to the house as a lovely young bride.

"She ran this house like clockwork," said Louisa dejectedly, commenting on Hepzibah's loyalty as the housekeeper silently packed her things. "I wish there was something I could do for her."

Louisa was at a loss as to what do for anyone. Even Jere-miah Land, given notice by the bank, stayed only long enough to present Louisa with a full accounting of the disaster.

With the lumber mills gone, the cotton mill closed, and the cider mill running decrepit machinery, the bank quickly gave up on its big plans for Marysville. Jobs vanished within a matter of months, and with them went all possibility of the town sustaining itself. Shops and small businesses boarded up their windows, while mill workers and their families packed up their belongings and headed elsewhere in search of work. For a week or so, the streets rumbled with buggies and loaded wagons leaving town. Then Marysville fell silent and empty—another sad, abandoned ghost of a town that had lived then died with the industries that spawned it.

The last thing Hepzibah and the maids did was throw dust sheets over all the furniture. The house looked, to Anne at least, as though it were filled with the crouching phantoms of its former self. Anne had been largely forgotten in the upset following the burning of the mill. She wandered about the house, distressed by Amelia's absence. Her defender had vanished overnight, and her safe haven was about to be taken away as well. Every room of the Thomas mansion now held a memory. Here were the seats around the fireplace where they had all laughed and drank hot chocolate after a skating party. The conservatory with its potted palms had been the scene of such happy studies; the summer kitchen, so alive with preparations for the picnic. Mrs. Thomas had been fair and just to Anne, admitting her back into her house after realizing Anne was not a liar, despite Hepzibah's vehement accusations. Mrs. Thomas had shown Anne a world of beautiful things, like concerts and silver tea sets, and the kind of laughter and joy she remembered feeling once upon a time with her own mother.

In the weeks since the fire, none of the children had the heart to keep up their lessons. Louisa, alternately in tears or cold fury about her prospects, was beside herself and didn't seem to notice. Anne's father, now in jail, made no help to offer. He now added the designation of "felon" to the original label of "wife murderer"—and the stigma settled squarely on Anne.

Violetta wouldn't talk to her any more and the two boys stuck together quietly by themselves. Though no one said it, they all knew Anne had led Amelia to the old grist mill. In their minds, their change in fortune was once again the result of Anne's heedless actions.

Watching Louisa clearly at her wit's end, Anne did not dare ask what was in store for her own future. It was bad enough that they all ignored her, but even Louisa's loyalty to Anne's mother Bertha seemed to evaporate in the midst of all the turmoil. It was clear that neither Jeremiah Land, nor Hepzibah, nor Louisa had any use for her.

"It's my own ill luck," Anne whispered nobly to herself. "The stars in their courses are crossed against me wherever I may wander!"

The eviction date had nearly arrived when Anne had a terrifying dream. She was lost inside a burning mill, choking on smoke and calling out, "Mrs. Thomas, Mrs. Thomas, I want to stay. Please let me stay with you!"

She woke up scarcely able to breathe, infinitely relieved to find herself in bed in the Thomas mansion with no clouds of smoke swirling about. Anne blinked in the darkness, calming herself enough to look across the room in case she had awakened Violetta. Oddly enough, Violetta's bed was empty.

"Hurry children! Run as fast as you can. Come on, Jock," urged Louisa anxiously as she ran across the driveway just below Anne's window. "Does everyone have their bags?"

Anne sprang out of bed and raced over to look out the tower window. Below her, running out from under the porte cochère, in just enough light to see, were Louisa, Violetta, Keith, and Jock. They hightailed it down the driveway, their luggage bumping against their legs as they scrambled into the obscurity of darkness. A sick feeling rolled though Anne, yet she wasn't the least bit surprised. She had known, deep down, that they were going to abandon her. It was no use running after them in her bare feet and nightgown, or calling out. They wouldn't answer and they wouldn't stop. If she even got close, they would drive her away. Once they were gone, there wasn't a soul left in the big house save Anne and Amelia's precious cat. Anne made up her mind she wasn't going to be afraid, though she was, and she wasn't going to cry herself to sleep. She crawled back into bed and hugged the pillow to herself, not even noticing how damp it had become close to her face. She imagined herself all alone standing on the prow of a graceful ship, sailing smoothly over moonlit seas. Old Blue Eyes curled up beside her and she allowed him into her dream. At any moment, the ship would arrive at an enchanted harbour with a castle on the hill above and a smiling crowd, with a retinue of trumpets, waiting for her to descend. There would be a great lady with silken hair the colour of wheat and wearing roses on her gown, who would greet Anne with open arms, ready to welcome the girl who was renowned for the incredibly blue eyes of her legendary cat. This woman who greeted her would look exactly like her mother. . . .

Anne woke up in the morning with Old Blue Eyes still next to her. The cat, much neglected since the disappearance of his mistress, sought her company and protection. Anne hugged it closely to her as she got out of bed. She would have to do her best for both of them.

First, Anne packed Gabriel's much-used carpet bag with her most precious treasures, his books. This left room for only a few clothes and a new set of memories. There was no trace of Louisa and her family in the house now except for rumpled beds and the partly built sailboat Keith had been working on to test out in the brook.

"I suppose she felt compelled to save her own skin again," thought Anne, attempting to understand Louisa's actions. Anne had heard so much about the Thomas debts by that point that she could imagine Louisa running and running for the rest of her life.

Down in the kitchen, Anne found some bread and a heel of cheese, which she shared with Old Blue Eyes. The cat fell upon the food as though no one had thought about feeding it for ages. Like the rest of the house, the kitchen was empty and still. Anne would even have welcomed a scolding from Hepzibah to break the loneliness. When the last crumb had been devoured, Anne found a wicker basket with a good lid and popped the cat inside. He seemed to be so glad to be going with Anne that he didn't even bother to yowl.

Carrying the basket in one hand and her carpet bag in the other, Anne set out across the garden in a familiar direction. She and her fellow refugee arrived at the grist mill just as Nellie was feeding her horses. The woman was dressed in her old hat and pants again, so different from the fancy blouse and skirt she had worn for the picnic. As soon as she saw Anne, she put down the pitchfork. With an enormous sigh, she motioned the girl inside.

"Come in, child. Come on in. Forgot all about ya, did they?"

When Anne told Nellie what had happened the night before, Nellie just shook her head..

"I know your dad's still in jail, but he would have tried to fix you up with somewhere to go if he was able."

Anne had heard nothing from her father, though she was sure he must know people who could have sent a message. Looking at the disappointment on Anne's face, Nellie knew what she was thinking.

"Oh, you can't stay with me, child. I'm squatting in an old mill. It's all I can do to keep myself going. I'll ask around about someplace for you to settle down in. A family maybe. Somewheres."

Nellie set off on her mail route, leaving Anne and Old Blue Eyes to their own devices in the solitude of the grist mill. The cat uttered a few mournful observations from his basket. Anne sat by the millstream, tossing in pebbles, wondering if an orphanage was going be her next stop. It surely was a trial to always end up being the girl that nobody wanted.

Eventually, the clatter of Nellie's wagon startled Anne out of her thoughts. Her heart beat anxiously as Nellie glanced at her over the backs of her team once she started to unhitch.

"You're in luck, girl. Got a place for you. Miles and miles away, but they offered to take you in."

Next morning Nellie hitched one of her horses to her two-wheeled cart and set out on a journey that took two days. They travelled out of New Brunswick into Nova Scotia by way of Amherst, then over to New Glasgow. They travelled along the sea road where the air was tinged with a bracing salt smell, and glimmers of water could be seen through the fir trees between the road and the ocean. Prince Edward Island was just off the coast, Nellie explained, and it was a place where the roads were entirely red. To Anne, it sounded like a fairytale spot. The cat rode along contentedly in its wicker basket and Anne's carpet bag lay at her feet. On any other occasion, the ride would have filled Anne with exhilaration. Today, though, she looked so glum that Nellie attempted to cheer her up.

"Open your hand. Look at the strong lifeline in that palm of yours," boomed Nellie heartily. Holding the reins in one hand, she took Anne's small hand in hers. Anne did have a vigorous lifeline running all the way across her hand and she looked at it with some hope.

"I declare you'll become a great lady one day," asserted Nellie. "Your open heart will allow you to float equally among everyone."

Anne felt a big lump deep in her throat. It was lovely to have such a fine prediction for the future, but she still had to cope with the immediate uncertainty of that moment. She wasn't a great lady yet, just a girl who once again didn't even know where she was going to sleep that night. The brave look Anne fixed on her face might have fooled some people, but it didn't fool Nellie. Every time Anne looked up at her with those large, expressive eyes, Nellie felt a pang right in the pit of her stomach. She tried to explain to the child why she was letting her go.

"I'm no good for you. You need a family. You need to be bought up by hand ... proper. The Hammonds are my friends. They own a small lumber business and they promised me personally they'll keep you till your pa lands on his feet." Nellie hesitated then added carefully,

"You'd be wise not to tell anyone he's behind bars neither."

Anne let out a long sigh, with no faith at all in her prospects. She feared she would be haunted by her father's unfortunate doings for the rest of her life. Bad luck, it seemed, ran solidly in their family. The possibility of finding any more kindred spirits seemed more remote than ever.

The cart creaked along under the dark spruce and fir trees, which seemed to grow thicker with every mile. The road they turned onto seemed little more than a track heading deeper into a dark wilderness. The trees here were of unrelieved density until the wagon suddenly emerged into a bright clearing around a rather weather-beaten saw mill with "Hammond" painted on a rough board above the door. Piles of lumber were scattered everywhere around the tiny building. Anne regarded it in dismay, fearing she was going to be put to work in a sawmill again.

Nellie drew up beside Pete Hammond, a gruff man in his late fifties who wore a flat cap and had a beefy face totally lacking in humour. He stopped yelling orders to his workers long enough to walk over to speak to Nellie.

"Hey, Pete," Nellie said, "here's the girl I was tellin' ya about."

Nellie hadn't told Anne what a rough taskmaster the fellow was. Anne would find out on her own soon enough. Mr. Hammond simply jerked his thumb over his shoulder.

"Don't look at me. You gotta take her inside ... to the missus."

He pointed to a hardscrabble house just beyond the mill on the other side of the stream. Clucking to the horse, Nellie drove on up to the yard, where a woman was hanging laundry from a wind-tossed clothesline. Anne peered about at the giant white pines pressing in on every side.

"It's such a lonesome place," she murmured in a small voice.

The screech of the great, whirling saw blades cutting logs into planks echoed back from all sides, sending chills down Anne's spine. Not another house or trace of human habitation was to be glimpsed in any direction. Behind Mrs. Hammond, the house was of unpainted boards weathered to an ancient grey. A number of small faces began to appear at the windows, staring at Anne with intense curiosity.

The enormous basket of laundry in front of Mrs. Hammond spoke of plenty of washing to be done. Mrs. Hammond, who looked quite overtired to Anne, stuck pins onto the clothesline with short, impatient stabs as though there weren't enough minutes in the day.

"Hello there," called Nellie as she drove up. "How ya doin'?"

The woman dried the dampness from her hands on her apron.

"I'm all right. What's this?"

"This here's the girl I was tellin' you about," Nellie said, drawing up the horse and cart.

"All right," said Mrs. Hammond, squinting at Anne.

"Take a look at her."

Nellie helped Anne down from the high cart seat. She stood apprehensively while Mrs. Hammond gave her a solid inspection. Anne was dressed very nicely, as befitted a child of the Thomas household. Her brimmed hat was of finely woven straw and the collar of her dress was delicate lace with tiny flowers stitched into it. But pretty mauve sleeves and an apron with flounces didn't impress Mrs. Hammond. "Well, she can help around the house, I s'ppose."

"She's a good worker," Nellie put in, lest the woman decide Anne wasn't up to the job. "I can vouch for that. She's got a good heart and she loves children."

Mrs. Hammond pursed her mouth and eyed Anne some more, perhaps trying to figure out how much work, per inch, was actually in the child. It was a good thing Anne was handy with children, she thought. She had eight—three sets of twins and two that had come singly.

"All right Nellie, that's enough applesauce." She looked at Anne, finally relenting. "Well, get in there and put your stuff in the driveshed. We won't tolerate any idleness in this house. You'll do everything you're told to do. You can stay up in the loft. Got no more room in the house."

She gave the child a little shove toward another ramshackle dwelling.

There was nothing for Anne to say to Nellie but goodbye as she picked up her carpet bag and headed for a shack that would be so different from the cozy bedroom she shared with Violetta. She stepped through a door that led to bales of hay, a wagon, and old machinery. Apparently, the animals lived at the back of this dwelling, too, in close proximity to the family.

From the small loft she had climbed into and arranged her

things, Anne watched Nellie leave. The last thing she saw was Nellie lifting Old Blue Eyes from the basket.

"I really wish you'd take this beautiful cat too," Nellie was saying.

Mrs. Hammond threw up her arms at the animal's aristocratic demeanour, knowing it had absolutely no business in her rough world.

"Oh no, no no! Put it back! Lord almighty, I've got young 'uns. Can't be taking on a cat like that! The girl's enough to feed these days."

"Okay," Nellie thrust Old Blue Eyes back into the basket and slapped the reins on the back of the horse. "See ya, now."

"I'm sure Mrs. Thomas's cat will find better prospects than I," Anne thought to herself mournfully. A gloomy yowl from the depth of the basket begged to disagree as Nellie disappeared down the road.

"I'll let you know if she works out," Mrs. Hammond called after the cart and went back to her laundry.

When Nellie had driven completely out sight, Anne looked around at the chickens and sheep and bits of old furniture and equipment. From the loud grunts, Anne surmised that pigs were not far away either. At least it wasn't the poorhouse. Behind her, nailed to the wall, was a dusty wooden shelf with a mirror above it. Anne wiped the dust from the discoloured glass and immediately spied the friendly, red-headed girl who had always looked back at her.

"It's been awhile, Katie," she told the solemn face. "At least we still have each other. If I hadn't lost myself in the beauty of Mrs. Thomas's world . . . but I do so love beautiful things. I'm sure I couldn't live here if I hadn't any imagination."

In a rush of loneliness, Anne reached out to touch the fuzzy image. Then, like a diminutive soldier once again going into battle, Katie herself sighed and turned away. Anne knew she was about to face the rigours of Mrs. Hammond's command.

"Anne! Anne Shirley! Get in here before I give ya a darn good whippin'," she screamed.

Nineteen

In the soft light of the bedside lamp on Marilla's desk, Anne chewed her thumbnail. She was determined to make this letter sound proper, despite the flurry of changes going on in her life. She had a desperate desire to meet her father, now in his eighties. She'd managed to establish an ongoing formal communication through the intermediary of his housekeeper. It turned out he was agreeable to meeting her. She awaited a time and place. Nothing was firm though. The housekeeper had mearly said Walter intended to write her soon. Anne imagined inviting him to Dominic's imminent wedding. There would be so much to discuss when they met, and family members she wanted him to meet. Anne knew this letter must not sound too anxious. She wished with all her heart that he would write her himself.

"Dear Father," she read aloud, "I do appreciate all the letters from your housekeeper, but I've yet to hear a reply from you. If you have changed your mind about wishing to communicate with me directly, at least let me know. Sincerely, your loving daughter, Anne."

After all these years, she still feared that he really had no desire to meet her, and that he was hiding behind the guise of a dutiful housekeeper as a way of being polite. The continual disappointment had been very hard to bear. In the last few weeks four letters had been exchanged, leaving Anne with the feeling that she was on an aimless pursuit. She had been too personal, perhaps, after all these years. If her father didn't want anything to do with her, she fervently wished he would just be honest about it.

Not that Anne didn't have a million other things to occupy her mind. In a fever of anticipation over Dominic's return, she'd planned all kinds of improvements and renovations to make Green Gables feel like home again. Unfortunately, she'd have to wait a while to unveil the results. Dominic and Brigitte were still waiting to find space on one of the crowded ships bringing so many Canadians home after the war in Europe. The wedding was going to have to be delayed until the couple's travel plans were firm.

The scent of newly mown hay drifted on the morning air as Anne made her customary expedition to the letterbox. It had been some time now since she mailed her last missive, so hope for a reply was growing. Dominic, at least, had been faithful in keeping her updated as to their whereabouts and travel prospects, and Anne was grateful now for his regular letters. Thrusting her hand inside, Anne pulled out a promisingly fat handful of mail. On the path back to the house, she quickly sorted out two letters from her daughters and a bill from Martha Gillis Real Estate, for services rendered in the aborted sale of the property.

At the bottom of the pile was a heavy envelope from the Harding Funeral Home in Fredericton. Anne could not imagine what business that establishment could have with her. Quickly, she tore it open and scanned the contents. It was, in a way, an answer from her father at last.

"I have just received your address from your father's next of kin," wrote the funeral home director, Mr. Harding. "He has only just passed away in his eighty-second year. If you care to pay your respects, you may contact me at the above address."

Anne packed a hasty suitcase, donned her dark suit, left a message for Gene, and headed for the ferry at Port Borden. Once on the mainland, she boarded the first train to Fredericton. As the train steamed through the falling darkness, Anne stared out of the window. Lights periodically threw her face into relief, illuminating her sadness and frustration. She could not even contemplate why her father hadn't at least said something to her, written some personal note before he died. She felt maybe it was just a selfish whim on his part. Walter Shirley probably had no desire to revisit his unsavoury past with a grown woman. She had long ago been forgotten by him, after Marilla's instincts prevented any further childhood communication. Yet this long-forgotten letter had seemed like such an olive branch from the depths of the past! Anne had come to earnestly believe in it as a gesture of fate, trying to make amends for the many bungled opportunities between a father and a daughter. Surely fate had not been toying with her, Anne mused as she waited. She realized now just how merciless fate could be. Destiny had clearly established that she and her father were never to meet, and this realization left an unfilled emptiness in Anne's soul. She had no idea why she was even driven to make this journey, except that she knew she must.

Once in Fredericton, Anne went directly to the Harding Funeral Home. The director met her at the door and conducted her to his office where she was seated in one of the firm chairs opposite his broad mahogany desk. He was a bearded old gentleman with a bald head, large ears, and a sympathetic manner. He leaned across the desk on his elbows as he spoke, inadvertently revealing to Anne things she had never known.

"Your father was a man who was a pioneer in our community," he said, "which enjoyed the results of his strong entrepreneurial efforts. You may or may not know he is predeceased by his wife, Louisa."

Anne sat motionless, listening, scarcely able to breathe. Her father had indeed married Louisa Thomas. Perhaps that explained why Louisa had been so forgiving of him long ago, and why she had smiled so blissfully on seeing him at the picnic. She must have already set her affections upon him. The same Louisa who had left Anne all by herself in the empty mansion while she and her children fled into the night had become involved in a lover's tryst with Walter! At that instant, she was able to see things from Amelia's perspective. She remembered the rustle of Amelia's dress as she'd turned away from discovering them together at Nellie's, as though Amelia had tried to hide her from the sight of something more illicit than a child could ever understand. Mr. Harding cleared his throat, worried Anne wasn't listening. She looked at him directly and he continued speaking.

"He had a housekeeper looking in on him in the same home he'd lived in, oh . . . for several decades. He was a chipper, good-looking old fellow," Mr. Harding said, struggling to keep his curiosity about Anne to himself. All sorts of queer upsets happened in families when someone died and relatives showed up who hadn't been heard from for years. He had just about seen it all and knew how to maintain decorum no matter what transpired.

"Sadly the will was never updated," Mr. Harding went on. "Of course, your father adopted Lousia's three children, Violetta, Keith, and Thomas. Louisa and your father also had a son of their own. However, we've had no dealings with the man."

Their own son. Anne's head whirled, causing her to worry she was going to faint. She had a half-brother she had never even known, someone of her own flesh and blood. Anne looked so awkward and forlorn that Mr. Harding rose to take her arm. He kept the dialogue moving as he helped her up. Anne rallied and nodded. She had accepted this commitment between herself and fate. She would see it through to its conclusion.

"When we informed the lawyer, Mr. Sproule, that we had made contact with you, we received instructions from the next of kin that you be the person to determine the disposal of the remains."

Anne was yanked back from her thoughts and speculations about her newly discovered brother. The man was telling Anne that the burial was being left to her, a decision that surely should have been made by the family who had lived with him.

Mr. Harding looked embarrassed, as well he might, at this edict. In truth, he was concerned that perhaps viewing her father's remains would be too much. Anne didn't know what to say. They had crossed the thickly carpeted hall and reached the room holding the coffin. Anne tried to smile, letting him understand that she was prepared to accept this gauntlet tossed at her feet. Just before they went in, the director paused and delivered the most crushing news of all.

"The next of kin have also requested that they . . . ah, wish to protect their privacy."

Anne breathed deeply. Violetta, Keith, and Jock wanted nothing at all to do with her. Mr. Harding's words sunk like lead into her consciousness. At their request, the funeral director was forbidden to inform Anne where any of them might be found. She wondered if they had found out about the letters Anne had sent. Heartlessly, they were shedding Anne and Walter Shirley like old clothes.

Amelia Thomas's words from long ago swirled in Anne's head. "Grown-ups will take advantage of a child's innocent heart. . . ."

The sting of this latest rejection felt as potent now as if she had suffered it back when Louisa and her children had abandoned her in Marysville. Anne stepped into a shadowy room, where Walter Shirley lay in a simple pine casket.

Discreetly, the funeral director turned back to his office. Anne was left alone with her father for the first time in forty-seven years.

The small backroom bore little resemblance to the splendid viewing rooms at the front of the funeral parlour. The lid of the coffin stood upright against the nearby wall. Large, dark bottles of chemicals sat on shelves and a big wooden cabinet full of mysterious elements occupied the corner. Apparently, Walter was getting the bargain service at Harding's. Anne was angry that that the stepchildren he had adopted, supported, and raised, after he married their mother, had so little regard for him.

Anne approached the open pine box fearfully, steeling herself to look at the man who had left her to survive on her own when she needed him the most. He lay in eternal stillness, waxen and peaceful. Mr. Harding had done a good job there. Walter had grey hair and a stout figure, but Anne knew him at once. She saw that his wrinkled face was seamed with laugh lines. He looked as though he had enjoyed his final years very much. As Mr. Harding had put it, "a chipper, good-looking old fellow" he remained.

For a very long time Anne stood in front of the simple coffin, trying to comprehend her life without him. One emotion after another welled up as she acknowledged this man who had given her life. She didn't know whether to grieve or shout at him. Tears began to run down her face—silent, painful tears. Stepping forward, she laid her hand on her father's.

She remembered reaching up to grasp his big, warm hand as a little, little girl. In her memory he leaned across her and gave

Bertha a tender kiss on the cheek. Until recently—when she'd started writing the play—Anne had been unable to acknowledge how much she still longed for that image of her parents.

With dignity and resolve, Anne set about seeing that Walter Shirley was properly buried. If he had been unable to do right by her, she was determined to do right by him. Days later, as she placed her hand tenderly on the mound of soil marking his burial place, Anne admitted that her entire life had been a search for the ideal parents and self-respect that had always eluded her. She realized now that fate *had* intervened on her behalf, a long time ago. She had lived a charmed life, with Matthew and Marilla Cuthbert and bore all the love they had to offer for a child like her.

Twenty

After ordering a proper headstone, Anne set out on the final leg of her unexpected but utterly necessary journey. She needed to find her half-brother. He was the very last connection to a past she'd never imagined she would be able to trace.

First, however, she needed to find Walter's house. Holding a scrap of paper with the address to which she'd written so many futile letters, Anne found the street and walked along, checking numbers until she came to a large stucco house with dark shutters and a good deal of fretwork decorating the verandah. A flagstone path meandered up through grass and an old garden that looked as though it had been neglected for years. The front door was wide open. A matronly, grey-haired woman in an apron was busy sweeping out a dusty foyer and setting cardboard boxes in the yard. A pyramid of old furniture and other rubbish already stood by the fence near the sidewalk, waiting to be collected.

Anne hesitated at first, but she slowly ventured up to the verandah. The woman in the doorway stopped sweeping and looked at her inquiringly.

"Hello," Anne said. "I'm looking for 78 Old Fort Lane—it's Walter Shirley's home—but I don't see any number here."

"And who would you be?"

Considering the reception she'd received at the funeral home, Anne decided on a more subtle approach.

"I...I knew the family when I was young," she replied, sadly looking at the piles of old things.

"Oh, well help yourself to any of that junk that you want," the woman told Anne genially. She was obviously not the questioning type. "I'm the new owner. I used to look in on him. We were great chums. The wife died years ago."

"He...had a son." Anne spoke softly, her heart in her throat. She prayed that this woman, if she had indeed been a real chum, would reveal everything she knew about Walter's family. The woman merely shrugged, gesturing with her broom.

"Never laid eyes on him. I dealt with a lawyer."

"Do you know how I can get in touch with this lawyer?" Anne inquired.

To her relief, the woman put the broom down quite obligingly.

"Sure. I got it right here on the papers for the deed."

Anne waited on pins and needles while the woman disappeared inside. It seemed to take an eternity to find what she was looking for. While she stood there taking in her father's residence, Anne glanced down at the pile of rubbish lying directly beside her. Among the junk, she spied a small, well-worn book sitting on a broken chair, clad in brown paper. She remembered her mother wrapping textbooks as such in class, in an attempt to preserve them from wear and tear. The writing on the brown paper was in an elegant script: *Paradise Lost* by John Milton.

Anne casually picked up the thin volume and opened the cover. Just inside lay the inscription she'd known would be there: "Bertha Shirley, Bolingbroke Public School, 1888."

A clatter of footsteps on the porch brought Anne back from the past. The woman smiled as she handed Anne an envelope with an address written on the back. Anne slipped it into her pocket.

"Thanks so much. Would you mind if I kept this old book?"

The woman flapped her hand magnanimously, glad to be rid of one more thing.

"It belongs to you," she said, utterly unaware of the truth behind her words.

Anne set off with purpose and, not much later, approached a law office in a large stone building. The words "Graham C. Sproule, Solicitor, K.C." were lettered in gold on a frosted glass pane. Opening the door, Anne stepped into a dark panelled reception area guarded by a very efficient-looking blond woman, hard at work behind her desk. She looked up as Anne approached, not hiding her annoyance at being disturbed.

"Hello," Anne began. "I wonder if I could speak with Mr. Sproule. I'm related to Mr. Shirley, who owned the house just sold on Old Fort Lane."

The secretary, a very modern young woman, didn't even have to consult any papers.

"I'm afraid that file has been closed. We are no longer retained to act on behalf of Mr. Shirley."

She fell silent, impatient to conclude her work and for Anne to leave.

"Well, someone must act for his estate. May I speak with Mr. Sproule?" Anne asked again doggedly.

The secretary shook her meticulously groomed blonde head.

"He's away in Boston on business. He won't be back for several weeks."

She began shuffling the papers on her desk into a neat pile, a clear signal for Anne to go away. Anne could not help but feel that the woman was keeping something from her.

"Can you tell me where I can contact Mr. Shirley's son?" she pressed.

"We don't do estate work," the secretary repeated, as though Anne was slow in the head.

Anne stood her ground. The secretary merely looked past her to the clock on the wall behind Anne, which had begun to chime. She stood up abruptly. Quitting time.

"Actually, the executor ordered the file closed," she said as she collected her jacket and purse from a coat rack in an adjoining office.

In a rush of frustration, Anne opened her heart, hoping against hope for an ounce of empathy.

"I'm Walter Shirley's daughter. I'm looking for my half-brother, Walter's son. Can't you help me? Please!"

The effect of such honesty was the exasperated twitch of two carefully plucked eyebrows. The secretary opened the door for Anne to leave.

I'm sorry," were the last words Anne heard before the door clicked shut. She stood alone in the hallway feeling like a desperate fool. If the secretary thought she'd discouraged Anne, she was mistaken. Anne only set her jaw and marched forward on the next leg of her pursuit.

Anne was not without resourcefulness. As a writer, she had spent days researching hordes of books and stories. Now, she undertook this much more personal quest in a similar vein. She went straight to the Fredericton City Archives, where she was immediately sent downstairs to search among the racks and racks of records. Anne soon found a ledger of wills on probate. Running her finger down the column, she eventually lit upon Walter Shirley's name. Opposite this inscription was a small sticker that read, "Pushed." She carried the ledger up to the clerk, a young man in shirtsleeves at a desk covered with paperwork, and pointed to the entry.

"Tell me, what does this sticker mean?"

"Oh. . . ." The young man took the ledger and peered at it through gold-rimmed spectacles. "That. The will's been probated. The funds have been settled and a receipt is waiting to be filed."

Finally, a piece of luck! Either a copy of the will or at least all of the information contained in it had to be available here on these premises.

"Who are the beneficiaries?" Anne asked carefully.

The clerk shook his head, looking quite bureaucratic.

"I'm sorry, that's confidential, madam."

Another brick wall! Anne knew this place was her final hope. Once again, her frustration burst through her restraint.

"I need help," she blurted out in direct appeal to the clerk. "Walter Shirley was my father and I'm looking for a brother who I never knew I had."

At first, Anne was certain the clerk was going to be as intransigent as the lawyer's secretary. The young man looked at Anne's trembling lip and the hunger in her eyes. He could see this woman was desperate for a crucial piece of information; as if her very life depended on it.

"Um . . . I'm not supposed to do this," he said slowly.

He hesitated, wavered a little, then checked the file number on the ledger and reached into a box in front of him. It took him only a moment to rifle through to the right pocket, from which he drew a card corresponding to the will.

"Ah yes . . . Walter Shirley. Dependents: Violetta Phillips, sole beneficiary: Violetta Phillips," muttered the clerk to himself.

Anne quickly wrote down Violetta's address in Boston. Her last name was Phillips and the address was plain as day: "Violetta Phillips, 115 Cranston Street, Boston, Massachusetts."

"Doesn't look like there is a son or any other next of kin," the clerk concluded.

He handed the card to Anne as if to convince her he was telling the truth.

"Everything went to Violetta Phillips, and not a son?"

There was no mention of Jock or Keith. Perhaps they had not survived the Great War; Anne might never know. All the clerk could do was nod. "I appreciate your efforts," Anne told him, truly grateful for his kindness.

"I'm sorry I can't be of more help," the clerk responded.

"Please don't indicate where you found the information, ma'am," he called over his shoulder as Anne slipped out of the stacks. She nodded in response. She wouldn't have dreamt of betraying the one person who had been willing to help her. She walked out of the city archives in a daze. She had another lead—the address of someone who would be able to tell her all about her brother—should she choose to.

Twenty-One

As soon as she could manage, Anne boarded the maritime train out of New Brunswick and travelled down the eastern seaboard into the United States. This was not a new journey. So many people from the Atlantic provinces had immigrated to Boston over the years, searching for work in the mills and fisheries, that the entire region felt like a close cousin. Like all Maritimers, Anne could never forget how the people of Boston had rushed to the aid of Halifax after the great explosion of 1917 when a munitions ship blew up in the harbour, levelling the entire east end of the city, and killing and injuring thousands of city residents. Boston had a relief train, the first of many, loaded with desperately needed supplies and medical help on the move within hours. Every year Halifax sent Boston a magnificent Christmas tree in memory of the occasion.

On this visit to Boston, however, Anne felt the shadows and secrecy that often imbued the city. It was fogbound and she spent a great deal of time in an old taxi, locating Violetta's address. Anne couldn't help but think about how Violetta, Keith, and Jock would have known her father far better than she. Finally, her search through the misty streets ended in a district that grew more affluent looking by the block. Soon, she was standing before an imposing brick house with a wide portico overhanging a magnificent semicircular drive. Violetta had finally achieved her dream of wealth and standing.

Girding herself, Anne walked up to the massive polished mahogany door and rang the bell. The door was set around a beautiful stained glass window, which reflected Anne in a myriad of coloured fragments. After a long time, an ancient maid in a cap and uniform answered. Anne looked beyond the maid into a spacious foyer panelled with polished wood. Carved Chippendale armchairs sat by the walls and a huge floral arrangement stood on a round table just beyond the foyer.

"Mr. and Mrs. Phillips are not at home, madam," the maid replied in answer to Anne's request. "You may leave your card."

It was the custom for callers who found the family not at home to leave an engraved card with their name on it so that their visit could be duly noted. The maid held out her hand for the card, but Anne was not going to be turned away that easily. Brushing past the servant, she stepped inside with an air of casual familiarity. First, she tried to find out about her unknown brother through a bit of subterfuge.

"I'm a dear old friend of Violetta's. I just wanted to leave her a note . . . for her and her brothers. There's Jock, Keith, and . . . oh dear . . . what's the other one?"

The maid looked at Anne blankly, as though she had never heard of a third brother.

"Do you have a pen please?" Anne improvised, grasping for something that would keep the maid busy for a moment.

Looking exasperated, the maid moved a few paces and looked up the stairs. Anne caught sight of a bent figure, leaning on a cane and making its way down the broad staircase.

"Who's there?" inquired a cracked old voice—one Anne could still recognize.

A leap of excitement shook Anne as the old figure continued down the stairs. Here was the first person from the old days that she'd the good fortune to meet again.

"Hepzibah? Dear Hepzibah! I thought we'd never see each other again!"

The old woman halted halfway down the stairs, her brows furrowed. Even under the creases of age, Hepzibah maintained her unsmiling, disapproving expression. She responded not at all to the involuntary happiness in Anne's voice.

"It's Anne—Anne Shirley!" she exclaimed, realizing that when Hepzibah had last seen her, she was a little girl in a pinafore and red braids. She might not recognize a grown woman in her fifties.

Hepzibah stood on the stairs, leaning on her cane, as if refusing to move any further. Her face became only harder.

"We've never met," she insisted with a vacant, hazy expression. At first Anne wondered if she had succumbed to senility but Anne persisted earnestly.

"I came with Louisa to Marysville—for a year—as a child. We stayed with Mrs. Thomas," Anne added, doing her best to jog Hepzibah's memory.

Although Hepzibah remained unyielding in her demeanour, something like an expression of alarm was creeping in among the wrinkles. She glanced toward the maid, who seemed to take a silent order. She opened a door at the side of the hall and stuck her head through.

"Robert," she called.

A grey-haired man of the same vintage, wearing a chauffeur's uniform, appeared.

"What's the problem, Miss Hepzibah?"

Hepzibah's eyes darted to Robert then back to Anne. She jerked her head at Anne quite rudely, and in that small motion, Anne saw a flash of total comprehension. Hezpibah was deliberately pretending to be in her dotage. There wasn't a thing wrong with her memory. Instantly, a bubble of anger swelled inside Anne.

"You know exactly who I am," she lashed out. "I want to see Violetta. My father has died and I need to know some things!"

Hepzibah remained unmoved. She waved her cane at the returning maid, indicating that she should hand Anne a card from the dish on the side table.

"You can write to Mr. Phillips at his downtown office. That would be best," Hepzibah instructed Anne.

The maid forced an elaborately embossed gold card into Anne's hand then shuffled over to the big front door, opened it, and waited pointedly for Anne to leave. Anne remained rooted to the spot, looking around in some faint hope that Violetta might appear from the depths of the house, despite the story about her not being home. But Violetta did not appear. Anne drew in her breath. She quickly concluded that Hepzibah probably thought that she was there to grub for a share of the inheritance, after all these years

"No one cared enough about my father to even see to his burial! Tell Violetta I don't give a damn about his estate or his money or anything...!"

"What business have you here, ma'am?" the chauffeur asked, with an edge of menace.

When he presumed to take her arm and propel her toward the door, Anne tore herself loose. Her face was burning. A fury like no other boiled up from deep inside—from a place that went all the way back to Marysville.

"I have a brother! That's my business! I have a brother," Anne thundered out, her eyes boring into Hepzibah. "And I want Violetta Thomas to tell me where he is! It's the very least she ... or any of you ... could do!"

Anne struggled to subsume the rage that engulfed her. She wanted to wring the knowledge bodily from Hepzibah, but the old woman remained on the stairs, as wintry as ever. The chauffeur spoke in slow, emphatic tones.

"There is no person by the name of Thomas that lives here ...nor Shirley. You must have been given the wrong address."

The hostility emanating from Hepzibah was palpable now and the two servants took their cues from her. The situation couldn't have been clearer: Everyone associated with Walter Shirley was determined to cut Anne off cold. The wall they'd put up was impenetrable—there would be no answer from any of them. Ever. She was clearly done.

Staring Hepzibah straight in the eye, Anne ripped the Phillips' card in half. Even before the pieces had fluttered to the floor, she had turned and was striding out the door, her head held high.

ANNE RETURNED TO FREDERICTON for one last visit—to her father's grave. The earth was still freshly mounded and the marker had not yet been installed. She laid a small bouquet of wildflowers on the mound and touched the soil with her fingers. Although her father remained an enigma, Anne knew fate had intervened in her life again. She thought of a quote from Shakespeare, "There is a divinity that shapes our ends." She wanted to know why Walter had written that letter to Marilla. Anne would never know whether he had really wanted her or if he had meant exactly as he had said—that it was his "duty to try to contact" her? So many unanswered questions plagued her. She wondered if he was relieved when he'd received no answer. Perhaps Louisa had influenced him to simply forget about Anne in favour of her own children. Violetta had certainly managed to get everything.

Unfortunately, the grave was incapable of answering back, and the moment left her feeling more empty than when she'd arrived. The question that tormented Anne the most was destined to remain unanswered forever. She would never know if her brother, her own flesh and blood, was out there somewhere, or whether he, too, had died or simply disappeared. Once again, fate had left her hanging.

Twenty-Two

Back at Green Gables, Gene was sitting on the verandah doing a crossword puzzle and listening to the radio. Anne had telephoned him at the hotel and left a message that she had missed him and would meet him at Green Gables that afternoon. As he waited, Gene quickly fell under the charm of the quiet old place. He loved the whisper of the breeze in the orchard and the quiet prospect over the fields. He was just trying to think of a word for a "feather scarf named after a snake" when a movement at the end of the lane caused him to glance up. Anne was standing completely still, suitcase on the ground beside her. She was weary, but breathing in the spectacular Island atmosphere appeared to be a tonic. She was relieved to be home at Green Gables.

"Hello there," Gene called out, his face creasing into a smile.

He hurried down the verandah stairs and across the grass to take her suitcase.

"Why did you leave that message for me to meet you here?" he demanded. "I could have easily picked you up at the station."

Anne approached slowly, her epic journey written on her face.

"I just wanted to be alone a little while longer."

They began to walk back to the house together in comfortable silence.

"I never got the chance to know him," Anne said eventually, staring down at the ground.

Gene could practically feel the exhaustion in her words—and the disappointment.

"You never needed Walter Shirley to be a part of your life," he offered, trying to give her some perspective.

His conviction made Anne smile and she brightened.

"I never wanted you to be a part of my life either. Now look at you!" She teased, slipping her arm through his.

Friendship and understanding passed freely between them, and Gene liked that. He and Anne sauntered up the front stairs of that welcoming white clapboard house with the green roof. Anne hadn't realized how much she needed the old place until she'd set foot in it again, barely a few months ago. After she unpacked and put on her slacks, she stepped out to walk about the farm, drawing solace from the familiar landscape. Gene kept by her side as they strolled through the lovely orchard of spreading apple trees, engulfed in greenery. For Anne, being surrounded by green was an omen; green was the colour of hope. Tilting her head back, she looked up into the apple branches she'd climbed in as a child. She especially adored spring, when they clothed themselves in lively clouds of fragrant white blossoms. Now, in fall, they seemed serene, lush with fruit. That serenity was in her bones now.

"I wonder if trees sleep and if they do, what do they dream?" she speculated, her reliable imagination springing to life. Gene glanced at the faraway look in Anne's eyes. He had learned so much about what moved her from the play she had written. These days, he looked at the rolling acres and the rambling farmhouse with entirely new eyes.

"So, how does it feel," he quipped, "to be Anne of Green Gables, rather than Anne of nowhere in particular?"

Anne's smile was full of laughter and heartache, but her face was radiant.

"All I can say is that when I arrived here, I knew this was my real home."

She remembered the exact feeling from so many years before—driving with Matthew over the brow of the hill and seeing Green Gables before her with its apple trees in bloom and the tidy white house set against an evening sky full of stars. "Matthew and Marilla were everything to me."

Anne and Gene sauntered back to the house through the long grass, enjoying every sensation of the evening air together.

Twenty-Three

Anne didn't have time to dwell on regrets about her father. She had just received a telegram from Dominic confirming that the wedding could now be set for the day after the couple was scheduled to arrive. They were on their way and would arrive in P.E.I. in one week's time. Anne had set to work putting Green Gables into a festive mood for Dominic and Brigitte's wedding and had invited nearly the entire town of Avonlea, as well as everyone else who was near and dear to her for Dominic's homecoming. She strung up large colourful paper lanterns all around the yard and hung bunting everywhere. There were even tents to shelter the ample refreshments. As the hour of the couple's arrival approached, people streamed on to the property to join in the extraordinary celebration.

Anne and her immediate family gathered on the Green Gables verandah for a photo. She was flanked by her two daughters, Rilla and Frannie, while their husbands stood directly behind. Little Timmy, all of two and now fully recovered from the mumps, chortled at his grandmother as he sat in her lap. Several other grandchildren were all struggling to stand still. Orchestrating the event was Elsie Barry. Her brother, John, held the brownie camera.

"Ready," cried Elsie. "Everybody say 'cheese'!"

John squinted into the glass viewfinder and pressed the button.

"That's great! Got it!" he told the anxiously smiling group as he closed the lid on the camera.

Instantly, Anne's family separated as the children raced off, darting and shouting gleefully all around the freshly painted farmhouse.

"Hey, enough, you three!" Frannie called out after their flying figures, worried that they were going to annoy the other guests crowding into the yard. "Behave yourselves!"

"Oh, let them burn off steam, Frannie!" Anne countered as she watched them indulgently.

"All right, mother, it's your bash!" Frannie replied. Her mother loved watching the children enjoy themselves.

"Children should have high spirits, don't you think, Tom?" asked Anne of Frannie's husband as they strolled through the front yard, holding Timmy in her arms. Timmy was a bubbly child with a cap of fine blond hair and a grin as wide as a railroad track. Anne adored him, as she did every one of her grandchildren.

"Frannie's a little anxious today. She wants any occasion for Dominic to be perfect," chuckled Tom, reading his wife perfectly. "You know how she always worries about Avonlea gossip."

Anne smiled. She no longer worried about Avonlea gossip at all. People could darn well think what they liked of her big party at Green Gables. Everything she had prepared was done out of an intense love for her son.

"Children can make as much racket as they want here," said Anne.

Anne, who always loved being stylish, wore a new suit of rich ivory and a very grand, wide-brimmed hat of ivory and cocoa-coloured straw. She outshone her daughters in their fashionable yellow dresses, but it was mainly because she was so radiant. Timmy began to tug at Anne's hair, threatening her wonderful new hat. Anne handed him back to his father and looked down the lane yet one more time for the much anticipated guests of honour, covering her anxiety by ruffling Timmy's hair.

"Enjoy him, Tom. He won't be little much longer." She felt bittersweet, knowing how much her youngest grandson had grown since she'd last seen him.

Just about all of Avonlea was on the Green Gables lawn, including Gene and the theatre troupe, who had just finished the season at the White Sands Hotel. Gene looked particularly natty in a suit and tie, which he had donned as a concession that only proved the importance of the occasion.

Anne circulated everywhere throughout the party, greeting old friends and guests until she found Gene chatting effusively with Elsie.

"So glad to see you here," Elsie laughed before she dashed off to converse with some of her own friends. Anne took Gene's arm and walked the length of the picket fence as they surveyed the crowd. "They're still not here yet."

Anne craned her neck to look down the lane. She had been on tenterhooks since getting out of bed that morning.

"While we're waiting, why don't you introduce me to all your neighbours," Gene suggested as a distraction

Anne took a self-assured breath and stepped back into her role as chatelaine of the party.

"Sure...Oh, Rilla, darling! Can you and James start serving the drinks now?"

"Alright, Mom!"

As Rilla hurried off to do Anne's bidding, Gene pointed to a very old lady in a wheelchair attended by another equally elderly personage. The two were holding court on the lawn under a tent, while a large contingent of Avonlea folk gathered in a circle listening. The pair talked and gesticulated, enjoying themselves enormously.

"Who is that ancient pair everyone is fussing over?" Gene asked.

Anne's face softened instantly.

"Why Hetty King. And that's Rachel Lynde in the wheelchair."

Hetty still had a straight back and authoritative manner, the legacy of all the years she'd spent ruling the Avonlea school with an iron hand. Rachel didn't look as though she needed the wheelchair at all but kept to it only to annoy Hetty. Rachel had lost much of the substantial figure she'd had when Anne first encountered her at the age of eleven, but her eyes were just as observant and she was just as interested in everyone's business. Her funny donut of a hat tilted jauntily forward, she was using the occasion to catch up on all the latest doings among her neighbours. It had been a very long time since Mrs. Lynde had called Anne "terrible, skinny and homely," provoking such passionate wrath on young Anne's part that the good woman had been certain Marilla had taken in an insane child who might burn the house down or poison their well.

"And the two of them over ninety if they're a day!" Anne laughed. "Rachel has no use for theatre people, so you shouldn't have to endure any of her nonsense."

Leading Gene by the arm in another direction, the pair regarded a knot of people standing beside some very shiny automobiles. One couple consisted of a chic woman with hair still as black as a raven's wing. Beside her stood a comfortable-looking man with one empty sleeve tucked into his pocket, an ongoing reminder of his sacrifice in the Great War.

"Isn't that Fred and Diana Wright over there?" asked Gene.

Anne waved, letting them know she and Gene were engaged in conversation. Diana smiled and waved back, winking at Anne.

"I think your Diana and Fred look far too tanned and sophisticated for Avonlea," Gene asserted.

Diana blew Anne a kiss, a simple gesture that contained all their decades of intimate friendship. She put her arm around Fred, who smiled at Anne as he continued chatting with his children and his neighbours. Anne teased Gene about his comment.

"That's rather green-eyed of you, just because she's my best friend. And they've been hopelessly in love for the last . . . forty . . . years. . . ."

Anne's voice caught in mid-sentence at the sight of a young man and a pretty girl walking down the lane to the farm. She stood still for only a second as happiness flooded her face. Then, abandoning all decorum, she ran down the lane with her arms wide open.

The handsome, dark-haired young man in military uniform ran equally as hard to catch her. The fact that his arm was in a sling did nothing to prevent their embrace. Anne clutched her son to her heart in a kind of desperation that was a mixture of delight and relief.

"What took you so long?" Anne cried, laughing and sobbing at the same time.

"You knew I'd get here eventually," Dominic whispered into her ear.

Gaining control of herself, Anne managed to let him go and take a step back. As her eyes took in the cotton sling, a trace of alarm crept into all the happiness.

"Oh, dear God! Look at you!"

Dominic registered the anxiety on his mother's face as she stared at his bandaged arm. He grinned wider.

"I'm okay. Really, Mom," he insisted reassuringly.

With a small sigh of relief, Anne turned to Dominic's companion. She was a slim, beautiful young woman who had been watching the fond reunion with an enormous smile. Now the smile turned to shyness as Anne took her hand.

"You're Brigitte," whispered Anne, positively thrilled. She took in the dimpled face framed by long brunette hair, drawn back in a fashionable clip.

"*Oui*, I'm pleased to make an acquaintance," Brigitte replied in a charming French accent.

Anne immediately hugged her, dispelling all the girl's fears about meeting her future mother-in-law. When she let go, she hardly knew which way to turn, she was so excited.

"Oh, I can't wait to hear all about how you two met and I want you to meet my good friend, Gene and . . . oh, all this is overwhelming. . . ."

Gene was already coming forward, hand extended in hearty greeting. Brigitte, having hung back, suddenly prodded her fiancé.

"*Attend, Dominic. Il faut que tu expliques maintenant.*"

Brigitte gestured to a point on the road behind them. For the first time, Anne noticed a young man in a business suit, lagging uncertainly at the gate. She didn't recognize him as anyone she'd invited.

"*D'accord,*" agreed Dominic.

Turning to his mother, Dominic pointed back over his shoulder.

"That guy back there . . . he got off at the Bright River whistle stop and asked the station master about directions to Green Gables."

Anne stepped away from Gene and glanced at Dominic, wondering why a total stranger would be looking for Green Gables.

"He just sort of followed us here," Dominic continued then paused considering the enormity of what he was about to say. "He, uh . . . he claims . . . he's your *brother*." Dominic's voice trailed away.

Anne felt her insides whirl. She stood for a moment, watching this awkward fellow somewhere in his thirties, who appeared almost frightened to move any further. In a split second, her entire life passed before her eyes. Letting go of Dominic and Brigitte, Anne slowly walked toward the young man. Dominic, Gene, and Brigitte stood watching the strange tableau unfolding before them like a pantomime.

They watched Anne cautiously approach the man, until they stood facing each other as he talked. Not many words were exchanged before Anne took his hand in hers, her other hand flying to her mouth. She shook her head as the fellow talked on, his hands sketching the convoluted course that had brought him to the threshold of Green Gables.

Gene, Dominic, and Brigitte were immobilized, each afraid to break the spell. Behind them, the family and guests who were ready to pounce on Dominic and Brigitte with greetings and congratulations also began to notice Anne and the mysterious visitor.

Watching in astonishment, they saw Anne suddenly throw her arms around the man and hug him close—as tightly as she had just hugged her own son. None of the guests had a clue as to what was going on.

Finally, the poignant embrace ended. With the stranger's arm across her shoulder, and her arm wrapped tightly around his waist, Anne led the young man up the lane to introduce him to the curious group of onlookers. She had difficulty speaking. This was such a personal revelation, and here she was making the introduction to nearly the entire town of Avonlea.

"This...," she faltered a little, but gained control of herself, "this is my...brother...everyone. My brother, Andrew. Dominic, he's your uncle..."

Anne took Andrew and Brigitte each by one arm and began graciously presenting them to all and sundry, her happiness radiating in an ebullient glow.

"Hey, everyone. This is my son's fiancée, Brigitte. She's going to be part of our family. And *this...this is* my brother...Andrew. ...Isn't it wonderful?"

Although Anne's quest for her father had become known among her daughters and several close friends, the sensation caused by the appearance of an unknown brother swept through the crowd, drawing incredulous gasps and cries. Instantly, neighbours and family swarmed around Andrew, shaking his hand and introducing themselves. There was so much patting on the back and waving of arms that Andrew looked utterly overcome by such a reception. Anne herself was in tears—simply breaking down in the wave of excitement.

Finally, Dominic extricated himself from the melee and found himself standing beside Gene, surveying everything from the periphery of the crowd. Dominic was as floored as everyone else at the appearance of this young man. Anne had never revealed one iota of her life before Green Gables to any of her children.

"Me, being an orphan," he said quietly to Gene, "Mom always made it plain about wanting to do for me what the Cuthberts had done for her, but I had no idea..."

"Neither did she," replied Gene, smiling at Dominic's bewilderment. "Her life is extraordinary. And the great thing about it is that she's completely unaware of it."

ANDREW WAS DRAWN RIGHT into the midst of the family and friends who filled the yard at Green Gables. Anne insisted he stay for Dominic and Brigitte's wedding, and completely reorganized everything so he would be a part of the wedding itself, as the newest family member. The couple's headlong rush to the altar was so romantic, and the wedding itself became legendary. The day after the garden party, Avonlea's white frame church was jammed with even more guests. When the doors were thrown open to let Dominic and Brigitte sweep out as newlyweds, they were all but submerged under a wave of rice and confetti thrown at them by the cheering and adoring throng.

Gene was waiting with their car, a large white Packard abundantly rigged with cans and a Just Married sign. Dominic and Brigitte rushed down the church stairs, laughing and shaking hands. Brigitte still clutched her bridal bouquet and wore a trim white wedding dress designed to also act as her going-away outfit. The pair did not want to wait a minute after stepping out of the church to start their lives together.

"Come on," urged Dominic to his bride, "toss it over your shoulder. That's the custom here. Whoever catches it will be married next."

With a sidelong glance that was so very French, Brigitte tossed the bouquet over her shoulder into a crowd of several unmarried young women leaping to catch it. One of them shrieked with triumph as she fielded the flowers.

The delighted girl danced up and down, waving her trophy to her friends. Dominic opened the back door of the car and chivalrously ushered Brigitte in and Anne ran to kiss her new daughter-in-law through the open window. Andrew intercepted Dominic as he made his way around the back of the car and shook Dominic's hand warmly.

"I felt I had to let you know that your mother was reminiscing during the ceremony about how you were lost as a kid and when she found you, what a roller-coaster of emotion it was for her. I feel the same way about finding her."

Dominic smiled, knowing exactly what Andrew meant. They embraced, then the groom climbed into the Packard.

Children, freed from the constraints of the ceremony, galloped wildly about as Rilla and Anne leaned into the car window to say their goodbyes.

"I wish Dad could have been here," Rilla said wistfully, missing Gilbert.

From inside the car, Dominic reached over to squeeze his sister's hand.

"He is here . . . in spirit, Rill."

The motor purred to life and everyone stood back, shouting and waving as the newlyweds were driven away. Out of all the enthusiastic faces watching and waving, the most emotional belonged to Rachel Lynde. She had witnessed several epochs at this wonderful farm and had even lived there for a time with Marilla, after her husband Thomas died. She understood its secret charm and power. Now all of the recent, fascinating events at Green Gables would provide fodder for weeks and weeks of mouth-watering discussion with Hetty King.

IN THE DAYS AFTER THE WEDDING, Andrew revealed his entire story to Anne. After the death of his mother, Louisa, he had fought bitterly with Violetta. There had been no reason to retain any connection. Andrew disappeared overseas to pursue his life and to do his part in the war. His personal circumstances had been completely disrupted by the titanic clash of nations that had just ended so violently.

Only when he returned did he learn of his father's sudden death. When he went to seek the details from Mr. Harding, the kindly old funeral director also told him about Anne. In utter disbelief, he discovered how all the Thomases had turned their back on Walter when he died, thrusting the responsibility for his interment on a woman who hadn't seen her father in more than forty years. Andrew learned it was Anne who undertook the burial and ordered the gravestone. Neither his parents, nor any of his half-siblings had ever even mentioned that Walter had another child. He was not only staggered to learn of Anne's existence, but also livid that his entire family had kept it from him. Andrew's journey to Green Gables had been fraught with a multitude of fears and hopes. He had no idea what to anticipate, except that the woman who claimed to be his half-sister had been concerned about finding him.

Like so many people emerging from the deprivation of war, he longed desperately for the closeness of a family. With his father dead, and Louisa's other children estranged from him, he felt completely deserted. To discover that someone had actually been searching for him cheered him and gave him hope. Anne's emotional welcome made him feel as if he'd found a soulmate; a sister whose regard for him was unassailable. He was just as thrilled to learn all about her astonishing life and to find that they had so many things in common.

Andrew didn't stay long at Green Gables after the wedding, but his departure was made with many promises to return soon. Anne wanted them to remain close and she intended that they would remain so the rest of their lives. Besides, Andrew was now an uncle to her children, and there was a whole tribe of young ones he needed to get to know.

On the afternoon of Andrew's departure, Gene dared to offer Anne a friendly kiss on the cheek before heading back to the White Sands Hotel to begin wrapping up his administrative duties. She had decided not to go along with him. Her life had been turned upside down over the last few weeks and she felt she needed solitude to recover. She had laid the past with her father to rest; the fictional play that he'd inspired felt like a distant chronicle now. It was a story that would prove to be moving and enlightening to others for years—as all good drama was intended—but it was now as redundant a belonging for Anne as the carpet bag she'd carried with her for so many years. Both were almost immaterial in this new chapter of her life.

LEFT TO HERSELF, Anne perched on the verandah rail, a cup of tea in hand. This had been her favourite spot as a child, and it remained an ideal place to contemplate events. She had her notebook in her lap and found she was able to add a vital new entry.

"Everything that has happened in my life," she wrote, "the good and the bad . . . is much more than I could ever have made up."

She gazed out over the soft, rolling farm fields and the trees now brushed with hints of autumn colour. So content was she with the spirit of this place that she could barely believe she'd ever thought to let it go. Green Gables was part of her soul.

"I do *long* to write and eventually I'll write about every part of my existence. My life has been . . . unexpected, exceptional, really. A life of self-doubt has granted me recurrent advantages." Anne smiled wistfully to herself.

"Eventually, the more love a person gives, the easier it is to find. That's the only part that matters. Nothing else." She wrote and then closed her notebook.

The breeze caught her hair and she took a deep breath. She'd known even before Andrew had appeared that the gnawing emptiness over her father would vanish in time. She'd been able to see the truth about her life in relief and to make it more perceptible through the surest means she could—memory and storytelling. She understood that it didn't really matter why Walter Shirley had let her go, or that they had never seen one another again, or that his family had determined not to acknowledge her. Matthew and Marilla, Gilbert, their children, and even the community of Avonlea, had given her an identity and a joy so great that it eclipsed the idealism of a life with her birth parents. She was rich in love, both past and present. It was an extraordinary gift that fate had bestowed upon her. She only had to see it. She opened her notebook again.

"And it's so much nicer," she wrote, "to be Anne of Green Gables than Anne of nowhere in particular."

Acknowledgements

I am indebted to the following individuals for their professional advice and assistance in bringing the film and book to completion: Gail Hamilton for helping to translate so descriptively the bare foundations of a film screenplay into a broad novel; Linda Pruessen and Carol Harrison for their sublime editorial dexterity; Michael Schwartz, Mark Reitsma, Dan Matthews, and the entire staff at Sullivan Entertainment, who have offered comments, editorial assistance, and have been endlessly patient in supporting me through the arduous process of creating a viable celluloid interpretation of Anne's enduring story; Gord McClellan, who helped me find the strongest storyline to present; Martha Mann for twenty-five years of bringing Montgomery's characters to life onscreen with her vast knowledge of period clothes and customs that have made such a strong imprimatur on the visual storytelling in both the film and in the text; Raymond Lorenz for his clever capacity at creating sets and adapting locations on an epic scale that made the background to the film and the interpretation of the novel so vivid; Yuri Yakubiw, whose ability to translate light provided scintillating depth to the images in the film and to the passages of the novel; Daniel Pellerin for creating such all-encompassing soundscapes on the Anne films; Shirley MacLaine and Barbara Hershey for knowing when and how to perform a line exactly as written and when to collaborate with a filmmaker until the dialogue becomes something much more powerful than may have originally been intended; Ivan Fecan for his vision and support in permitting me to bring hundreds of hours of television to viewers around the world based on my depiction of small-town Maritime Canada; Michael Levine for championing our Anne and Avonlea films and books over the years with skilful assistance; and, as always, Trudy Grant for inspiring me to embark on turning our recent Montgomery centenary celebration film into this novel and numerous other projects, and our three children who have motivated me in writing for films, whether they know it or not, and who have come to the conclusion they do enjoy some of my work now that they are grown up.

Lastly, to Lucy Maud Montgomery, whose journey through life as a magnificent storyteller provided me with the impetus to begin to question what Anne would have been like had she grown up to become an author like Montgomery herself, and how Anne as a child might have looked had Montgomery delved even deeper into her own personal back story in the creation of her illustrious heroine. With enormous gratitude at having had the privilege of creating a body of work inspired by one of Canada's most pre-eminent and enduring authors.

—Kevin Sullivan

KEVIN SULLIVAN is a writer, director, and film producer, known around the world for his beautifully executed and highly praised period movies such as *Anne of Green Gables*, his movie adaptation of Timothy Findley's *The Pianoman's Daughter*, and such classic television series as *Road to Avonlea* and *Wind at My Back*. Having won hundreds of international awards, including three Emmy Awards, a Peabody Award, a Prix Jeunesse, and four Cable Ace Awards, he has established a strong brand based on visual style, quality of writing, and outstanding performances from award-winning performers, including Colleen Dewhurst, Christopher Reeve, Eugene Levy, Michael York, Stockard Channing, Ryan Gosling, Sam Waterston, and Christopher Lloyd. His most recent film is *Mozart's Magic Flute Diaries*. He is also the author of several books, including *Beyond Green Gables* and *Anne of Green Gables: The Official Movie Adaptation*. Sullivan's library of movies, books, and music are available at www.sullivanmovies.com.